BLADE BORN
A BORDERLANDS NOVEL

KORY M. SHRUM

An Exclusive Offer For You

Connecting with my readers is the best part of my job as a writer. One way that I like to connect is by sending 2–3 newsletters a month with a subscribers-only giveaway, free stories from your favorite series, and personal updates (read: pictures of my dog).

When you first sign up for the mailing list, I send you at least three free stories right away. If free stories and exclusive giveaways sound like something you're interested in, please look for the special offer in the back of this book.

Happy reading,

Kory M. Shrum

DEDICATION

To everyone who has read a version of this book
in the ten years I've been trying to write it.
Thanks for sticking with me.

CHAPTER 1

MIDNIGHT IN THE GRAVEYARD

T he wrought-iron gate prevents me from entering the graveyard. It's ten feet tall, too high to climb without levitating, and I don't have a feather stone for that. I yank at the bars, but a thick chain latched together by a padlock, bigger than a balled fist, clanks against the bars. The muscles in my back stiffen at the sound. I look up and down the dark streets encircling the cemetery.

Orange lamps spotlight wet pavement. Nothing moves.

"No magic," a voice rasps over my shoulder.

The phantom glows white-blue. She hovers above the ground, suspended mid-air. Her hair floats around her head as if she's submerged underwater, an invisible current languidly tossing her locks.

Her eyes are ink-black pools set in a luminous face.

My dead sister isn't nearly as translucent as one might expect a ghost to be. The moon is full tonight, and her form seems to be collecting all the moonlight into itself. During a new moon, or the barest sliver of a waxing crescent, I can put my hand through her and read its dim palm lines without squinting. She hates that.

"It's rude to put your hand through somebody."

Of course, I could dispute the *body* part.

I don't. I try not to give Phelia a hard time. Not just because she's my sister, or because I love her—both true— or even because she's dead.

I try not to tease Phelia because her death was my fault.

And because I can't look at those glowing cheeks and liquid eyes without feeling like I owe her.

But I'll lick a demon's back before I ask the aunts about ghosts. If they even suspect that Phelia haunts me or Rowan House, they'll banish her. *Three twists of a witch's tit*, as Aunt Arty says, and it'll be done before I can say *Ocimum tenuiflorum*.

As creepy as it is having a glowing, translucent person follow me around, I can't bear the thought of losing her.

Again.

I heft my backpack up onto my shoulder and turn back toward the gate. Phelia flitters impatiently.

"No magic. They can taste your magic," she says, twittering back and forth. "It's like a field of narcissus in spring. Rose water. The sky at dawn. You will call them to you."

I let go of the lock. "See if I leave Kipling open for you again. You sound like a walking sonnet. Come here." I wave her closer. Phelia's body illuminates the padlock in my hand. I trace the keyhole with my nail, flecks of iron sticking to my fingertips. "Maybe I could—"

My free hand closes around the cord at my neck.

"Yes!" Phelia agrees. "Use the key."

I reach into my shirt and grab the necklace nestled there. Two items hang at the end of a frayed rope, a gray smoky quartz and a tarnished skeleton key made of actual skeleton. Sure, it's weird having a dead guy's finger between my boobs, but it's hard not to appreciate the convenience.

Skeleton keys are made from the finger bones of the innocent. This man hanged for a crime he didn't commit. And the frayed rope laced through the bone key—it's the rope that took his life.

Besides, it hardly looks like a finger anymore. If I squint, it only looks like a piece of ivory polished smooth, a beautiful triquetra looping at its crown.

I suck in a breath before slipping the skeleton key into the lock. "But this is magic too."

Magic attracts demons. Especially mine.

My eyes sweep the dark graveyard again, straining to catch any sign of movement. Any darting shadow. Of course, by the time you can see a demon, it's usually too late.

Drizzle splatters across my cheek and exposed neck. The wind kicks up and a chill runs down my spine, icing the droplets there. The little hairs behind my ears prickle to attention as the lock clicks open and the chain groans. As soon as the lock opens, so does the gate. It swings wide with a metallic wail.

The creep factor goes from a mild four to a solid eight.

Don't work yourself into hysterics, Aunt Demi would say.

If I want to catch a demon and make it back to Rowan House before the aunts find my bed empty, I'd better hurry. The smoky quartz can only do so much to hide me from Aunt Arty's omniscient eye.

Phelia giggles. She has a habit of giggling. I'm not sure if it's because she was only ten when she died or if it's a ghost thing, the giggling.

She skips through the graveyard. Twirling. Dancing. She casts a blueish glow on every tombstone she passes, like a shifting lantern.

I tuck the skeleton key and crystal back into my shirt before the rope cord gets too wet from the intensifying drizzle. "You'd think dead people would have a little more respect for cemeteries."

"Catch me, Amelia!" she trills. "Catch me."

A nervous tension makes my heart flutter at the base of my throat as I follow her deeper into the dark. Mist rises from the earth as the rain falls, and it's like watching specters emerge from graves. Foggy phantoms called up to join my sister's dancing.

Hysteria, I warn myself. Hysteria won't help me do what I need to do.

I wipe rain out of my eyes and cut around a stone angel. Too bad angels aren't real.

It'd be nice if a pretty boy with gossamer wings and a sword could swoop down to vanquish the demons preying on the innocent.

While angels may not be real, demons certainly are. And I am going to catch one.

Tonight.

Blinking back droplets, I find my sister, bright and ephemeral before a grave marker.

She's stopped dancing.

I don't need to see the engraving to know which grave she's standing on. Beside her, I bend forward and trace the stone etchings with my finger. A cold tremor vibrates through my bones.

Ophelia Rowan Bishop

2000–2010
Beloved daughter, sister, niece

My chest compresses. "I'm sorry, Phe—"

She doesn't hear me because she's already moved further down the row to a fresh grave, taking her light with her so that I can no longer read her name. I slip the heavy pack off my shoulder and set it at the base of her headstone. I follow her to a mound of disturbed dirt, heaped like a body under a sheet.

"They're coming for this one," she whispers, her transparent toes grazing the churned earth. "Hide!"

Fear kicks me in the gut and ice-cold adrenaline pours into my nervous system.

"Hide now!"

As soon as Phelia calls the warning, I cast my mind out and find them. Like red sparks in the darkness, I sense the demons rushing toward me. They move like a pack of wild dogs.

Five?

I concentrate.

No. *Six* demons. Two of them are a mated pair with a shared mind.

Great. Just *great*.

It's worse fighting mated pairs. They coordinate their attacks without any body language to signal their intentions. A pair alone would be trouble. A pair with a four-demon-strong entourage is excessive.

Odd, actually.

I scramble to my feet and turn full circle. I need a stronghold.

Next to the stone angel is a crypt with a good view of the fresh grave. I dash for it. I slip into the stone shelter, scuffing my boots on the gritty floor. Leaves from last autumn crunch underfoot as I push the monstrous door closed behind me. I climb up on a bench to peer through the stone hatch work.

"There's too many," Phelia pouts. "We're toast."

My sister, brighter than a morning star, trembles beside me.

"It's not *your* entrails they'll be slurping down," I grumble, unhappy to be sharing my hiding place with a disco ball.

"You need your chevalier. You're stronger together." Phelia reaches out for my hand, but hers passes right through mine. My heart hitches, clogging my throat. It's suddenly hard to breathe.

Sometimes Phelia can throw books or move small objects, but no matter how many times we've tried, how hard we've concentrated, we can never touch each other.

I let my hand fall to my damp jeans.

"My chevalier." I dab rain from my face with my sleeve. "He told you to call him that, didn't he?"

She doesn't blink.

Until I perform the fivefold kiss, the ritual that would bind us together forever as hunter and keeper, Alex won't be my chevalier.

He's been pressuring me to bond with him ever since I killed my first demon at thirteen and started hunting with the other demon-killing witches. But to bond with a keeper —to bind my magic to his—is to sign his death warrant. And I won't do it.

I love him too much for that.

The ghouls slink into view. Their ape-like trot slows as soon as they see the fresh grave. Blood-red eyes and snarling snouts snap. Their hunched forms of gray flesh work their way down to the corpse, digging like dogs. They claw the dirt with long, sloth-like talons.

Now that I can see them, I can smell them. Funny how that works. They reek like roadkill warmed by the sun. Their shrieks are worse, high and sharp, like nails on a chalkboard. Like a strangled pig.

Thunder cracks open the sky, and a sharp stab of lightning breaks apart the April clouds.

The rain comes. Real rain. Not the light drizzle that's been following me around all night.

Getting a ghoul into a bell jar will be hard enough, and it's not even the demon I need. What I *really* need is a puppeteer. The kind of hell spawn that enters people and controls them like meat suits.

Full-fledged demons are hellbound. Lucky for us, the most powerful can't cross to Earth, but they can send their spirit, their soul or part of their essence, as long as they find a suitable host. They need a body to move around on this plane. Hence the name puppeteer and why they are the worst of the worst. They are the top of the demonic food chain. Ghouls, like all carrion, are on the bottom.

But believe me, demon-hunting witches like myself have our hands full with even low-level demons. So, it begs the question why I'm out here in the cold rain, trying to catch one with a blessed bell jar.

No. The real question is what I *wouldn't* do to save Alex's life.

A ghoul's head snaps up. It peers into the dark, one grizzled corpse limb bobbing up and down in its mouth as it chews. When its eyes fall on the crypt, it stops chewing. Two more stop munching and look toward the crypt too.

"They can see my light." Phelia's face erupts with an

enormous smile. "Oh, maybe you'll die! Maybe it'll be horrible!"

"Phelia." I give her a low, warning growl.

A second ghoul lifts its head and sniffs the air. The third bumps the fourth and they begin to saunter slowly toward the crypt. My heart kicks the bottom of my throat.

"Don't stay in the crypt," I whisper. "In case I'm wrong about the entrails thing."

I flash Phelia a forced smile, all bravado, and shove against the crypt door. Without stopping, I burst out into the rainy night, running as fast as I possibly can toward the cemetery's gate. I'm already calculating the distance between me and the bell jar in my backpack while rehearsing the spell I need to pull this off.

But I keep forgetting the third verse.

Separate earth from sky. Separate—

What in the Maleficarum was that next line!

I hear the ghouls gaining on me, but I don't dare look back. I whip around the stone angel and snatch up the backpack beside Phelia's grave without stopping. I blink rain droplets out of my lashes and press on.

The sound of their limbs slapping the muddy earth reminds me of a herd of wild horses. Despite my efforts to concentrate, the furious pounding causes me to look back and gauge my breathing room. They move like monkeys, swinging their hips up beneath their shoulders in a sort of gallop. The closest one is practically on top of me.

I pull my athame, a long, tapering blade, out of my hip holster. I just need one ghoul alive. Pity the first five who come at me.

It leaps.

I crouch and thrust up into its underbelly. My fist connects with its body, my blade buried to its hilt. The ghoul howls and rolls away. I struggle to keep hold of the rain-slick blade but manage it. The ghoul hits the earth, screaming. Its flesh smokes. It's the oil on the blade, a mix of myrtle and mint. Nothing fancy to witches, but because of their purification properties, it burns demons like acid.

The second ghoul launches itself and I brace myself for impact.

I wait.

And wait.

But the second ghoul never lands.

Instead, a bright light rips through the darkness. Something grabs hold of me, but it doesn't have the long, sloth-like claws of a ghoul. It has arms and hands that shine like moonlight.

Phelia?

No. The hands are too big. A body even bigger than my own. A man's hands.

Then he throws me.

My body is flung up into the sky. I drop the bell jar but not the athame.

Oh my Goddess, I'm flying.

Or maybe the man still holding me is flying—if this creature can be called a man. My gaze falls on the deathly white hand tight around my waist.

Vampire? Incubus? I start through a list of creatures that might try to abscond with a woman in the night.

I can't twist my wrist enough to stab him, and when I squirm, trying to break his hold, it's a joke. I don't move an inch. So, I call my magic, but before the white-hot tingle seizes me, I hit the ground with a thud, dropped unceremoniously.

I'm on my hands and knees, no longer in the cemetery.

My right hand aches from hitting the earth while still holding the blade.

A burst of light catches my attention. It shoots through the cemetery like a comet blast. My eyes dart toward another burst of light, but it's already burned out before I can get a good look at its source. He's moving too fast, whatever he is. Another blast hits a ghoul, and it wails as its body disperses in a cloud of ash. The light he's shooting is killing them.

Incinerating them.

"No!" I shout through the bars. "I need one of those!"

The beams of light cease and the cemetery falls dark. I start to wonder if maybe I should've kept my mouth shut.

I pull myself up by the bars of the wrought-iron fence and peer into the darkness. I twist the athame nervously in my other fist. I cast my mind out and feel the magic.

I sense something...strange. Magic, but it's none I recognize.

The ghouls are gone.

And Phelia is gone, too, but that isn't surprising. As much as she might hope that I die so that we can have endless playtime, Phelia tends to run at the first sign of trouble. Perhaps she isn't interested in seeing me actually die. Can't blame her. Sometimes I still find myself replaying her death over and over in my mind.

I sense one ghoul left in the cemetery.

A yelping shriek shatters my concentration. Another horrible, hissing whine makes my flesh crawl like the time I heard a fox tearing apart a rabbit in the woods outside Rowan House.

I hold my breath, straining to hear another sound.

Then he's there. It was pitch black one moment, and now he's right in front of me, this pale stranger.

He didn't make a sound. I can't even find him with my mind. I'm forced to rely on my eyes, which is a pretty limited way to see the world.

Still, I take him in.

He's tall, beautiful, with very sharp cheek bones. He looks unreal. No one is that pretty.

I'm more than a little dazzled until I realize he's holding the dropped bell jar out to me.

"Oh," I stammer.

I accept the blessed jar through the cemetery's bars, unable to look away from his face even as the weight of it settles into my hand. The glass is cool and slick from the rain, but I only register this from somewhere far, far away.

I'm more interested in his bright eyes shining in the darkness. As feral and inhuman as a cat's. And the light isn't reflecting off his skin the way it should. He's standing too straight. Like a tree. But when he was fighting the ghouls, he hadn't seemed stiff at all. He was water. Waves overtaking a shore.

Looking at him, staring into those flame-like eyes, causes a strange fluttering in my chest.

I recognize the heat sliding over my skin too. That pulsing tune vibrating along my nerve endings.

I can feel his magic. His *magic*.

Inside the bell jar black smoke bubbles beneath the glass, pinging from one side to the other. It's the ghoul's demonic essence free of its body. It's exactly what I need to get started with my save-Alex plan.

Movement catches the corner of my eye and I gasp. The stranger is right beside me, somehow having escaped the cemetery and its gigantic fence in an instant. I hadn't even seen him move.

"I'm sorry," he says. His voice is like music, like wind across my cheek. It's pretty, like a song.

Then his arms are around me. One slides under mine, the other presses into the small of my back, lifting me off my feet.

He kisses me.

More heat flushes through me, intensifying. The tingle starts behind my teeth, a slight vibration over my tongue, and then it's everywhere. In the tips of my fingers, under my skin and between my toes. I'm drowning, unable to breathe, and he won't let go. His kiss only deepens, the hand at the base of my spine squeezing me possessively.

I hear a lock click, the sound of something snapping open deep inside me.

He pulls back, his eyes reflecting moonlight like an animal's.

"We cannot wait any longer," he says, and he sounds sorry. "We're out of time."

For a moment I can only stare at him, dumbfounded and blinking. Then I recover my voice. "Uh, in my culture, we don't jump right to the kissing, we—*Whoa.*"

My words break off as the world tilts and all thought leaves me. All my focus shifts to keeping my body upright. If I didn't know any better, I would say I'm drunk. My body sways and I wrap my fingers around the fence's bars and hold tight until the world stops spinning. I'm holding on to him as if I might fall over.

"What did you do?" I ask. Is this his magic? "What did you *do?*"

Demons howl in the distance. Why wouldn't they? The night is drenched with magic.

I steady myself, knowing I'll need my wits to fight any demons drawn to it.

"I hope you can fight because—"

He's gone.

I'm alone in the pouring rain and foggy night, my body vibrating. I'm clutching the fence like it's a lifeboat in the middle of an endless sea. It feels like he's still kissing me— all heat and white-hot breath skittering up and down my spine. I'm shaking.

Holy hellebore.

Maybe angels are real.

CHAPTER 2
THE COVEN CONVENES

At the edge of the cemetery, beneath an enormous willow tree, a squat shed stands with a battered green door and cinder block walls. I insert the skeleton key into the lock above the shed's rusted handle. I wait for the key to warm in my hand, for the storm-sky smell of magic to rush up around me, and then I turn it.

Instead of opening the shed to reveal gardening tools or buckets, or whatever the caretaker must need to keep the graves presentable, it's my bedroom.

My moonlit bed is still unmade, covers rumpled, pillows in a heap. The enormous desk taking up half a wall is littered with books and odd bits of unfinished spell work: dried herbs, half-burned candles, clay figures, bell jars, oils, stones, and a heap of notes. A battered armchair serving as Jinx's scratching post sits in the far corner of the room.

And that's the magic of the key: open any lock, any door, to anywhere.

I cast one last look over my shoulder at the foggy cemetery to be sure I'm not being followed. Whatever kind of major magic that guy has will certainly draw some big, bad, and very hungry demons.

I have no intention of being here when they arrive.

My strange, pale admirer seems to have truly gone. I don't understand what's just happened, but I also don't have the luxury of obsessing about it. I step across the threshold into my bedroom at Rowan House, nearly fifteen miles away, and throw the door shut behind me.

The second my soggy backpack slips off my shoulder, a hand clamps over my mouth. A large arm wraps around my waist, pinning my arms against my body. Without thinking, I call my magic. It uncoils like a snake ready to strike at my command.

The husky voice in my ear purrs a warning. "Easy there, Bishop. You'll need me alive to cover for your ass."

I relax, going soft in Alex's arms. He releases me and I turn to find him grinning.

His father is French and his mother is Haitian. Their union gifted him with a lovely dark complexion—a night sky without stars. The more time he spends in the sun, the more his soft curls turn golden brown. And it's getting long, his hair, so he's taken to pulling it into a ponytail at the nape of his neck the last few months—something he started around Thanksgiving.

Tonight, his shirt is Caribbean blue and sitting tight across his shoulders and chest.

I punch him in the arm. "I was about to shatter your kneecaps."

He snorts, his grin spreading wide enough to activate his dimples. "Lucky you didn't. Or I might have to tell the aunts you snuck out. Pain has a way of making me *very* vocal."

Alarm rockets through me. At the shock of being seized

in my own bedroom, and because truthfully, I'm still reeling from that kiss, I overlooked an obvious fact.

There are voices.

An excited murmur rumbles on the other side of my bedroom door.

"What happened?" I tiptoe across the dark room and peek through the crack. Because of the second-floor landing and rails, I can't see much.

"Emergency coven meeting," he says. "Someone rang the alarm thirty minutes ago."

My heart is pounding in my chest. I run through a rather long list of unsanctioned magic I've performed lately, wondering if any of it would warrant an inquisition.

Alex sees me chewing my lip and squeezes my shoulder. "I don't think it's about you. Unless you have something to confess?"

"No, not really," I say.

"Fine. Don't tell me why I covered for you." He doesn't sound mad, but Alex doesn't anger easily. It's the mark of a good demonkeeper. You can't be a slave to your emotions and battle demons.

"I'll tell you. Eventually," I amend. I already feel guilty. I don't like keeping secrets from Alex. It's one of the reasons why our relationship is so easy. I don't have to pretend with him. But if he knew what I was attempting to do, he'd try to stop me.

"We better go down. I've already stalled for too long." He steps forward and starts picking leaves out of my hair. "Pull this mess into a ponytail. That'll hide most of it, but you stink."

I elbow him hard in the ribs. He coughs up a laugh.

As soon as he slips out of the room, I snatch the pack out from under the bed and stuff it in the closet, between a box of winter clothes and a stack of old photo albums. I cast an invisibility charm. It makes the bag hard to see. Even if someone is looking for it, their eyes will slide right over it. I do this to Aunt Arty's car keys, too, whenever she pisses me off. I'm not usually a fan of passive aggression, but between witches it's essential. Direct aggression escalates quickly at the dinner table if everyone starts hurling hexes.

I grab fresh clothes and sneak into the bathroom at the end of the hall. Five minutes later, freshly scrubbed, I head downstairs.

As soon as I hit the bottom step, I know something horrible has happened.

My eldest aunt, Arty, serves as the leader and head spokesperson for our coven, so Rowan House would be a natural choice for a meeting place. But if this were mere coven business—or a demon that needed to be dealt with —only the hunters would be here.

And yet our den is overflowing with people.

Doors open and close constantly. The back door. The front door. Closets. The pantry. A hundred witches are crammed into the space and not half of them hunters.

I make polite apologies as I shoulder my way through the crowd toward my aunts, noting the tang of magic hanging in the air.

A warm hand clasps my forearm and pulls me forward.

Alex helps shuffle me toward the hearth, an enormous fireplace made with old stones. It stretches all the way to the top of the vaulted ceiling. Supposedly these ancient stones were given to us by the fey—who first taught witches to use magic. The hearth is the center of every witch house and the source of its power. It makes Rowan House more than a collection of walls and doors. It makes it alive. If we ever have to move away, the stones will be the first possession we're sure to carry with us, as cumbersome as they'd be.

When my Aunt Demi sees me, her long raven-black hair rippling over her shoulders, she reaches out to intercept me from Alex, pulling me up onto the stone ledge. "Stand with us, Amelia."

I do as I'm told even though standing in front of all these people like I'm about to give a speech is the last thing I want to do. Give me a horde of demons any day. Public speaking? No, thank you.

Arty watches me with a stare that could neutralize acid. She's clairvoyant, seeing the present and future with her mind's eye. If I wasn't wearing the smoky quartz around my neck, a talisman that's supposed to blind her to my actions, I'd be certain she knew all about the cemetery and what I'm up to. Even with the smoky quartz guarding me, I have to repress the urge to squirm under her glare. Over the roar of my pounding heart I ask, "What's going on?"

"Show her," Arty says. Her short spiky hair gives the impression of a rooster's comb, swooped back over elfin ears. Her hands sit folded one on top of the other on the head of her carved wooden cane. Beneath her bony fingers, I can just make out the shape of the snarling jaguar cut into the wood. "Get it over with."

Demi pulls me close against her and whispers into my ear, "The Priest family has been murdered."

Before I can react, Demi's power washes over me. As her cool hand cups my cheek, I'm flooded with her memories, but also her soothing energy.

The vision begins with Jinx leaping onto Demi's chest, his furry black paws swiping gently at her face until she gets up and follows him downstairs to the hearth. In the vision, the fire is burning blood red. A distress call from the

Priests' hearth spirit. Demi wakes Arty and they travel by key to the Priests' house to find it in ruin. Half of it is burned to the ground, giant holes punched through walls, plaster dust and wood scattered over beautiful antique furnishings. Their personal library is scorched black. The ash of burnt pages rises into the air on a breeze from the shattered windows.

Everyone on the property is dead.

Mr. and Mrs. Priest and their bonded demonkeepers. The wives and children of their keepers, throats torn out in their beds, pillows bloodied. And four of the five Priest children, all girls, burned and blackened.

Thirteen dead in all.

Demi takes her hand off my arm suddenly, and I stagger. Arty's hand is on my back. She whispers, "Steel spine, girl."

I suck in a breath as Demi places her hands on me again. No horrible visions this time. Instead, she floods me with love, warmth, safety. The terror and fear subside, but my cheeks are still wet with tears. I look heavenward, trying to calm myself. I tell myself to count the birds.

At least thirty birds, familiars of the witches gathering, perch on the wooden beams running across the vaulted ceiling. They chatter excitedly. Birds and cats are the most common familiar a witch can have since both are half in and half out anyway—already straddling the line between this world and the next. But plenty of people have other animals too, usually a native species connected to the lands they call home.

I spot Mrs. Weatherly's heron and Mr. and Mrs. Longbourne's doves. I see my own blue jay, Dragon, and Aunt Arty's speckled screech owl, Orion. The type of familiar a witch has says a lot about her. An animal only joins you in spirit if it recognizes something inside you that it admires.

Blue jays are supposed to be fearless. Faithful. They symbolize longevity, endurance, and strength. Resourcefulness. Boldness. A ferocity of mind.

I'm not convinced any of that describes me, but Aunt Arty likes to say, *You don't know when to quit, do you?*

No matter how hard I concentrate on Dragon's beautiful blue-gray feathers and his long, elegant tail, I can't chase away the image of the Priests' two youngest girls found dead, their skin charred black like burnt paper.

Every time I blink I see them, just ten and six, found holding hands.

My mind can't process the idea that the Priests are dead. I just saw them. I spoke to January, the eldest, two days ago.

Take this book, she'd begged. *I think Melody is messing with things she shouldn't.*

"Melody?" I ask, except it comes out choked. Melody Priest, the middle daughter, was the only one I didn't see in the vision.

I blink as if that will bring the world into focus. It doesn't.

"Missing," Arty says, her hawk eyes watching me. "And we are banning hunting until we know what's going on. Do *not* go out on your own again until we know more."

I don't miss the *again*.

So much for discretion, I think.

I spot Alex in the crowd. Concern radiates from him. He can see my tears, no doubt. He takes a step toward me, but I shake my head. I mouth the words, *I'm okay*.

His shoulders don't relax.

"Do you hear me?" Arty hisses. "It isn't safe to be out alone, reeking of magic and—"

"It's never safe," I say.

She clicks her tongue. She's done this since I was a kid, her way of telling me how much I annoy her.

But thankfully, she turns those sharp eyes toward the people crammed into Rowan House.

"Thank you for coming." Her gravelly voice projects easily over the crowd, which falls silent at once. "We'll get straight to it then. Just after midnight, we received a distress call from the Priests' hearthstone and went to investigate immediately. We found the Priests dead."

Voices cry out. Disbelief circulates through the crowd and the heat from all the bodies seems to magnify.

Someone says, "*All* of them?"

"Melody is missing," Aunt Demi clarifies. "But all the other souls have passed. And the entire compound has been incinerated."

Disbelief folds into alarm, and all I can do is stand there and play the part of stoic leader. This is what the aunts have groomed me for. As the only daughter from a First Family, I will be expected to do as they do now—lead. In times of crisis or when decisions must be made for the covens, the responsibility will lie with me.

This is even truer now. In the wake of the Priests' deaths, the Priors, Hatts, and Bishops are the only First Families left. And now I'm one of only three remaining daughters, along with Perdita and Colette Hatt. One, or all, of us will be expected to lead the coven.

I hope the Hatts like to rule because I despise politics. I only want to be out hunting.

When it looks like the room is going to devolve into full-blown panic, Arty slams the butt of her cane into the floor, banging it like a gavel. The room hushes immediately.

Demi unleashes her magic too, casting calm across the room with a simple charm muttered under her breath. Faces soften. Shoulders relax.

"Was it demons?" Mrs. Weatherly asks, clutching her gray tabby, Charm, to her chest.

"We believe so," Arty says, leaning into her cane. "Even without the ash and sulfur residues, the violent nature of the attack was"—her eyes fall on the younger children in the room, all still in their pajamas—"what we've come to expect from demons."

"How could one demon kill an entire family?" someone asks.

"And the Priests aren't weak! Little Elei could've taken on a demon alone if she had to!"

My heart twists at the image of Elei shielding her little sister's body with her own. Elei died protecting her sister, which is more than I could do for Phelia at that age.

"We believe it was more than one," Demi adds, still pouring relief and ease into the room.

Despite her best efforts, half the faces in the room go pale.

"Unheard of!"

"Impossible."

"Only carrion runs in packs, and they can't leave the in-betweens!"

"How did they even enter the Priests' house?"

"It's warded!"

"No evil can pass the hearthstone! Why didn't the hearth protect them?"

Arty brings down her cane again. "Until we know more, there is no point in all this speculation. And every second we waste here flapping our mouths costs us. Melody could still be out there. She might be severely wounded."

"Why can't you see her, Artemis?" Mrs. Weatherly asks.

An unsurprising question. Everyone in the coven has relied on Arty's all-seeing eye at one time or another.

"I don't know," Arty admits. "Either she's dead or she wears a charm. It's also possible she's using magic to hide herself. Maybe what killed her family is still in pursuit of her. We will know when we find her. Send your familiars. In any case, they can do what I cannot."

The birds on the rafters above ignite with their own urgent chirping. The Rowan House windows fly open and a flurry of flapping wings overtakes all other sound. Feathers fall on the crowd as birds rush into the night. They're followed by several cats—some of them quite fat—leaping out the low windows. My jay and Arty's owl are amongst the first out. An orange tabby that had been washing its ears beside Jinx hops down from the chair and prances across the hearth before jumping out the nearest window.

Demi nods to Jinx. "You too."

The black cat meows indignantly, as if to say he's done his part for the evening, *thankyouverymuch.*

Demi points to the window until Jinx, with an upturned tail, follows his ginger friend.

"Volunteers will return to the Priests' home with Demi and I to retrieve the bodies. We will dispose of them after all evidence is collected."

"We will honor them, of course," Demi interjects. She's always trying to soften Arty's business-first tone. For Arty, it's what needs to be done. She rarely cares how anybody *feels* about it.

Squeezing the head of her cane, she barrels on. "Everyone else, if you discover something, contact one of the First immediately. If you are not a hunter and you find a demon, do *not* approach it. If you *are* a hunter, I still recommend that you back down."

She gives me a sharp look.

"At least for now, until we know what is going on here. There is one more thing I must tell you, I'm afraid."

The steadily growing whispers hush again at the threat of more bad news. All eyes are on Arty.

"Their keepers were emptied," she says plainly. "We will need to consult the records to see how many demons were loosed. Then we will send out the hunters, when it's safe."

Emptied. I grit my teeth. All those years of sacrifice, of hard work, and for what? Just to have the demons let loose on the world again? This news will devastate Alex.

I find him slipping out the side door by the kitchen. He's with Lance, his boyfriend, another demonkeeper.

Everyone is talking over each other in a torrent of voices, but Arty is doing her best to pitch hers above the rest. "If you're volunteering to return to the Priests' house to collect evidence and prepare their remains, step forward."

I watch the door close behind Alex.

A few witches move toward the hearth to meet with the aunts. Most slip away back through the closets and pantries chattering nonstop to each other. I jump down off the hearth, hoping to catch up to Alex.

Arty grabs my hand.

"Don't go far. We need to talk," she says with all the ominous foreboding she can manage, which is a lot.

"I won't." I pull away, hoping I'm in trouble for anything but running around a graveyard alone at night while another family was being murdered in their beds by demons.

I weave through the crushing bodies of departing witches, mumbling polite goodbyes as I pass. I'm three feet from the back door when Dean Prior steps in front of me.

Dean Prior, the only child of Ysabel Prior, another powerful hunter from a First Family.

She's friends with my aunts. I like her. So it's a marvel that she bore such an insufferable son.

Hellebore. I don't need this right now. I need to catch up to Alex to see how he's taking the news. He was friends with the Priests and their keepers, the same as me.

"Are you all right?" Prior asks by way of introduction. He blinks his big blue eyes at me and juts out his lower lip. He thinks it's cute. I think it's nauseating.

"Fine, thank you. If you'll excuse me." I step around him, but he blocks my path again.

"It's just that I saw you crying after your aunt told you the news," he goes on, deliberately ignoring my clear attempt to escape. He flutters his eyelashes as if this will make a difference. On Colette Hatt, maybe. Not me.

I unclench my jaw. "Yes, well, anyone with emotions will find the image of burned and mutilated children upsetting, Prior."

"Don't call me Prior," he says, forcing another pout. "We aren't *just* hunters to each other, Amelia. We're so much more than that."

I debate between locking his knees together or his lips. I can probably only cast one charm or the other before someone notices. Everyone notices when I use magic. The aunts can cast a hundred charms under their breaths and no one bats an eyelash. I say the first word of a curse, and everyone's head turns. Arty says it's because I lack control.

Demi claims it's because my power is raw. Whatever the reason, it's annoying.

A rattle of the kitchen trash draws my eye. I peer around the island counter in time to see Prior's familiar, a big and bullish badger, digging through our garbage. When his head emerges, two chicken bones protrude from his mouth.

I *hate* Prior's familiar. It's unfair, I know, to detest an animal. But the badger is as much of a bully as Prior is. I once saw him try to eat Jinx. *Eat* him, headfirst. He'd only let go because I'd sprayed him ruthlessly with the water hose. If Jinx hadn't gotten up the birch tree in time, I'm convinced I would have witnessed the cat's murder.

"Prior, please do something about your badger."

He speaks as if he didn't hear me. "You're not worried you'll be attacked, are you? You know I would never let anything happen to you, Amelia. You're too important to me."

He takes my hand in his and I notice the black smudges on his fingers. It leaves sooty prints on the back of my hand. Maybe he's been up to a bit of spell work himself tonight.

I smile up at him and twist his index finger until he howls.

"We have rules about touching women without their consent. I *know* your mother taught you better."

His face is red and his jaw working.

"You're my *intended*." His composure slips. He takes a breath and slicks his hair back. "Is it a crime to be worried about my future wife?"

I snap my fingers and his knees lock together. Prior loses his balance and falls forward, slamming his shoulder hard against the edge of the countertop beside us. When he opens his mouth to squeal, I snap my fingers again to seal it shut.

The stragglers still standing at the back of the room, nearest the kitchen, feel my magic. They turn and look at me with creasing brows. Beyond them, the aunts are staring right at me over a sea of heads. Arty's brow rises. Demi's draws together.

Sweet silverweed.

I'll pay for this later. But right now, I don't have it in me to care.

I step over the boy writhing on the kitchen floor and through the back door out into the night, determined to find Alex before anyone else can stop me.

CHAPTER 3
ALEX'S DILEMMA

Rowan House is high in the Smoky Mountains, so it is even colder up here than it was in the cemetery. Every breath I take burns my chest. I whisper a spell, and heat blooms in my navel and washes over me. The fact I can remember this spell now and not when I was in the cemetery lets me know just how nervous I was about enacting my plan.

And *now* I have a ghoul in my freaking closet.

I follow a path of paving stones to the forest. The manicured lawn surrounding the mountain chalet gives way to unruly trees. The moon is still bright, so I'm able to see the outlines of basswood, sweet gum, black birch, and white ash trees leaning into one another as I wind my way into the forest. The scent of pine sap is thick in the air. I step as quietly as I can through the brush, moving toward the pulse of Alex's magic.

His concern burns like a flare in my mind, signaling distress.

I throw one leg over a log and use my hands to heft myself over the fallen tree trunk. My palms come away damp with moss and rainwater. More eerie mist hangs in the moonlight between the trees. I divert left off the path, still following the pulse.

Then the trees break open and two shadowy bodies take shape in the mist.

I creep closer, as close as I dare, before crouching behind a red maple tree. It's big enough to hide me from the pair as I strain to hear what's being said.

"That's *why* you should be with me," Lance hisses. His voice is high, his frustration nearly a growl. "I don't understand why you won't just—"

Alex murmurs something too low for me to hear, but his deep voice is unmistakable. How many times has he uttered reassurances to me in that tone?

Since Phelia died? Countless.

Lance throws up his hands. "Sleepovers aren't enough anymore, Alex. I want you *there*. I want you in *our* bed. *Every* night."

Another reassurance from Alex vibrates through the air.

Lance yanks himself out of Alex's arms. "But you're *not* her chevalier. You'll never be."

My heart skips a beat and guilt as sharp as ice cuts through me.

Lance turns to leave but Alex catches his arm at the last minute and pins those hands to his chest. He lets go only to run a hand through his own hair. When Lance tilts up his chin to look Alex in the eyes, they kiss.

I duck behind the tree, my face burning. I feel like a creep.

You're not her chevalier.

Lance is talking about me. How many times has Alex asked to be my keeper? And how many times have I refused him? He's my chevalier in every sense of the word

—except the one that matters to the coven. We hunt together. We look out for each other. I can recognize his magic in a room full of spellcasters—just as he knows mine.

And I would die for him without hesitation. He's family.

I could have bonded with Alex years ago. But when I was initiated into the rank of hunters after my first demon kill at just thirteen, he was still training. As the youngest hunter the coven has ever seen, no one expected me to bond with a keeper in the beginning.

Still, everyone expected me to choose Alex. Eventually.

We'd been friends forever. We grew up together here on the Rowan House property because Arty's chevalier is Alex's dad.

But then two years turned into four. Then into six.

And Alex is still a trainee.

My reluctance to bond with him or anyone is seen as equal parts arrogance—like maybe I think I'm too good to work in partnership with anyone—and rejection.

People have begun to think there's something wrong with Alex. Even though any witch who stands within a hundred yards of him can sense that his magic is strong. If he weren't so loyal to me and if the other unbonded hunters weren't so worried about offending me, a Bishop, he would've gotten snapped up ages ago.

But as much as Alex might believe that binding our magics together will make us stronger, faster, unstoppable in the fight against demons, I can't overlook the cost of that bond.

Bonding with Alex will make me his executioner. I *refuse* to let that happen.

Lance pushes past me, following the path back toward Rowan House. I remain pressed against the tree and try to still my thrashing heart as cold moonlight slides over my skin.

It takes a great deal of will to keep every muscle perfectly still until he's out of earshot.

I'm about to sneak back myself when Alex says, "It's rude to eavesdrop, Bishop."

I step out from behind the tree to face him. I grimace. "Sorry."

I go to him like a dog with a tail between her legs. His short curls are springing up around his face in the humidity. A few damp tendrils stick to his cheeks. His mouth is ruddy from all the kissing.

"Seriously, I didn't mean to be a creeper. I just wanted to know if you were okay. Why did you guys come all the way out here? Did you miss that part about a murdering pack of demons being on the loose?"

"Yeah, but I'd rather be out of earshot of everyone else when my boyfriend yells at me."

I purse my lips. "Sorry I ruined that for you."

He squeezes the back of his neck. "He still wants me to move to the Hatt compound."

"So do it," I say.

"I don't want to. I belong here." He gestures in the direction of his dad's cabin just on the other side of these trees, less than a quarter of a mile from the back door of Rowan House.

I get why Lance is mad at me. Because Lance is bound to Perdita Hatt, he lives with her as is custom. Since Alex is unbound, there's no real reason why he can't go live with his boyfriend.

He—like most people—thinks that Alex is more vulnerable as an unbonded demonkeeper. That by holding out on him, I'm putting his life at risk. And no doubt the Priests' murders probably solidified these beliefs. I'm sure that it's also annoying because clearly, I'm ruining Lance's chance at domestic bliss.

"You should move in with him," I say. "I'll get you guys a puppy. To celebrate."

He puts his hands on his hips. "I don't want to move in with him."

"I thought you were in love."

"I am, but I'm *twenty*." He says this as if I don't already know. "No one has to live with their boyfriend at twenty. And when will it be my turn?"

"Your turn to what?" I ask.

He smirks. "To catch you making out with someone in the woods."

Alex is trying to direct the conversation away from Lance and their problems. I see what he's doing and I go along with it.

"Don't hold your breath," I say.

"You're too picky."

"Selective," I say.

He folds his arms. "No one is perfect."

"I don't need someone who's perfect. I just need someone who doesn't act like they're twelve."

"Maybe you're into older men." His grin grows wicked. "I've seen the way you smile at Ibis."

I snort at the mention of the mysterious shopkeeper on 42nd Street. "Maybe I just like guys who like books. Or wear glasses. Why does it have to be that he's older?"

Alex's grin only deepens. "So you *are* into him?"

"Shut up." I aim for a lighthearted tone, but my voice is flat. Humorless. I mean, Ibis is hot in a bookish way, but have I truly been as into someone as Alex and Lance are into each other?

The sharp cheek bones and bright eyes from tonight's cemetery dance flash in my mind. My whole body heats at the thought of that single kiss. Of the way I'd leaned so hungrily into it, pressing my body into his as if it's all I've ever wanted to do.

Okay. Maybe.

Maybe I could be that into someone.

Alex's frown falters. "What did Demi show you?"

I shake my head. I can't bear to say it.

On the best of days, I hate talking, but it seems especially useless in moments like this when no words will do. Instead, I lift my hand in question. It hovers six inches from his exposed neck. I'm searching his face, trying to read him as easily as he reads me, but I'm not as good at it. I wait for a visible sign, a signal that I have his permission. Finally, he nods, and I place one cool hand on the side of his throat, my thumb resting on its hollow.

I show him everything as it was shown to me. The Priests' house. The wreckage of the slaughter. The bodies, especially those of the Priests' keepers. That is what he cares about most. The residual magic that shows the keepers were emptied *before* they were killed, meaning all that sacrifice was for nothing.

His eyes pinch closed and he places a hand over mine. A silent *Please, stop.* I shut off the vision, but I've got tears in my eyes again. Neither of us says anything. He takes a step away from me and turns, giving me his back. I let my hand fall and give him the space he needs.

My stomach hardens into a cold stone. A pit.

"I'm sorry." My voice cracks. "We'll find out what did this. We'll make sure it never happens again."

After a long pause, he nods, still struggling to find his voice.

I understand. It sucks. It sucks when you do your very best. When you fight like the world depends on it and yet it still isn't enough.

The strongest witches hunt the demons that plague this world. The keepers can contain them, but we can't kill them. They feed on magic. They can't be killed by it.

That's why we need the demonkeepers. A hunter's magic is offensive, made for attacking. The keeper's magic is passive. They heal, restore balance. Their tremendous regenerative powers allow them to house demons in their own bodies, using their brand of magic to suppress, neutralize, and control them. And a demon can't feed on that kind of magic.

So the best we've managed in all these centuries of war against the demons is containment.

The hunters fight them, weaken them, and then the keepers absorb them—then there's one less demon in the world to hurt anybody.

But when a demonkeeper can't hold the demons any longer—maybe their limit is thirty demons or a hundred and thirty, it doesn't matter—the end result is the same.

When that moment comes, when the demonkeeper is finally overpowered by the sheer number of demons inside them, then a witch has the responsibility to track, trap, and kill her possessed keeper.

When the keeper's soul passes from this world, it will incinerate the demons.

That momentary exposure to the divine light that emerges at death is the only way we know how to truly kill a demon. Even our best alternative, a blessed bell jar, is a conditional and temporary solution.

Snobby, elitist bastards like Prior think keepers are weak because they don't use offensive magic. Alex can fight like a warrior, with his fists and a blade. But his magic is for healing and containment.

I think their magic is amazing. It's so much harder to contain and transmute darkness inside you, to heal what has been broken, than it is to throw a hex or a spell. I believe that without keepers, demons would run this world.

But yeah, that's the hunter-keeper reality. That if I bond with him, I will one day have to kill him.

Kill him. Alex. *My* Alex.

Kill him as if I don't love him.

As if he's not my best friend. As if he hasn't been there every day of my life through every loss and heartbreak.

I can't do it.

I can't—I—

"Don't worry." Alex wraps his arms around me. He can sense my despair, no doubt, but has no idea what's causing it. "We'll stop whatever it is before it has a chance to hurt anyone else. Lance thinks it was a full demon. Or some monster we've never seen."

He rests his chin on my hair.

I open my mouth to protest, but then I remember the stranger's feral eyes flashing, his power to incinerate ghouls with a blinding light and make girls magic-drunk on kisses.

"It's possible there are creatures we've never heard of." I absorb his warmth in the chilly evening.

That gets his attention. "Creatures you've never heard of? That a *Bishop* has never heard of? With your extensive library and obsession with history?"

I stare up at the moon and wonder how many witches have done the same throughout time, wondering and wishing as I am. Praying for a miracle even as hopelessness devours their heart.

He arches a brow in question. "Is this about the cemetery?"

I turn away.

He grabs my shoulders and spins me back to face him. He holds me at arm's length. "Are you *sure* you don't want to tell me what you're up to?"

He looks half playful, half truly desperate.

Sure! I'm launching a dangerous and suicidal mission to save you from being torn apart by demons. Also, I made out with a stranger.

When I still don't answer, he shakes his head and says, "Fine, but if some monster rips my throat out because you didn't warn me, I'll be right there with Phelia, haunting your ass."

"Way to play the guilt card, Laveau."

And it works.

"Okay, *okay*. I did see *two* things of note tonight when I was in the cemetery. First there seems to be an unusual uptick in demon activity, which is probably connected to the Priests' murders. And second there was this shiny—guy."

He arches a brow. "I'm listening."

I tell Alex what I saw. Or at least, I give him an edited version. I describe the man and his abilities the best I can, but I conveniently leave out all the details that might suggest *why* I was there in the first place. And, of course, I leave out the kissing.

My meager explanation only stokes his curiosity.

"Wow. He sounds hot. Was he hot?"

I do some sort of weird, noncommittal shrug.

He holds his hands up. "*Wait.* He shot *light* from his *hands*? Before jumping over a nine-foot wrought-iron fence and disappearing? And you just happened to see this because you went for a moonlit walk in the rain because you couldn't sleep. *That's* your story?"

"It's a good story."

He barks a laugh. "It's pathetic. You better come up with a better one before Arty gets ahold of you."

I remember my aunt's warning glare back at the house. *Don't go far. We need to talk.*

"You know, if we were bound together, you couldn't do that," he says. "Run off into the night alone. If I could find you anywhere using the bond, you'd be safer from...What are you doing again?"

"Nice try. No more questions."

"Whatever it is, I forbid you from getting hurt." His smile becomes sad and soft at the edges. "You are not allowed to die, too."

Too. Because I'm not the only one who loved Phelia.

"Gah! Hunting demons alone in a cemetery? *Really*, Bishop?" He puts me in a headlock. "What did I do to deserve such a reckless friend?"

"Something horrible." I push against his elbow, trying to squirm free. He just picks me up in a bear hug and squeezes me harder. Wheezing, I pant, "You were probably Hitler in your past life. Stalin. Christopher Columbus."

A noise catches our attention. We stop grappling with each other like children and turn toward the sound. Lo and behold, there's Prior. Gawking at us, jaw working.

Alex releases me.

"You got something to say to me, Prior?" I call out to him.

He doesn't answer me. He only turns away and slinks back into the shadows.

CHAPTER 4
DREAM A LITTLE DREAM

I'm standing in a moonlit field. Heavy armor sits across my shoulders and back. It shines like a river at night, reflecting the moonlight pouring down on the field. I have a helmet that covers the side of my face and head, a slender piece of metal stretching over the bridge of my nose. A massive crest of blue jay plumage spills from the helmet and down my shoulders like a wild mane.

I have never felt this powerful, this strong in both body and magic, in all of my life. I know I'm dreaming. And knowing that you're in a dream makes it easier to accept whatever happens next.

Part of the strangeness of this dream is that my vision is better at night. With these amazing eyes, I'm looking at a damaged gate in front of me. It stands several hundred feet tall. It's made of stone, crowned with two carved herons turned toward one another. They mark the entrance. The stone gate is covered in spiderweb cracks because something enormous has slammed into it from the other side. Worse, its magic is failing. It's the loss of the ward that concerns me, not the damaged stone. If the magic keeping this gate sealed breaks, my people will be slaughtered.

Even in the dream, I can feel them. My people. They've been hidden away, kept safe from battle, but still they call out to me.

Be patient, I whisper to their fearful hearts and minds. *The moon is with us now.*

Queen Sephone, The Living. She hears us, they reply. *Per Sephone's power, by her grace and will alone. Per Sephone we are beloved. She will guard and keep us until sleep. She will guard and keep us until Queen Naja, The Child of the Dreaming, reigns again and—*

They fall back on these old prayers.

"What's disrupting the ward, my queen?" my lieutenant asks. I do not turn my head to look at him. But somehow, I know his voice as well as my aunts' or as well as Alex's or Phelia's. It's a voice I've always known, and in my heavy armor, I'm glad to hear it beside me.

"Deception. Trickery. They want us focused on this gate. Why?" I ask.

"You think they aren't really here? On the other side?" He speaks in the same sweet, melodic voice.

Look at him. Show me his face, my dreaming mind begs.

But I don't so much as peek at him from the corner of my eyes. *Why?*

As soon as I think the question, I know. If he's hurt from battle, if she sees him bleeding, it will upset her. And the queen can't be distracted now. Her will alone is holding the fragile magic of the gates intact. If she loses focus, all will be lost. And her lieutenant knows this too. He hangs slightly back, so that she cannot even see him in her periphery.

"Ciel?" I whisper. I am the queen again. That's her voice sliding over my tongue and lips. "Are you hurt badly?"

"It's nothing," he says. "I'll go check the Southern Gate."

I cast my mind out over the fields, over the bodies of the slain monsters who managed to slip into our world. A hawk consents to be my eyes and I slip into her mind. She doubles back high over the Southern Gate so that I can see it for myself.

Only I can't see enough.

A thick fog hides the stone wall of the Southern Gate, hides the encroaching fields. The moonlit lavender fields shine as the hawk glides silently overhead.

Wake up, Amelia, some part of me begs. *Don't look. Wake up.*

But I don't wake up.

"Something is wrong," I say to my lieutenant. "I can't feel them."

All the soldiers I sent ahead to the Southern Gate are silent in my mind. And they shouldn't be. I should feel them as well as my own heartbeat.

Don't send him to the gate, my dreaming mind begs, the half-awake and wiser part of me. *Don't send him!*

But the dream rolls on and the Southern Gate materializes before me. Its high stone arches are whitewashed and iridescent in the full moon's light. Two stone vultures frame the gate, again turned toward one another. They stand watchful, peering down into the black passage.

A broken gate.

A *wide*-open gate.

Bodies of the dead—my dead—lie scattered in heaps like overturned earth. My power touches each one, looking for the souls within. But they are gone, eaten by the monsters who breached our lands. And without a soul, I cannot resurrect them. They are truly lost to me.

A loss as sharp as a blade through my heart.

Dark shapes shift in the fog, and I know we are not alone. The army at my back bristles, but I touch their hearts and calm them. We cannot attack blindly. We wait to see the challenge clearly.

The Lord of Hell steps forward.

In full armor, he stands at the edge of the mist, only half revealed. The fur along his back and legs is the same silver-gray, his eyes fiendishly gold, even in this light. He makes a small gesture and the mist dissipates, revealing the mass of a great and terrible army at his back. Grotesque and half-formed creatures crowd around him, jostling one another with eagerness.

"You've brought all of Hell with you," I say calmly.

I am not afraid. Not for myself.

"Unlike my predecessors, I would never make the mistake of underestimating you," the invading king says, his voice surprisingly beautiful.

In one swift motion, with speed I can barely register, the king shoves his blade through my lieutenant's chest and rips out his soul.

Before I can bring the wrath of the heavens down on him, he holds the dancing flame of it out for me to see. "You can save him!"

He cries this paltry offer as if he wasn't the one who tried to end my lieutenant's life.

The small, bright orb of his soul pulses beautifully in the monster's palm. The blue crystalline energy swirls, alive. It burns brighter, even more precious to me because of the darkness surrounding its tender flame.

"How *dare* you." My voice is murderously cold.

White-hot magic erupts around me, ready to extinguish all life on the field. The army at my back inches forward, and the king's army does the same, the beasts snapping their jaws in anticipation. My aching heart screams its own battle cry.

...Ciel, Ciel, Ciel, Ciel...

"Before you lay my army to waste with a single word from your enchanting lips, remember that the heart of me remains in my domain," the king says, his gaze measuring my every movement. His fur bristles in the wind of my power as I struggle to control myself, the power that wants to devour him. "If you kill this makeshift body, I will not die."

I stare into those yellow eyes and feel a hatred unlike any I've known before. I'm practically burning with it.

"If you cast me back to Hell, I will take him with me. Then it will be *you* marching on my gates, will it not?"

"I wonder why you took the trouble to come here at all. Has Hell outgrown its boundaries?" A cold disdain drips from my words.

"I don't want Elysium, or even the gilded city of Elysia," he says, offering me the beautiful flame. "I want only you."

The world trembles.

No.

I'm trembling.

"Amelia."

The dream fades and my eyes open. It's Demi shaking me awake. Her raven-black hair falls into my face. All the Bishop women have the same dark, bird-like features inherited from our mothers, but Demi's sharp eyes and hooked nose seem larger than usual as she leans over me.

At first, all I can do is blink at her. The dream, despite all its depth, lingers, and I'm desperately grasping at details, any details. But it's like trying to hold on to sand. The harder I squeeze the faster each grain slips through my fingers.

Yet I do hold on to two startling facts.

First, the lieutenant in my dream is the stranger who kissed me in the cemetery. I saw his face clearly the moment before the invading king slid a blade through his chest.

The second fact: now I know his name.

Ciel.

See-elle.

And there is something so familiar about it, like remembering a song I loved a long time ago, forgotten until someone played the melody.

Now the lyrics are rushing back. Like they've been on the tip of my tongue for a long time.

"Are you okay?" Demi asks. She places a hand on my knee and squeezes me. "Your magic's—"

Just beneath the surface. Yes, I know. I can feel it. But it's fading now.

"I'm fine," I say, and sit up, my back against a soft mound of pillows. Of course, I wonder if this is a desperate lie I'm telling myself. I got kissed in the cemetery and now I'm dreaming about the guy. Have I been bewitched? Is this some kind of spell? Fairy tales warn us about magic kisses for a reason, you know.

The couch across from me is vacant. Alex and I waited up for the aunts to return, but clearly he snuck away without waking me. Not surprising since he has breakfast every morning with his dad. It's a promise between them.

Without the crush of bodies, my aunts' den looks quite different in the daylight. The grand room with its cathedral ceiling is lined with glass windows, and the mountains stretch beyond the forest. This view gives the impression that we're high in the trees.

Despite the cheery spring light on Demi's face, she looks exhausted. When she draws her ash-stained clothes around her, I catch a glimpse of her strong, olive-skinned calves.

"Did you find Melody?" I ask, dragging a hand over my face as if this will clear the last of the dream clinging to me.

She shakes her head. "No. We'll have to keep looking."

"Alex and I can go out," I say. "He's the best tracker. You should have started with him."

"No," she says, her mouth pressing tight. "We won't have any of you out there until we know what we're dealing with."

"But I want—"

She cuts me off without missing a beat. "What *I* want is for you to tell me what happened with Ysabel's boy. You're too old for me to apologize on your behalf anymore, Amelia. No one is going to believe in your *accidents* any longer."

I'm not sure what to say.

"Please," Demi adds when she sees my hesitation.

I arch a brow. "He called me his 'intended.' *Again.*"

She doesn't even look surprised. "We told his mother that you've refused his offer."

"Yes, well, I don't think she's told Prior. He won't give it up. If he doesn't quit, I'm going to throw him off this mountain and have Dragon peck out his eyes on the way down."

"He's ambitious."

Anger explodes behind my eyes, red hot and dangerous. Dishes in the kitchen rattle on the shelves. Demi places one hand on my leg and the fury melts from my body just as quickly as it came. At first, this angers me more. *Who does she think she is, trying to take my anger from me? I deserve to be mad!* But as my rage increases so does her strength. She matches me pitch for pitch, and I know she isn't even trying.

"I'm sorry, but I can't let you bring the house down. Even if you *are* entitled to your feelings."

All I'm left with is a weak retort. "I'm no one's trophy."

A flash of the king's face and his golden eyes burn in my mind. I suddenly sympathize with the queen more. It seemed she'd been dealing with an entitled jerk as well.

"You're *our* trophy. Our darling girl." Demi flicks her eyes to indicate Arty as the other half of her *we*. She pushes the hair out of my eyes and uses this touch to send me her feelings. Fear. Concern. And an overwhelming wave of gratitude. *We are so lucky to have you. It could have been you dead in those ashes. I don't know what I would do if it was you. If we lose you too—*

I flinch.

As suddenly as they came, her thoughts and emotions disappear. She cuts them off midstream, the second she realizes I'm in her mindscape. She meant to send me her feelings, not her thoughts. She's done this ever since Phelia and I were little girls. It was her way of making sure we knew how loved we were. How better to know someone loves you than to feel that love coursing through you. But she hadn't meant to send me the fear or her dark thoughts.

"I'm sorry," she says. "But we *do* love you."

"I'm not marrying him," I say, trying for levity. The night has been bleak enough.

"We'd never force you to."

"Good," I say, lifting my chin. "Because I'm not."

And I mean it.

He only wants me because I am a daughter from a First Family. He wants me for the power my family commands politically. For the status our children would have. Prior himself descends from a First Family through his mother, Ysabel. But witches are matriarchal. We follow our mother's line. His children will bear their mother's last name. Prior can only hope to maintain his power and influence if he marries into another prominent line.

After the deaths of the Priests, Prior has only three remaining choices. I'm not interested. Perdita Hatt is already engaged. That leaves only Perdita's younger sister, Colette, who actually adores him. I'm not sure why he doesn't expend his energy there instead. If Melody is alive she could be a fourth option—but I doubt that Melody, wherever she is, is thinking of anything as ridiculous as marriage right now.

"Doesn't Lady Prior have family in Europe? He'd have more choices if he went abroad. Let him go torture someone else for a few years."

"That's not a bad idea," Demi says. "I'll speak to Ysabel again."

I lay my head back on the sofa cushion. "If he won't go there's always a love spell. If we make Prior fall in love with Colette, then he won't be my problem anymore."

She frowns. "Love magic is forbidden, Amelia."

I'm grinning too much. And the more I grin, the more horrified Aunt Demi looks.

"*I* won't cast a love spell."

"Amelia—"

"I won't. Probably. I'm just saying it's *very* consensual. On Colette's end."

My aunt mutters something under her breath as she pushes away from the sofa. I stand and stretch. All I want to do is go upstairs and crawl into bed. I haven't slept enough.

My burning and itching eyes say so. But maybe a biscuit with butter and honey will be good before I fall into bed.

I'm halfway to the kitchen when Demi turns, listening to something only she can hear. Then she says, "Artemis wants to see you in the library."

My stomach turns on a dime. I swallow, hearing a click in my throat. "Of course she does."

CHAPTER 5

WE WITCHES THREE

B efore I even reach the library door, I hear the *tap, tap* of Arty's cane. The steps are sluggish and clumsy. She's tired then. All that searching through the rubble must have left her hip aching. This means she'll be grumpier than usual.

Lovely.

Her left knee and hip were broken years ago in a fight with a demon. She's lucky. After all, most hunters come away with worse injuries. In my most morbid moments, I wonder what major injury I'll sustain first. Will I lose a finger or my whole hand severed at the wrist? Maybe an eye? I might look cool with an eyepatch.

If I manage to die and keep all my parts, it means I got off easy. Just ask my mother. She died hunting. And when the demon was done with her, we didn't have much of a body to bury under our sacred tree. I suppose death by demon is better than losing a daughter. At least my mother was spared that misfortune.

I knock on the library door and it opens on its own.

Like the rest of Rowan House, the library has the same

chalet look. High ceilings with long wooden beams running across the top like rafters. Windows letting in all the light include a window seat for reading. Something large like an eagle cuts a dark shape across the spring sky. The walls that aren't windows have built-in bookcases from floor to ceiling.

The room smells like books, old books. The red leather chairs and a cream-colored loveseat angle toward the windows. Shadows dance over the red Tapiz rug.

Behind the enormous desk, Arty sits reading from a thick book. Her black eyes meet mine over the rim. "Start by telling me why there's graveyard dirt all over your room."

I don't say a word.

The fireplace ignites on its own, a fresh flame leaping from the smoldering cinders.

I roll my eyes to hide my creeping panic. "Don't be dramatic."

"You smell like Hell. With a capital *H*."

"You aren't smelling so fresh either." I sit in the red leather chair opposite her on the other side of the desk. The fire roars at her back. I refuse to confess.

She isn't going to give up either. This is usually the problem with our conversations. "Visiting your sister's grave isn't a crime. You can see her whenever you want. I just wish you'd do it in the daytime when it's safer. Surely you know the danger of roaming the in-betweens alone at night. You reek of magic. A demon is bound to notice you."

Does she really think I was only visiting Phelia? Or does she suspect more and this is just a lure?

"Especially now that we have something dangerous on the loose," she adds, unblinking.

I arch an eyebrow. "Last night you said it might be more than one."

Arty regards me with a heavy stare and I'm suddenly very grateful for the smoky quartz crystal hanging around my neck.

If not for the cloudy gray stone, I'd be just as vulnerable to Arty's omniscient gaze as everyone else. Demi gave me the crystal. *Every witch deserves the freedom to make her own choices—and mistakes.*

"Well?" I press. "Do you really think the demons are working together?"

Because it's been to our advantage that they're like cats. Lawless. Uncoordinated.

"I don't know," she says at once. "I can't see."

My blood freezes. "You can't see? The demon? De*mons?* Or you didn't see the attack coming?"

"Any of it. I haven't seen any of it." Her eyes fall to the quartz around my neck. "Quartz burns them. So it must be magic. A deliberate shield of some kind. I think."

"You *think?*"

"If I *knew* I wouldn't be sitting here pretty as a peach, combing my books, now would I?"

I let it go. Her frustration sparks in the air. In this way, Arty and I are just alike. We hate not knowing. For a clairvoyant as powerful as she is, this must be pure torture.

"You should go to bed," I tell her. "You're exhausted."

Arty grunts and hobbles across the room. She pulls a book from the shelf and tosses it onto her desk with a heavy thud. A moon dial and a handful of citrine stones bounce.

"There's the other matter to discuss. Not only were you in the cemetery in the middle of the night, *alone...*" she begins.

I fall back into the chair and get comfortable. I brace for the approaching lecture.

"You cast to harm in our house during a coven meeting," she continues. "That's a direct violation of our neutrality laws."

"Prior started it."

She sighs. "I wish you would run instead of fight."

"You didn't teach me to run."

She opens her mouth to argue but nothing comes out. Her face pinches in pain. And for a long moment, she only stands there, a hand flat on the pile of books in front of her. She motions for me to come around and sit in her chair. I do, if a little confused, feeling the warmth of the fire as I slide into the high-back seat.

"Let me teach you something else then." It's her pedantic voice. "First line of defense is knowledge. I want you to find answers to the questions I wrote down here."

She taps a piece of paper on the desk. I read the list.

Demons who target the First?
Demons of fire?
Non-demons that may target the First?
Consult lunar, solar, and water calendars. Cycles? Anything due to awaken from dormancy?
The strength of fifty demons?
Can blind a clairvoyant?
The fey???

I look up, unable to hide my disbelief. "The fey? You're reaching."

No one has heard from the fey since the beginning. They're little more than, well, fairy tales now. Supposedly, it was the fey who brought the magic and taught a handful of human families the power to protect themselves and their communities. These families were called the First, or sometimes the First Families, because they are direct descendants from those original lines. The magic handed down from fey to witch was supposed to be stronger than the offshoots that came later.

But no one has seen the fey since—if they ever saw them at all. I have doubts that's where the magic came from. Why? Because we also have legends about how the moon turns into a black cat and prowls around once a month, which is why we have the new moon. So, forgive me if I don't believe every tall tale I read.

"And you can't mean *fifty* demons," I say. "If this attack really had the damage of fifty demons then it must have been a group of them, right? A pack?"

Arty isn't listening. She's turned away from me again, pulling books off the shelves.

I look harder at the shaky script. It isn't the steady, looping letters I'm used to seeing. And I know Arty's hand-writing. She's penned my every lesson since I could read.

She was trembling when she wrote this. "You're in a lot of pain."

"We all must get acquainted with pain, Amelia. There is no better teacher."

I close the books and try to stack them neatly. "Can I ask you something? Can someone bewitch you with a kiss?"

Arty arches a brow.

What worries me is the dream's connection to Ciel. I can't help but feel that his kiss started this.

I push despite her suspicious gaze. "Like, can a creature kiss you and you start thinking about them all the time? I guess I'm asking if there's any magic in kissing? Can some-thing happen if you're kissed a certain way?"

"Are we calling men creatures now?" Arty's brow arches

even higher. A knowing smile crooks the corner of her lips. "The short answer, Amelia, is *yes*. Kissing can lead to things. We had this discussion when you were nine. Do we really need to have it again? Is this about Prior's boy?"

"Goddess, no. If you ever see me kiss him, assume I'm possessed." Embarrassment heats my cheeks. "Never mind. Forget I asked about the kissing."

"*Sure.*" She throws a few more books on the desk in front of me before limping out of the room.

I listen to her cane on the stairs, to the heavy way she leans into it, pausing on the first landing. The first real pang of worry runs through me. She went very easy on me just now.

She's only done that twice before in my life. The day she found me screaming on the riverbank, when Phelia died. And on the night I killed my first demon. It had been Arty who reached me before the others. Arty, who found me soaked in blood, who ran her hands over my small body searching for a wound. I can still clearly see her face, seized by relief once she realized not a drop of the blood was mine.

In the quiet library, I read at her desk. I take notes as I go, but with the lovely heat of the fire at my back and the spring rain beginning to belt the large windows, exhaustion overtakes me.

I doze off, reentering the queen's dream.

I only *just* make it to the Southern Gate, see the invading king's golden eyes, when voices wake me. I lift my head from the desk.

Someone is in the hall outside. I open the door and see the aunts putting on their coats.

"What is it? What's happened?" I'm squinting, my voice thick with sleep.

"We found Melody," Demi says, pulling her trapped

hair free of the coat's collar. "While we're gone, please make the spare room ready for her."

I freeze in the doorway, my hand on the handle. "What room?"

Arty doesn't even look up. "The only bedroom in this house we aren't using."

"*Phelia's* room?"

"Melody is going to need it more," Demi says apologetically. "She may be with us for a very long time."

CHAPTER 6
THE FIRST TEST

I decide I'd rather try my luck with the ghoul than clean out Phelia's room. One look at her closed bedroom door is enough to send me to my closet for my backpack.

Thanks to the skeleton key around my neck, when I open my closet door for the second time, candles spring to life in the Bishop vault. One after the other, wicks ignite, until all eighteen candles along the walls are burning. Then the candelabra overhead does the same. The vault's inner chamber glows with the dancing light.

I step through and close the door behind me, noting the sharp temperature shift between this deep underground chamber and my warm bedroom miles away.

The fire dancing along the wall seems brighter because the walls and floor are painted black. This vault serves as an interrogation room. A windowless bunker without an exit.

The demon vault can only be entered by skeleton key, and only by a *particular* skeleton key. This vault belongs solely to the Bishop family and is accessible only with our keys. For this reason, I only have to worry about the aunts finding me.

Of course, this also means that if something goes horribly wrong, I'll be trapped down here with only demons for company. Indefinitely. Because who knows when the aunts might think to look in the vault for me.

In the center of the candlelit room is a demon trap: blood, crushed stones, and chalk mixed into the concrete to make a permanent mark on the floor. The octagon mark is meant to bind a demon to the spot while we ask it questions.

I pull the blessed bell jar filled with black smoke from my backpack and place it at the edge of the demon trap. The glass clinks as I set it on the concrete floor.

I also lay out the plastic-wrapped book January Priest gave me and place the athame by its side, safe beyond the marked border of the trap. I wait for my eyes to adjust. Once they do, I'm able to see the room more clearly. A path leads between two rows of shelves to the back of a separate antechamber. There are rows and rows of these shelves. Boxes of unused candles, empty bell jars, salt, and drying herbs—everything a witch might need to control a demon, in addition to her own power, of course.

I slide the jar into the center and unscrew the cap. As soon as the black smoke billows out, I slide the glass away so it doesn't get trampled or smashed. I'd like not to waste a jar if I can help it.

The black smoke solidifies into a suggestion of a body.

Bulbous yellow eyes fix on me and the ghoul lunges, its jaws snapping. The stench of death hits me. My stomach turns. Carrion always smells bad, but I'd forgotten how much worse it is in this closed space without circulation.

The ghoul reaches the edge of the trap and hisses in pain. Steam rises from its flesh like water thrown on a hot grill. It stumbles back with a whimper.

"Yeah, well, that's what you get for trying to eat my face." I go down to my knees in front of the book and slide the athame closer.

I try to conjure the courage to read the book.

It isn't the idea of reading it that makes my pulse climb into my throat.

When January Priest gave me the book, I wasn't sure why it was wrapped in plastic. But as soon as I tried to read it, I figured it out *fast*.

This isn't just a spell book. It's a book that *bleeds*.

The plastic sticks together as I peel it apart. I have to use my nails to separate the fine layers and expose the book's cover. It looks even more horrifying in the candlelight.

The pages have a rubbery texture like raw chicken skin, and already my fingertips are coming away red with the blood that never stops welling up from the binding. If I'm to believe the rumors, this book is all that's left of the demon Belphegor.

Surprise, demons are a cutthroat class of creatures, and no sooner than one king is made, there's another demon trying to usurp him. One such king, Asmodeus, had a faithful servant named Belphegor. Belphegor fell asleep on the job and Asmodeus was almost killed by a usurper seeking to dethrone him. Even though he failed to protect the king, Asmodeus insisted that Belphegor honor his pledge to serve him for all time, but since he was a useless bodyguard, he would fulfill his oath as a different kind of protector—a guardian of the king's most potent spells. To punish his servant, he turned Belphegor into this spell book, leaving enough of him alive to bleed for all eternity.

I don't know if any of this is true, but the book does bleed, the paper does feel like skin, and when I press my fingers to the cover, I swear I feel a throbbing heartbeat. Frankly, that's enough for me.

And why, *oh why*, Amelia, would you read such a book?

If there is a spell anywhere in the universe that might tell me how to actually kill a demon, I think it'll be in this book.

Look at me giving it a go.

My fingers flip the wet pages. My eyes glance over spell titles as I turn page after page:

The Enemy of My Enemy
Death Draught
PACT TO PACT
Terror Heart
A Soul, Halved
To Send A Clay Envoy

Finally, I find one that looks promising. Ashes to Ashes.

The spell talks about demon bodies and how to destroy them.

I swipe my hand across the bloody page until the words are clear enough to read. I read fast because more blood is already welling up. I'm sure there's a simple spell to stop the bleeding, but I don't know it. Unfortunately.

If one has not THE blade
Render dust to dust
And ashe to ashe
Unname the body
And the spirit cannot last

I think that part says *THE* blade. It's hard to see in the dark.

I put the book down and wipe my bloody hands on my jeans. The hissing ghoul paces the demon trap as I consider the book's advice. *Unname the body...* This makes me think of a similar spell in one of Arty's books. That to neutralize a magic, we fight it with its contrary. For fire magic, we call water.

But what's the opposite of a ghoul?

A ghoul is a demonic spirit that creates its body from graveyard dirt. So, everything I'm seeing is dirt, shaped into the corporeal form of the ghoul by its magic.

Graveyard dirt's magic can be neutralized with sea salt.

I clamber off the floor to get a fresh bottle of purified moon water and salt from the equipment shelves. My footsteps echo off the walls, and I realize how cold my hands are. I open and close them, trying to encourage circulation, before kneeling in front of the trap again.

I pour salt along the concrete floor in a thick ring. Then I open the jar of moon water and begin with a simple purification ritual.

During the spell, the salt rises from the floor and floats toward the ghoul. The demon slams its clubbed feet against the concrete and squeals like a pig in a slaughterhouse. The second the salt connects with its skin, the screams intensify.

It thrashes in the trap. I close my eyes and keep focusing on the spell, on saying the words clearly and correctly. I'm binding the salt to the body of the ghoul, making it as much a part of its corporeal form as the graveyard dirt.

I open my eyes and snort. Then the snort rolls into full laughter. The demon looks like a donut. It's still a ghoul, but the salt is now mixed in with its dusty form so perfectly, it's like it's rolled in powdered sugar.

I lift the jar of moon water and splash it onto the ghoul, ending the ritual.

I expect it to howl. Something as pure as moon water—the witchy version of holy water—should send it into a frenzy. But it doesn't. Its body is hunched as if waiting for the pain, and when it doesn't come, the ghoul looks up as surprised as I am that the moon water didn't hurt.

Silverweed.

I've screwed up. I didn't kill it. I *purified* it. Which means these markings on the floor can't trap it anymore.

I dive for the athame the same moment the ghoul lunges. It sails out of the trap in a single bound and then it's on me.

Rock-solid muscle slams into me. My shoulder blades connect with the unforgiving wall before I can get a firm grip on the athame. It clatters to the floor, out of reach.

The ghoul sinks its fangs into my arms.

I scream.

Magic leaps from my skin like a solar flare, burning bright. The ghoul is lashed and falls back hissing, probably more out of habitual reaction than actual pain, because light shouldn't affect it anymore. And I'm right—it was surprised, not hurt. It recovers too quickly.

I barely have time to grab the athame and slice the air wildly, hoping to hit my mark. I slash the ghoul's neck, and it staggers, its claws scraping along the floor. It unleashes another ear-splitting scream of frustration.

It scampers over the open book and launches itself at me. I thrust the blade, aware that my arm is now pulsing in time to my heart. My skin is turning hot then cold. A small tremor starts in my limbs.

It's the ghoul's venom injected into my system by its bite. It's a ticking clock.

I stumble toward the bell jar, and accidentally kick it. It rolls along the floor away from me. Lovely. The ghoul sees its chance and dives for my calf, snapping at me with its exaggerated jaws. I land a kick to its nose and it falls back howling.

Finally, I scoop up the jar and open it.

A vacuum-force suction erupts from the jar. Instead of trying to bite me again, the ghoul is scampering away. It tries to dig its nails into the unyielding cement, but it's too late for that. It's sucked into the jar, dissipating into black smoke once more as I screw the blessed lid into place. The only difference now is that when I hold the jar up to the candlelight, a mound of sea salt shines at the bottom like silt while the black smoke lazily rolls along the sides. Let's hope that since a bell jar is bewitched to hold anything—evil or good—it will hold a purified ghoul.

Panting, I fall against the nearest wall, my breath labored. A sharp pain is shooting through my chest, and my left arm has gone entirely numb. The floor is a mess with salt, moon water, and blood, from both me and the oozing book. The book itself has been kicked into a corner and is still bleeding onto the floor.

Project Save Alex, take 1, is a total failure.

I didn't expect to solve my problem on the first go, but

I'd hoped it would at least end without me covered in blood.

With a great deal of effort, I drag myself up and hobble toward the storage shelves in the antechamber. I place the ghoul out of sight. Irrationally, I'm mad at it for not dying and refuse to take it home with me.

I'm still mad as I begin packing everything up.

It's hard to do with one hand. Yet I manage to wrap the book in its plastic again and stuff it back into my backpack. I return my athame to its sheath. I've hidden all evidence of my efforts in case the aunts pop in.

I'm at the supply closet, packed and ready to get out of here, but I hesitate.

I can't go rushing back to Rowan House. If I show up bleeding and poisoned, the aunts are going to ask too many questions. Maybe they're not home yet, but I don't know.

And the effects of the ghoul venom are *really* kicking in.

I can't stay here. I can't go home.

That leaves only one option.

I slip the key into the large keyhole, leaning heavily on the door, my breath tightening into strained pants.

When I pull open the door, there's Alex stretched on his bed, one hand behind his head like a pillow. He's reading something. I can't read the title given my blurry vision, but I can still see the soft light from his lamp falling across his bed.

Here he thought he'd get to do a little light reading then go to sleep, and look at me, about to ruin everything. He sees me in that instant, and frowns over the top of his book.

"Amelia?"

He's using my first name. I must look worse than I thought.

I stumble through the doorway, clutching my wounded

arm as fresh blood bubbles up between my fingers. The gashes are deeper than I thought. I kick the door closed behind me. It's a pathetic kick, but no point in worrying about that now. I can barely drag myself across the carpet to him.

"Hey," I say. At least, I think words are coming out of my mouth. "Are you busy? 'Cause I could use a little help."

CHAPTER 7
PAST NOT FORGOTTEN

Alex springs up from his bed, the abandoned book falling to the floor. "You're bleeding."

"Sorry." I fall to my knees. The gravity is a little better down here.

"Badly."

"I'm *sorry*." What does he want from me? "I'll pay for the carpet, *Laveau*."

"What happened? What bit you?"

Thankfully, I don't have to come up with a lie, because this is the exact moment when I slump completely face first onto his bedroom floor. He doesn't even catch me and slow my fall. What a gentleman.

His large hands slip off the backpack and turn me over. He rips the sleeve off my shirt, what's left of it anyway, tearing the fabric in a jagged line up to my elbow.

I feel him call his magic. It's all sea breeze and salty sunshine. Very tropical. I wonder if he's brought the Caribbean with him somehow. He hovers his hand above the wound.

"Don't." I grab his wrist. It's a pathetic grip. "Don't waste yourself on me."

"Healing you will be easier than explaining to the coven why you died on my bedroom floor."

"So, this is about you." I don't know if he's heard me. His fingers are pressing into my throbbing arm, inspecting the wound. I hiss. "That's fine then."

"Is this ghoul venom?" He fingers the puncture wounds the ghoul's teeth have left in my arm. "Or are you trying to turn yourself into a vampire? This isn't how you do it."

"How would you know?" I grit my teeth. "Do you know any vampires?"

"Maybe."

Keepers have tremendous healing ability. When they take demons into their bodies, they use this healing power to fix the damage the demons cause on the inside. Of course, a chevalier will use that healing power to heal their witch too.

But Alex isn't my chevalier.

He doesn't owe me this.

"Stop," I croak as his hands grow warm on my arm.

"Shut up," he says. His tone is soft. Incredibly kind.

The more demons Alex takes inside him, the harder it will be for him to heal himself and me. And that's what he's thinking about now. About the day he'll be useless to me.

I squeeze his hand. "You shut up. I'm always going to need you, you idiot."

"Get out of my head, Bishop," he says, but he's smiling.

The itching fire in my arm weakens. The heat folds into cold. I'm shivering. My teeth chatter.

He frowns. "I've closed the wound, but the venom is everywhere."

"P-pesky cir-circul-latory s-system," I say, the words clipped and quivering through my chattering teeth.

"It would be easier to pull all the venom into your stomach and then have you puke it up."

"C-can't w-wait."

"Sit up." He slips his arms under mine, hauling me into a sitting position. My back rests against a bed post. He steps out of my line of sight for a moment and then reappears with a small black trash can, the interior lined with a white plastic bag. "Hope your aim is good."

"I'll aim f-for y-you," I say, trying to keep my tone light. I can't stand it when he looks worried like this.

He kneels in front of me and puts his hand on my stomach. "You'll be okay."

He closes his eyes. His thick brows knit together in concentration. He's murmuring something under his breath. I can't focus on what he's saying because I'm preoccupied with the crawling army of fire ants marching up and down my skin.

The venom pools in my stomach, forming a hard, writhing knot.

The first time Alex had to save my life was just after he dragged my body from the river, the day Phelia died. He's extracting the venom from my veins the same way he pulled water from my lungs then. History repeats itself, one way or another.

"Into the trash can, please," Alex says as he slides his hand away. He's angling the mouth of the can toward my face as if he doesn't trust me. There's something in the trash already—a rotten banana peel? That sour scent is the tipping point. I grab the side of the can and hurl into it.

Four times.

"Better?" Alex asks when my stomach stops spasming and I finally put the can down beside me.

I slump against his bed. My teeth have stopped chattering, and I'm no longer shivering like I just crawled out of a lake of ice. But in return, my back, head, and throat are sore and achy. And my limbs feel weak and useless.

"Dare I ask how the hell you ended up in a fight with a ghoul? Were you in the cemetery again? I can close these puncture wounds but most of this is demon blood."

"Observant," I say, frowning at my hair. It's matted with blood too. Gross.

Alex's irritation grows. "Look. I want to respect your privacy. You've got something going on and you don't want to talk about it. Fine. But a whole family was murdered last night, and you said yourself that demon activity was escalating. The aunts have forbidden hunting and yet the very next night here you are, out there—"

I could tell him I wasn't hunting, that I was in the vault, but that hardly seems important right at the moment.

He throws up his hands. "Something is going on and now is *not* the time for you to be your usual reckless self. This is why we should bind our magics. If I was your keeper I'd know if you were in trouble. I wouldn't have to hope you made it to me. We wouldn't lose precious time. Just tell me why you're so against it."

I've been honest with Alex about nearly everything all my life. My reluctance to explain my objections to him becoming my chevalier is probably infuriating.

"What if I make a promise?" I ask.

One brow raises, skeptical.

"I'm serious. What if I make a *promise* to tell you everything, if you just give me a little more time?" I offer my hand, and it's thrumming with magic. I know he can feel it because the skeptical brow softens. He knows if I make this kind of promise, I can't break it.

"How much time?" he asks, his hand hovering over mine.

"A month."

"A month!" His lips press into a displeased line. "You could be dead in a month."

"Take it or leave it, Laveau."

He rolls his eyes and clamps his hand over mine. We shake and the magic warms our grip.

"Now. Can you please just"—I wipe my mouth with the collar of my bloodied shirt—"give me a mint?"

He opens a desk drawer, searching. His desk is much tidier than mine. It has a respectably clean surface: all pencils in the pencil cup, all the books stacked in a line along the wall between two brass bookends meant to look like a lion—one side a head, one a hindquarters and tail.

And there are four pictures. One of Alex and Lance. Lance is tucked into the crook of Alex's arm while kissing his cheek. Alex holds up the camera in a traditional selfie pose. They're adorable. The second is one of Alex and his dad, fishing of all things. They're both holding up an enormous fish. Alex holds the tail and his dad holds the head. They're grinning like fools. The third is a picture of his mother balancing a cup of tea on her knee while a baby Alex sleeps against her chest, his thumb in his mouth. She's smiling down at him.

The last photo is of us: me, Alex, and Phelia. We're maybe five or six years old and covered in mud.

I remember that day.

We were playing tag. Alex was it, and Phelia, the unscrupulous competitor that she was, tripped me. I fell face first into the mud and Alex tagged me, exactly as Phelia knew he would. I was so mad that I threw mud into her hair. She got mad and threw mud into my face, and after that there was no going back. We brawled ruthlessly in the mud, the three of us, pulling hair and screaming like little banshees until my mother dragged us apart.

"What are you staring at?" Alex asks, trying to follow my line of sight. He's holding the tin of mints out for me, shaking them in my face to get my attention.

"Mom took that picture." I nod toward the three of us as I take the mints. I shake out a handful of the little white pellets into my palm before popping them into my mouth. Who am I kidding? I shake out a few more. "I was thinking that it's probably the last photo she took."

Alex looks over his shoulder at the photo. "Do you want it?"

"No. But I need your help." Because I've realized something. Phelia's room is a treasure trove of the past. It's sat mostly untouched since her death. When she died, I moved from the bedroom we shared into the bedroom I have now. Slowly, I took my things from the room, piece by piece, but I left everything of hers undisturbed. So it's going to be full of more than photographs that will make my heart hurt.

"The aunts asked me to clean out Phelia's room for Melody," I tell him.

His eyebrows rise. "Are you okay with that?"

"Her whole family was murdered." I toss him the tin of mints. "The least we can do is give her our guest bedroom."

"But it isn't a guest room. It's Phelia's room."

He's pushing me to be honest with myself. But I don't have it in me right now. I'm covered in gore and I ache.

"Will you help me go through it?" I ask him. *Because I don't think I can do it alone.*

His lips soften into a sweet smile. "Of course."

. . .

Alex lets me shower and change into clean jeans and a t-shirt before we get started. Less questions that way, should the aunts show up. *Oh, that bloody, shredded shirt? It's nothing! I fell down some stairs, into a pile of...*Okay, my story needs work.

We stand in the center of Phelia's room. It's the same as it's always been, with one exception. It's so much smaller than I remember, easily the smallest room in the house. When we were little, I thought the room was enormous. We would run from wall to wall until we were breathless, and now I can cross it in five or six strides.

A double bed with rose-patterned sheets sits in the center of the room. I remember the greatest threat to us as children was the idea of separate beds. *If you girls don't stop giggling and go to sleep, we're getting separate beds!* An easel with an unfinished drawing of the trees—Phelia's—sits in one corner. Dolls and plastic swords are strewn about as if we've just stopped playing. A wooden horse with red runners waits at the foot of the bed. The wall that isn't a window looking into the forest is lined with bookshelves. It's mostly my mother's books. The aunts put them in our room when she died, precious heirlooms meant to replace the guide and teacher we lost.

Inadequate, if you ask me.

"Where do you want to start?" Alex asks. He leans into the doorway.

I bend down and pick up a sword. "I was a pirate for Halloween that year. Do you remember?"

"You were a pirate every day for about six months. That's what I remember. You only gave it up because Demi gave you that gladiator costume."

I swat his legs with the plastic sword, and he dodges me easily, pulling his long legs up to his chest one after the other.

I stand from the pile of toys where I crouch. "Let's start here."

It doesn't take us long to box up the toys, mostly because Alex is working faster than me. Every one I pick up conjures memories. Of birthdays. Of Yules. Or special days that were special only for small reasons. Like the first time I caught a frog and brought it home.

Then we move on to the books, most of them given to us when our mother died.

A stranger can tell a lot about my mother based on the books she read. With dozens of books on herbs and herbal medicine, and quite a few on botany, it is easy to see she was into plants. At the first sign of a cold, she had Phelia and me chugging honey and tea brewed from some kind of herb. When we got burned, she'd tear off a piece of aloe from a plant in her window and smear the goop over our injuries.

Mom made lavender sachets for our pillows if we couldn't sleep. If Phelia was prone to illness, I was the one always having bad dreams. She'd rub my back with chamomile oil until I fell asleep. When it was really, really bad, I'd wake up beside her still holding me, and be so happy that she never left me during the night.

A few of her books are handmade journals full of remedies. It seems Mom tried different herbs for different ailments and recorded the results.

But there are diaries too, full of personal entries from her life.

"Set these aside. I want to read them," I tell Alex, starting a pile of the handmade journals. We stack the remaining books into a cardboard box. I'll add them to the library later.

We're down to just the junk we've dragged out of the closet and thrown onto the floor to sort. We've made such great progress because Alex isn't letting me dwell. When I fall into memory, turning an old cornhusk doll over and over in my hands, he asks, "Do you think we should put the clothes in plastic bags? We're running low on boxes."

And just like that I'm back on track. He's gentle and patient, even though I know this can't be easy for him either. My family is his family.

In the pile of closet belongings, I find an old shirt smeared with mud that had been thrown into the back and forgotten. It was the shirt I'd been wearing when Phelia died. A white t-shirt with a rainbow across the chest, dirtied forever by the harsh mud stain.

Alex hadn't wanted to go to the river that day, but we'd begged and begged. And let's be honest, Phelia and I often ganged up on Alex and bullied him into doing what we wanted. Because it was spring, it had been raining for days, just like now, but by noon the sun had come out. As soon as the sun poked its head around the last cloud, we wouldn't let up. *Take us, take us. Please.* Because Arty and Demi were hunting and it was just the three of us in Rowan House, bored out of our minds. And also because Alex knew how to get to the river, because he was—and still is—the better tracker of the three of us.

We weren't supposed to leave the house, yet twenty minutes later we were waterborne.

Phelia used to pinch my legs under the water and say, "What's that?"

With wide eyes, she pretended to search the waters as fiercely as I did for a snake, a fish, or maybe even an undine water demon—anything with a mouth big enough to be a problem.

"I think I saw something black," she said, in a grave and serious tone. She moved her hand just beneath the surface so that I'd think it was a snake cutting the water.

Of course, I believed anything she said. "They're really poisonous!"

"Not poisonous, *venomous*," Phelia quipped, always relishing the chance to correct me when I misspoke. "Snakes can't be poisonous."

We searched and searched until Phelia suddenly gasped and disappeared beneath the water. When I was practically in tears, thinking she'd been eaten alive, she popped up laughing and spit water into my face like a fountain's stone cherub.

"I hate you." I started wading back to Alex, who waited on the rocks.

"Amelia," she called. "Amelia, I'm just playing."

"Play by yourself."

"Fifteen minutes," Alex said. He looked up from his book, shading his eyes from the last bit of sun with his hand. "If we don't get back before dark, they'll know we snuck out."

Ten minutes was all it took.

The river was high from a week of rains, which we liked, because we could push ourselves beneath the water, hit the sandy silt bottom, and leap up like frogs after a moment of weightlessness.

It had a feeling of taking off, of strong legs propelling us through the water into the sunlight.

That's what we were doing—jumping up and down—when Phelia was knocked off her feet and swept into the current. One moment we were jumping *up, down, up, down,* throwing ribbons of crystal water in our wake, laughing ourselves breathless. The next, I came up alone. Something sharp had scratched my arm, and I leapt up afraid it was a real snake bite.

Wiping the water out of my eyes, I inspected my arm and found only a long, angry scrape blooming on my skin.

"You promised not to trick me!" I whined. "You scratched me really hard."

I stared at the green-gold river water where Phelia had been just a moment ago. I ran my hands through the water but didn't feel her. Turning a complete three-sixty, I still didn't see her. My heart took off like a rabbit.

Phelia was gone.

I was about to scream to Alex when Phelia popped up from the water several feet downstream. We had not seen the downed tree branch tip over the side of the dam and sink for a moment. The large limb only scratched me, but it had pushed Phelia completely off her feet, slamming into her small ten-year-old body full on, the current on its side. The rains usually knock trees into the water, but we were always very careful to swim out of the way if something too big spilled over the ledge.

But in our jumping, we hadn't seen the branch fall. Nor did we see it disappear beneath the surface. For all our gifts, all our magic, we hadn't sensed a thing. We were just children, caught off guard. The limb, though slow, was still heavy enough to pull her under the water.

We weren't ever supposed to pass a certain point in the swimming hole because we knew the danger of being too close to the ledge. Beyond the safety of our little cove, the ground dropped away suddenly, going well over our heads. The current sped up.

Phelia understood this and was trying to escape the

current dragging her toward the drop. She had to escape it before she reached the limestone ledge that would disappear beneath her, throwing her onto the rocks below.

She knew this and came up screaming.

I dove without thinking. I quit gripping the sandy silt with my feet and let my body be swept into the current completely, moving with the water so that I could get to her as quickly as I could. This worked. As soon as I reached her, I grabbed her slender arms and yanked her right, toward the embankment.

Though Phelia and I were just alike, I have always been a little bigger, a little stronger.

Phelia leapt and I pulled. *Leap. Pull. Leap. Pull.* We were moving toward safety, but it wasn't enough. Phelia was choking on water and each jump was a little more sluggish than the last. She was getting tired of fighting the current. So was I.

Alex came then.

Our screams had pulled him from the book he'd buried his nose in. He hit the river at a run, great arches of white water spraying upward in his wake. He was taller than us, but this close to the ledge, the water rose halfway up his chest. Still he'd pulled with all his strength.

Then Phelia slipped from my arms.

And I yanked myself from Alex's embrace in order to grab her, pulling us both under. I could have lost them both that day. We could've all died. But Alex found his footing and managed to regain his hold on me. He dragged me screaming onto the stones.

Phelia was gone.

I was coughing water, half drowned, and Alex used his power to pull it from my lungs.

But it didn't matter, because Phelia was *gone*.

Now I stare at the old t-shirt, wondering what it must have been like for my aunts to find her body on the riverbank a mile downstream. What it must have been like to bury a child you loved.

I scratch the dried mud with a fingernail, but nothing comes off. It's part of the shirt now. Too much time has passed.

There were a thousand things I did wrong that day, but they all boil down to one truth. I wasn't enough. I hadn't been paying attention to the danger. And when the crucial moment came, I wasn't strong enough to save her.

"I shouldn't have taken you." Alex's voice is so low I can barely hear him. "When you asked me to go, I should've said no."

"It's not your fault," I say. "I was the one who wanted to swim."

I ball the shirt in my fists and throw it toward the trash pile. Neither of us says anything for a long time. We sort the pile of knickknacks with blind fingers.

"Ah!" Phelia squeals.

Alex and I both turn and look at her, bracing for her reaction. We wait with bated breath. I'd hoped she wouldn't show up until after we were done packing up the room.

"What have you done to my room?" she asks.

"We're going to let Melody stay here," I say, giving Alex a look. He nods, reassuring me that I'm not being cruel. "She's homeless and her family is dead. She needs somewhere to stay."

I expect Phelia to protest.

Instead, she rushes to the bed and tries to grab her stuffed animal. When her fingers slip through it, she moans and takes to pointing at it furiously. "You have to take him! You can't leave him here. Mr. Snorks doesn't like strangers!"

Alex grins. I elbow him in the side as I get up and cross to the bed. I pick up the cheetah lying against the pillow. Then I sit it on top of the pile of Mom's journals.

"Better?" I ask, gesturing at the going-to-my-bedroom pile.

But she isn't even looking at me anymore. Her arms are out at her side like airplane wings and the strange sound she's making with her mouth could be mistaken for an engine.

"There's so much room," she squeals with delight, running from wall to wall like we used to. "I love it!"

I catch Alex smiling. But that touch of sadness stays on his lips as his eyes track her around the room.

CHAPTER 8
NEW ARRIVAL

We put the stack of journals on the floor by my bed. I like to read before I go to sleep at night, and this is the perfect place for rolling over and grabbing one off the top of the pile. Because let's be honest, there are few things worse than lying down after a long hard day, my body sore and aching from chasing some demon, only to see my book resting on the chair across the room, taunting me to get up again.

Mr. Snorks gets the honor of prime pillow placement, and the plastic pirate sword gets propped against the wall.

Alex and I drift off reading my mother's journals and sleep until almost noon.

It's Demi's voice that wakes us. "Amelia! Are you home? I could use your help!"

We find my aunt in the kitchen. Grocery bags sit on the island.

"Where's Melody?" I ask.

"With Artemis. They're on their way." Demi pulls out two cartons of berries, a couple of leeks, and a loaf of bread. I assume she wants help putting the groceries away, but she stops me after I take a carton of eggs out of the bag.

"No, I'll unpack. I want you to light the hearth. Please. They'll be back any minute." She slips the carton of large brown eggs into the fridge. "I'm not going to have time to finish cleaning."

She hands me an apple we've cold-stored since fall and a small bouquet of daisies. I sigh, resigning myself to the role of vestal virgin.

Alex is failing to hide his smile.

"Shut up," I say, and this only makes him grin more.

I kneel in front of the hearthstone and place dried orange peels and kindling onto a log. I use the blessed flint rock to spark the kindling and then blow on the rising smoke, trying to encourage it to light.

"Come on, say the rhyme." Alex nudges me with his knee, but is careful not to touch the hearth himself.

"There once was a boy from Nantucket," I say, "whose face I dunked in a bucket."

"No, the other one," he chides.

"Shut up or I'm going to use you as kindling."

"You have to say it. She won't clean your house if you don't say it."

"I'm going to make *you* clean the house if you don't shut up."

That's the condition of using hearthstone magic. The hearth fire must be lit by an unmarried witch of the house to which it belongs. One witch, Agatha Dumbwaithe, had fourteen children, *fourteen*, just so she would have a steady stream of children to light the hearth. *Someone* hated housework.

The fact that you can only get a spirit to clean your house if you're single seems like all the reason to stay single forever, if you ask me. I'm going to have to meet someone really amazing if it's going to enslave me to toilet scrubbing and window washing.... or I could find someone who's into cleaning.

I ignore Alex's teasing and blow on the cinders. When the fire grows high enough that a strong, rolling heat warms my skin, I throw the apple and daisies into the flames. I turn my back so I don't have to look at Alex while I awaken the stone. I clear my throat. He snickers and I elbow him hard.

Bluebells and daisy shells
May I be like thee forever
A crescent moon
Unknowing too
Freedom and will I treasure
Heartstrings sing
Long and lovely in spring
Innocent through each endeavor
May I be like thee forever

The flames turn from orange to cheery yellow. A sigh circles the room. The carpets soften. Pillows fluff. The breeze seems to suck up any dust and stagnant air. Windows sparkle. Plants that were looking saggy now plump up, verdant again. The kitchen smells like cookies, though the stove isn't on. Even the light changes to a soft warm glow. All over the house there are the soft sounds of objects being shuffled away. If I peek in my room, I'll find the bed made, my drawers straightened. Even my desk, in its eternal chaos, will be put right again.

Alex snorts. "Unknowing."

"You're awful."

"What do you think this 'innocent endeavors' part is talking about?"

"I'll tell you when you're older." He's annoying me, but really I'm relieved. I got off easy. Sometimes the hearth makes you put flowers in your hair and *dance* before she'll clean.

Demi steps into the den, wiping her hands on a towel. She nods in approval as she surveys the den, the kitchen and hall leading to the library and upstairs. She opens the pantry to find boxes of food arranging themselves neatly on the shelves. "Very nice. Thank you, love."

"When are they supposed to arrive?" I ask as she steps forward and brushes my bangs out of my eyes. She hates it when my hair is in my eyes.

"Five minutes ago. I hope there isn't a problem," she says, frowning at the grandfather clock beside the sofa. It's almost seven. "Listen, I have one more job for you. I want you to go to Perdita's ball tonight."

"No," I say, outright.

"Yes," Alex agrees, at the same moment.

We exchange a look.

"I can't believe she's still going to have it. A family died. Our friends *died*." I cross my arms over my chest. "Who cares if she's engaged?"

"Now they're calling it a celebration," Alex says. "They're celebrating that Melody was found alive."

He's doing a terrible job of hiding his excitement. I know why he's excited anyway. Lance will be there.

Demi steps closer to me, lowering her voice. "I know

you don't like social functions, but I need you to be our eyes and ears. Arty and I aren't invited."

To say I don't like social functions is an understatement. Everyone but me seems to view these parties as a chance to prove who is the biggest snob. They stand around, putting each other down. I hate it. If I go, *if,* I'll be lucky to get through the night without hexing anyone blind.

"What am I looking for *exactly*?" She better have an amazing reason that will inspire me to go to this dreadful party.

"We found...for lack of a better word...*evidence* of magic at the Priests' house." She's whispering, and both Alex and I have to lean closer just to hear her.

"Of course there was magic," I say. "The Priests would've fought for their lives."

The image of little Elei's body draped over her sister's flashes in my mind.

"No, not the Priests' magic," Demi says.

Alex and I exchange a glance instinctively.

"Someone else was there," he says, maintaining the whisper.

Why are we whispering? We're the only ones here. I say, "Another witch was in their house?"

"Yes," Demi says, her lips pulled into a grimace. "We're beginning to suspect the worst."

Betrayal. Witch against witch. An intra-coven war.

"We need you to go tonight," Demi says, her tone still grave. "Take Alex and listen to what everyone is saying. Ask questions and see if anything seems off to you, trust your intuition. And take this."

She digs into her pocket and pulls out a large green-gold beetle. "Keep it on you. When someone is lying, you'll feel its wings flutter."

She puts the scarab in my open palm. Light shimmers across its folded wings. It's dried out, practically mummified, and thankfully not alive.

"It's an enchantment that makes it move," she says.

Alex's eyes fix on it. I hold it out to him. "You want it? You're a better interrogator than me."

"No, you'll talk to more witches than I will."

"If I talk to more people it's only because you'll be off sucking Lance's—" My voice breaks off when my aunt's eyes meet mine.

"—face off," I finish lamely. "You know I hate people. And talking."

"But you'll go?" Demi asks, still watching me carefully.

I groan. "*Fine.* But if I end the night in a duel, you can't get mad at me for it. Deal?"

I'm being dramatic, but it doesn't earn me so much as a smile.

Her face remains pinched with concern. "I don't need to tell you to be careful. If someone is targeting First Families, we are in as much danger as the Priests." Her eyes cut to Alex. "Look out for each other."

Ayck! Ayck!

The sharp bird call jerks my gaze up to the wooden rafters. A darting blur of blue-gray feathers flits by, weaving through the beams. I square my shoulder, making enough room for the jay to perch. But before he reaches me, he spreads his wings and drops onto Alex's shoulder.

"Hey!" I cry out. "Whose familiar are you?"

Alex reaches into his pocket and fishes out two peanuts in their bulky dry shells. Dragon takes one shell in his black beak and the other in an outstretched claw before flitting back up to the rafter, where he begins to crunch loudly. The house cleans away the shells before they even hit the ground, throwing them right out the open window.

It isn't until the peanuts are gone that he comes to me. His claws clamp on my shirt, helping establish his perch on my shoulder. He rubs his crest against my cheek and ear.

"Oh, now you love me," I say. "Thanks a lot."

Ayck!

He smells like mountain air. He sees the beetle in my hand and snaps at it.

"No, not for eating." I move the beetle out of range. "I need this to find out who wants to kill us."

Ayck! Ayck!

"What do you think of all this?" I ask him, scratching his chest. "Do you think someone wants to murder us in our sleep?"

Ayck! He raises his beak in a silent demand for more scratching.

"Why don't you go snooping around too?" I lower my voice to whisper conspiratorially, "Jinx and Orion are probably on it, but you're the smartest and cleverest familiar ever to live, aren't you?"

Dragon puffs out his chest. *Ayck! Ayck!*

"Okay, off you go. Find out who the traitor is, but be careful."

Dragon takes one more peanut from Alex's outstretched fingers and then his little claws shove off my shoulders. Wings brush my cheeks as his sleek body shoots up through the rafters toward the attic, where he has an exit hatch that he uses as his own personal door to Rowan House.

The hearth fire sighs. It's the buttercup-yellow glow fading to the normal red-orange flame. The cleaning must be done, and just in time. The pressure between the walls changes.

"They're back," I say. The distinct ripple of magic that accompanies the house doors changing shimmers through me. Sure enough, Arty's *tap-step-tap-step* sounds in the library a heartbeat later. Shadows cut beneath the door, which we can see from where we stand in the den.

The library door opens, and for a moment, it just stands like that. Then the dark wisp of a girl appears with Arty at her back.

Arty pulls her into the hallway toward us.

She's filthy. Her clothes are smattered with mud and crusted earth as if she crawled from her own grave. Her face is streaked with soot, nails dark with grime.

Demi rushes forward and takes the other arm. They steer the silent, unblinking girl toward the chaise lounge in front of the window and sit her there. A moment later, she's wrapped in a blanket with a warm cup of tea in her hand.

Demi prattles on with the reassurances. "And we've gathered up some of your things and we'll have them brought right to your room. Just sit there and rest. Get warmed up. It's such a chilly April this year, isn't it, Artemis?"

Arty's grunt could be mistaken for a yes.

The aunts look at us. They're waiting for us to do something. Alex stiffens beside me. He gives me an elbow. The girl—if that's what she is—doesn't see this. She doesn't see anything. She's looking into her tea with large black eyes.

There's something about her skin. I can't explain it, but it isn't...sitting right on her bones. It seems thin in places, thicker in others, as if the thing underneath is malformed. I turn my head, the way Dragon tilts and turns his when inspecting something.

I have to get her in just the right light to see it—but it's there. An impostor. A monster hiding inside.

"That isn't Melody," I say.

Demi cries out, "Amelia! Apologize!"

"Use your eyes," I say, turning to Artemis. "Look at her."

"Get over here. Right. *Now*," Arty hisses, and tap-steps from the hall.

I cast a glance at Alex and see that he's as horrified by my behavior as the aunts. He's actually scowling at me as he kneels down in front of Melody, cooing at her like a lost child. For a second, I thought he saw what I saw, but I realize he didn't.

Arty leads me into the library and shuts the door.

"I know this is an adjustment, especially for you, giving up Phelia's room. I know it can't be easy." The tap of her cane is a little harder than usual. "But that is no excuse to behave like that."

"I'm not being mean." I cross my arms. "That isn't Melody. Did you even look at her?"

"I lost the use of my hip, not my eyes, girl."

"Can't you feel it?" I know I'm not crazy and I'm not going to let anyone convince me that I am. "That's some serious demonic energy. Maybe she's possessed."

Arty massages her brow with bony fingers. "Amelia, we checked for that. We practically drowned her in blessed moon water. She's clean."

"She's not. And I'll be the first to remind you after she murders us in our beds and we're all here, haunting Rowan House for eternity."

"Hellebore. No talk of ghosts. You know I hate ghosts!"

I stiffen, hoping Phelia didn't hear that. I put my hands on my hips and turn away from her.

My face is hot. My pulse is quick. My temper is only outmatched by Arty's, so if I don't want this to turn into a screaming match, I have to choose my next words carefully.

And this is important. Our very lives might depend on it. Arty has to hear me, not shut me out.

"You have always told me to trust my instincts, that no matter what the magic says or my head says, to trust my gut."

"Yes, but—"

"And I'm telling you she's dangerous. She's dangerous to *us*."

"Amelia." Now she just sounds tired. "We can't turn her away. If we turn her away it will look terrible."

"I suppose *that's* okay then, as long as the coven *approves* of our impending murders." If I roll my eyes any harder they're going to fall out of my head.

I step toward her. I want her to look into my eyes. She has to know I'm serious. Yes, okay, packing up Phelia's stuff wasn't fun. I keep thinking about it, turning it over in my mind like a puzzle box, but it is what it is. I'll get over it. But not this. It's like seeing jagged rocks below a cliff that my loved ones insist we must jump off simply because of propriety. It's ridiculous.

Sometimes I hate being a witch.

"Maybe she killed them," I say.

"Amelia!"

"Or something we've never encountered made her do it. I don't know, but I know what I see."

"What do you see?" Arty asks, her gaze snapping up to mine.

"A viper in the garden as bare ankles approach."

This is an old saying, but a powerful one. A reminder to trust the witches around us rather than disbelieve them.

These words do exactly what I hoped they would. Arty's face softens, grows serious rather than irritated.

"It doesn't matter if I'm not sure what I'm looking at," I

say. "I'm trying to tell you I see something. It's your job to hear what I'm saying."

She looks away, falling into her own thoughts. Finally, she looks up and says, "When I was trying to key into Rowan House, it wouldn't let me."

My heart skips a beat. "What do you mean it wouldn't *let* you?"

As far as I know, a door never refuses. By definition, a door opens. It's all it wants to do—open.

"The skeleton key kept taking me to the vault. I kept insisting on Rowan House. When I finally got it to open, Rowan House rejected me. Rejected me!" She barks a surprised laugh. "I had to offer my blood to cross the threshold."

"The house is trying to protect us," I say. "Unless you're going to say we're both wrong—me *and* Rowan House."

Arty looks ready to believe me. Her mouth is open as she thinks. Then she shakes her head. "We can't turn her away. There are already too many rumors."

"What rumors? And since when does the great Artemis Bishop give a damsel seed about what people think?"

"I suppose you'll hear all about it at the party tonight. Demi told me you were going." She taps the side of her head, showing me how Demi told her. "Be careful."

"*You* be careful," I say, jabbing my finger at the door and the girl out there.

Arty falls into another deep thought. "Keep your enemies closer. That is what we will do until we understand what's happening. I'll take your claim seriously—"

"Hear that, Rowan? She'll take our claim seriously," I say. The walls groan.

Arty scowls. "If what you're saying is true, it is even more important that we keep her."

"Because we're insane?"

"Because we're the strongest." Arty leans onto her cane. "She might overtake a weaker family. Would you sign someone else's death warrant? Would you send her home with Alex? With Perdita Hatt?"

"So we *are* the craziest."

"We'll blood seal our doors," she says, finalizing her plan with a nod. "Then she can't kill us in our beds. As she did the Priests."

Except for Elei, I think. She woke up and knew something was wrong, and tried to hide herself and her baby sister in the kitchen pantry. But why did they stay in the pantry? Why didn't they run to our house, or any house for that matter? Were they too scared? They were little kids. I know firsthand that little kids in trouble don't always make sound decisions.

Or were they fooled by a monster that wore their sister's face?

"Tell Demi the plan. She needs to watch her back."

Arty taps her temple again. "Already did."

"And I'll be sleeping with my athame. So don't either of you creep up on me in the night."

"Duly noted. But if I think better of it, I will take her to the vault. I promise."

My hand is on the door handle when Arty calls my name one last time.

"Amelia, if you can't be civil to the girl, just avoid her. In the event she *is* possessed, then Melody is still in there, and suffering the loss of her whole family as well as her body. No need to be cruel."

CHAPTER 9

FULL MOON BALL

Blood magic is powerful magic, but it also comes with a blood price. I want to blood seal the door now, before a minute goes by, but when I do, it will knock me unconscious for a while. It's unavoidable, unfortunately. And it's better to get it done now than after Perdita Hatt's ball. It would be my luck that I return home exhausted, forget about the blood seal, fall straight to sleep, and get murdered before I even begin to dream. Even if not-Melody chose not to do it with her own hands, there are other ways to kill a witch. While I'm at the ball, she could sneak into my room and bewitch my pillows to suffocate me. That's the kind of luck I've come to expect.

It would be nice to have Alex watching my back while I do this, but he's gone home to get ready for the ball.

I attach the leather sheath to my hip and pick up the athame. I do this because the second I finish with the blood seal, that's right where the athame is going, and it's going to remain *glued* to my side until all this is over. I'm not going to be one of those idiots who are caught unawares at the wrong moment. Of course, after the failed ghoul killing this afternoon, I guess there's plenty of evidence that I *am* one of the idiots.

With the heavy handle in my palm, I cut my fingertip with the blade.

I press the bloody fingerprint to the wood floor square in the center of the frame of my door. Then I let the extra blood drip into a respectable puddle, the size of a quarter. I say the prayer, repeating it three times.

Shall nothing cross
that crosseth me

Shall nothing cross
that crosseth me

Shall nothing cross
that crosseth me

The blood glows red, and the red light spreads from wood trim to wood trim, filling the frame. It shivers along the walls, ceiling, and floor as the room is sealed. In theory this is enough, but I'm not one for theories. I repeat the blood seal on the two windows and my closet for good measure.

After I recite the prayers for the windows and closet and have watched the walls glow red four times over, I know the room is truly sealed. Let's just hope a seal is enough to deter whatever is squatting inside Melody.

The exhaustion of the blood price hits me hard. I have just enough left in me to slip the athame into its sheath and stumble toward the bed. I don't even feel my body connect with the mattress before the darkness overtakes me.

Already I'm back in the dream. But despite this knowledge, I slip in deeper, either led by my curiosity for the rest of the queen's story or because of the false safety a dream promises. The belief that nothing bad can happen because it's only a dream, right?

"State your terms clearly," the Queen of Elysium says. *I* say. The blue jay plumage brushes my shoulder in the breeze.

The king stands before me, the flame of Ciel's soul dancing in his paw, his long black claws like a cage around it.

"I will give him back to you, return him unharmed, if you would do me the honor."

"What honor?" I ask, the first cold tremor of fear running through me. Real fear. "Your kind has no honor. You are like a child using words you do not understand."

The king's gold eyes flash, but he doesn't lose control of himself. "The honor of giving you a new name."

My blood ices like the northernmost river of Elysium, the Styx, which cuts through the celestial Forest of Temperance, a land of snow and ice.

A name. Mother, help me. He would give me a name.

The king is speaking again. "I would name you Sephone, The Living Goddess, Queen of Elysium, Ruler of Elysia, Wife of King Vinae." He adds the final title as if it is anything but the abomination it is.

"You would name me Queen Sephone, Wife of King Vinae," I repeat, my skin frozen.

"And I would be King Vinae, Husband of Sephone of Elysium," he adds companionably. His fangs glow white in the moonlight and the fur running along his back shines like silver, ruffling in the wind.

"Is that all you want?" I ask, unable to hide my disgust. I can feel the sneer on my face.

"And all the privileges owed to a husband," he adds, looking at me through long lashes. "To be clear."

"I will not love you."

"I did not transverse two worlds, destroy your gates, and kill hundreds of your people for your *love*," he says. Then, as if he realizes that this isn't the way to woo someone, he adds, "I will win your affection in time. Or at least your loyalty."

"I need time to consider your offer."

"You will leave with me tonight," he says, the first hints of his own temper showing.

"No." My magic is already rising. "I must bury my dead, those who cannot be resurrected. I must repair the gate, and I must solidify the governance that will run in my absence. I cannot leave any sooner than five nights."

He considers this.

"Three nights," the king says. I note the angry flush along his jaw.

"But the gate will take at least—"

"You will not fix it. Leave that to your sister. As long as you are my wife, your people have nothing to fear from me. Our marriage will be a peace treaty between our people."

Already he is seeking to control me through my love— not for him. That will never exist. But of my love for the people in this walled realm. My people, hiding in the temple of Elysia, our great city. And above all, through my love for the soul he holds in the palm of his hand.

"My sister is still a child not fit to reign. You will give me five nights." Though no number of nights will heal Ciel's broken heart—or mine. And my heart is breaking. I can feel the wound open and pulsing in my chest. "Five nights, a fair and merciful number from a generous husband to his wife."

"Five nights and the unharmed soul of your beloved. Do we have a deal?" the king asks, dangerous words from the one who rules Hell. But the truth is, I would have accepted far worse from him or anyone who stood between me and Ciel.

"Yes." I call my power around me like a shroud.

The moonlight seems to come from within my own skin. The wind kicks around me and the moon appears to grow in size as I draw upon its strength. "Let it be known that I am Sephone, the Living Goddess, Queen of Elysium, Ruler of Elysia." I take a breath. "Wife of King Vinae."

Vinae's grin makes my stomach turn.

"My love," he says in a tender voice that sickens me. He steps forward. He offers the dancing blue flame of Ciel's soul. I cup it in my hands as if it were a wounded baby bird.

Vinae kisses me.

I don't fight him—yet. I know the customs of Hell well enough to know the demons seal their deals differently than we do. Maybe because their words are not as honorable as ours. Whatever it is, I know the kiss is only political, if a little hungry.

He smells of flint rock, woodsmoke, and fur.

Something sharp pierces my lip—his fangs, I realize— and when he pulls back, his lips are bright with my blood. With a sinister smile, he licks his lips as if truly enjoying the decadence. "Let it be known that I am King Vinae, Sovereign King of Hell, Son of The Morning Star, Devoted Husband of Queen Sephone."

An iron fist has closed around my heart.

"Five nights and then we return to Hell. Together," he says, and it is all I have in me not to collapse into my fear.

With the taste of blood on my lips, I watch Vinae turn and drive his army back through the broken Southern Gate, the great stone vultures surveying the carnage gluttonously as they go.

The king and his army take position just on the opposite side of the gate.

And there they will wait for five nights.

Five nights.

Five.

"I am sorry," I whisper. My power carries Ciel's soul back into his body. My hands travel over his flesh, searching for wounds. My fingers probe the unbroken skin, finding wounds in the gaps between his armored plates. But there is only one that matters: where the king's blade entered through his back, straight through the armor.

I bend forward and kiss this wound, tasting the blood on my dry lips. It's magic, this kiss. It will awaken his body and soul again. This kiss will remind him of who he is.

I roll him over into my arms.

"Ciel, my love," I whisper, calling him home. "Come back to me."

Ciel's eyes flutter open, and I place a bloodied, battle-worn hand on each side of his face. The blood under my nails is dark as the dirt in the Elysium fields.

"Sephone."

"Hello, my sweet one," I say, and hold him close. I'm trying to block out the cries of my people, which are swelling in the darkness.

My queen, my queen. Per Sephone's grace, it cannot be.

In every corner of this realm they heard my proclamation, my acceptance of the new name. And they mourn me.

Tonight, in Elysium, all hearts are breaking. Not just my own.

They are right to be afraid. Because while looking into the king's eyes, I learned the true name of Vinae. I know there is only one way to escape the name he's given me—death.

And one such as I—I...

I do not die so easily.

Ciel pushes himself up onto his elbows, and when satisfied with this progress, up onto his feet. I rise with him, stumbling, clumsy in a way I am never clumsy except in the days before my stasis, in the nights before I slumber for a millennium and have The Great Dream while my sister, Naja, rules.

Ciel licks his lips and tastes my blood there. Then his soft fingers are on my face, wiping at my cheeks.

"Sephone," Ciel whispers, his face a mask of horror in the bright moonlight, his thumbs brushing at my tears. "Sephone—what have you done?"

I blink my eyes open and keep blinking until my bedroom comes into focus.

The afternoon light has disappeared, and the room is thick with shadows. Crickets chirp in the flower beds beneath my windows. The clouds break and a bright beam of moonlight cuts across Alex's cheek.

"We're late," Alex says. He smells like soap and cologne. He's even fixed his hair and changed into a sleek black suit.

I note all this with a dreamy vagueness. My fingers are on my lips. I can feel Ciel. His body heat. His smell, which is unlike anything else I have a word for.

Alex looks at my fingers pressed to my lips and cocks his head. Then he grins. "Did I interrupt a good dream?"

"He has beautiful lavender eyes and skin like moonlight."

Alex bursts with laughter. "He does sound sexy. Tell me more."

"Shut up." I wave him off, sitting up.

"Seriously, get ready. We're late."

"I'm not changing."

He arches a brow. "We'll see how long Perdita lets that slide."

I shrug on a leather jacket over my t-shirt and jeans and lace up my boots. The athame is still on my hip where I left it. Knowing there's not really anything else I can do to prepare myself for the unpleasantness of the night, I sigh and pull the rope cord over my head. I put the key between the door and jamb and wait. When I feel the vibration radiate up my fingers, I put the quartz and key back around my neck and open the door.

Couples in fine tuxedos and oversized gowns twirl in the swooping arc of the waltz beneath the domed arch of a ballroom.

I shut the door, sealing us in my room again.

"Come on, it won't be so bad." He reaches for the door, but I stop him.

"It's ridiculous," I say.

"You're a lovely dancer."

I glare at him. "I'm not dancing."

He tilts his head. Something he does whenever he thinks I'm being unreasonable. Which is often. "Your aunts need you to investigate. You have the fancy beetle in your pocket, don't you?"

I do. I can feel its stiff legs poking my thigh through the thin pocket.

"So let's go." Alex reaches around me and eases the door

open again. "You have work to do. And I have an angry boyfriend to woo."

With a groan, I open the door again.

Before I lose my nerve I step past several brooms and a mop bucket into the Hatts' ballroom. Alex closes the door behind us, leaving us on the top step of a landing. It seems that marble stairs are coming from all directions, all leading down to the large ballroom in the center. I feel like I've stepped into a Victorian novel.

"Is this supposed to be a costume party?" I whisper to Alex. "Because I'm pretty sure these dresses went out of style two hundred years ago."

A man in a three-piece suit with a top hat and tails trots up the stairs toward me. Goddess, no. I don't want to be announced. But he's already turning, already throwing his deep baritone voice over the music, a hundred conversations, and swishing skirts.

"First Daughter Miss Amelia Bronwyn Bishop and her companion, Mr. Alexander Desmond Lambert-Laveau."

The music stops.

The dancers stop.

All at once heads turn toward us.

I consider throwing myself down the stairs. A broken neck is surely reason enough to go home. But Alex must sense my dark thoughts, because he slides up beside me and takes my arm.

Two figures cut through the murmuring crowd. The woman, who can only be mistaken for a bewitched cupcake, is Perdita Hatt herself. The beautiful guy she's dragging in her wake is her fiancé, Abel.

My desire to run intensifies. But Alex won't let go of me. In my ear he whispers, "Steel spine," in a pretty good imitation of Arty's gravelly tone.

"You're *enjoying* this," I hiss in disbelief.

"I never claimed to be the misanthropic curmudgeon that you are. I *like* people."

"I can't believe you're going to abandon me here, of all places," I mutter.

He forces a tight smile. "And I can't believe you went hunting without me and got bit by a ghoul."

Touché. I can't even argue my case because here's Perdita and Abel at the base of the stairs. Her giant dress almost knocks me back onto the steps as she takes my hands in hers and kisses each of my cheeks. Her white lace gloves scratch against my palms.

"Amelia!" she cries as if I've only just been discovered after decades of mysterious absence. "It's *so* good of you to make it. You do me *such* an honor."

I will give him back to you, return him unharmed, if you would do me the honor.

My queen, what have you done?

I blink against the encroaching dream, trying to focus on the task at hand. I blink until the room comes into focus again. The ballroom with its swirling dancers, soft candlelight, and overblown grandeur seems like an illusion.

Finally, I manage to find my voice. "You can thank Alex. He insisted we come."

"Oh, Alex!" Now it's his cheeks she's assaulting. "Thank you so much."

Alex tolerates this. "I'll leave the three of you to it then. I trust she's in good hands?"

Alex literally hands me over to Perdita, who almost squeals, "Oh yes! We'll take great care of her."

"Where are you going?" I ask, horrified that Alex is going to leave me alone with this walking tub of frosting and her pretty mannequin.

"To apologize," he says. "For what, I'm not sure."

I follow his gaze to the upper landing. Lance is standing there, looking incredibly handsome in his tight dark suit, a goblet in one hand. Their gazes lock.

"That's some heavy eye contact," I say. "You'd better go."

And he does, without even looking back, leaving me entirely at Perdita's mercy.

"I'll make sure you have a wonderful time, Amelia," Perdita says, squeezing my hands. "Tell her, Abel."

"Absolutely wonderful," Abel agrees like a parrot. "The best of times. A night to remember."

Just before he reaches the steps, Alex turns and mouths, *Beetle.*

"After all," Perdita says, "we First Daughters have to stick together. Abel."

Abel turns to her, an arm across his chest. He looks more like a butler than a fiancé. I try to remember a time when he wasn't following Perdita around like a shadow.

"Tell Elizabeth that Amelia must have a dance card."

"No—" I say. Some traditions deserve to die.

"Oh, you must dance with *someone*, Amelia." Her blond curls quiver. "I know you know how to dance. You danced quite lovely at your First Moon ball. I was surprised, to be honest. I told Abel it must be because you fight so well. Didn't I, Abel?

When a witch comes of age, she is given a party to commemorate the occasion. I hadn't wanted it. It was another reminder of something Phelia would miss out on because of me. But the aunts insisted—even Arty, who might be the only person who detests parties even more than I do.

"We'll fill your card with all the most eligible bache-lors," Perdita is saying. "Dean Prior. He's very handsome."

"Very handsome," Abel repeats without any feeling at all. Maybe she removed his brain when she accepted his engagement. Perdita frowns up at him, but he only blinks his big cow eyes.

"I'd rather shrink my own head than dance with Prior," I tell her.

"Oh. I thought you liked him." Her pretty eyes flutter nervously.

"I loathe him."

She pulls at one of her ribbons. "If not Dean then who do you like?"

The image of Ciel, bright and unbidden, flashes into my mind, his hand pressing into the small of my back, his mouth hot on mine in the cold cemetery night."

We cannot wait any longer. We are out of time.

"No one," I say, my face flushing. "I don't like anyone."

The scarab twitches in my pocket and my cheeks grow hotter.

"I think it's ridiculous that women are expected to find a partner and have children just because of our bloodlines. All I want is to be a hunter," I add.

"And a fine hunter you are." Perdita smiles beatifically. "*But* there are *so* many lovely boys here. All from fantastic and connected families."

"Did you hear what I said?"

Her eyes continue roving the room, taking inventory. "Even some of the families from the Greater European covens accepted my invitation."

That would be a no, then.

"There must be forty boys our age here, and almost none of

them are engaged. Well, Victor Hornsby is engaged to Hannah, but that's what I'd call a *soft* engagement. His parents encouraged the match. As a First Daughter, you have so much more to offer. If you liked him, it would be nothing to separate the pair."

"Absolutely nothing at all," Abel says with his blank cow eyes.

Goddess save me.

"The only other matter is your dress," Perdita says.

"I'm not wearing a dress."

"*Exactly*," Perdita says as if I've just kicked someone's cat. "And your hair."

"There's nothing wrong with my hair."

"It's a very lovely example of a beach wave," Perdita agrees, her tight curls quivering. "But this is a formal evening ball, Amelia. We should put it up."

"Perdita, no—"

Perdita bounces, a flurry of pink ruffles. "Oh, it'll be *fun*. Like when we were little girls."

"You've forgotten about the ribbons," I say.

When we were little girls, one of Perdita's enthusiastic glamours had me growing ribbons out of my head for a month.

"Oh, I've gotten *much* better since then," Perdita assures me. "I haven't had an accident in *ages*."

She snaps her fingers and her magic leaps across my skin before I can conjure a counter charm. Unfortunately, because glamours aren't really harmful, it's difficult to protect against them. It's hard to convince the magic I'm in danger when the threat is tulle and lace.

Rich cream fabrics spring from my hips, falling down over my legs. My boots soften to satin slippers, giving the soles of my feet direct contact with the cool marble floor. My waist is cinched tight with a snug-ribbed corset. A cool breeze slides across my neck and chest, so I don't even need to look down to know she's given me an uncomfortable amount of cleavage.

I check my neck for the key and quartz, and they're still there, at least.

"Oh, Amelia, you're so *lovely*."

"Absolutely lovely," Abel parrots.

"Abel, the dance card."

"The dance card," he says, and departs, leaving Perdita and me at the center as couples twirl around us.

"My athame, Hatt."

"It's still there," she says with a sniff. "Under your skirts. And I gave you pockets. I know how much you like pockets."

I search yards of fabric and find the desiccated scarab in my left pocket. And my blade sits on my right hip, but I'd never be able to lift these skirts and reach it in the event of danger.

"I'll have to burn a hole in this dress to pull my dagger."

"Pull a dagger?" Perdita gulps air. "At my engagement party?"

"A whole family was just murdered. Did you already forget?"

"Of course not," she says, her brow scrunching, giving her doll face a bit of maturity. "But that doesn't have anything to do with *us*."

The scarab doesn't twitch. Either Perdita truly believes the attack had nothing to do with the First Families or she is very good at lying to herself.

The music changes and Perdita's face lights up.

"Oh, I love this song! Dance with me until Abel comes back."

I'm about to run, truly run for the door, but she's

already slipping a gloved hand in mine and pulling me into the dance. Lucky for her, I know the secondary part.

"Do you think it was an accident then?" I ask on the first twirl. If I don't focus on getting answers, I will murder her here and now.

Perdita shrugs one bare shoulder. "Maybe the Priests did a spell wrong and it backfired."

"Do you really believe that?"

Another shrug. "I don't think it was demons. I think it was an accident."

I'm waiting for the scarab to flutter, but I still don't feel anything.

"I suppose if you thought we were in danger, you would have canceled the ball," I say, thinking aloud.

"Oh, Papa didn't want me to cancel the party," Perdita says on the second twirl.

A soft flutter catches my attention.

I push my luck. "He didn't?"

"Oh, no. Papa thinks it's important to celebrate our strength in times of darkness. It's what the Priests would have wanted."

Another fluttering, stronger this time. Definitely the scarab. Of all the things to lie about. Why is she ashamed to admit that she didn't want to cancel her party? Maybe because it would make her seem callous? January Priest was supposed to be her friend.

"You know, if you don't want Dean for yourself, would you mind terribly if I struck a match between him and Colette?" she asks.

"Please," I say. "The sooner they're married the better."

Perdita practically bounces in her slippers. "They'd have *beautiful* children."

The thought of breeding makes me shudder.

A bee lands on Perdita's shoulder and she bends her ear to it as if listening. "Excuse me, Amelia. Colette needs help with her dress."

The song ends and Victor Hornsby appears to replace her. He bows and offers a gloved hand. He might be the first person in the room that looks more uncomfortable than I do. But he's handsome enough if you like black hair, black eyes, and sharp features.

"Good evening," Victor says, his grin tight. He doesn't even show teeth.

"Congratulations on your engagement, Victor," I say. "Many long days and nights to you both."

The formal blessing is a little awkward on my tongue, but I couldn't think of anything else to say to him. And then I remember that I didn't congratulate Abel and Perdita. Their fault.

If they hadn't been so overwhelming, I'd have remembered.

Victor visibly relaxes. "Thank you. I'm glad you approve. I have to tell you, when Abel insisted that I dance with you, I was worried Perdy was scheming again."

"Imagine that."

He laughs. "I think she lives for it, the matchmaking."

I gesture toward my dress. "Whatever gives you that idea?"

"You look very lovely," he says with a charming smile.

"Settle down, Hornsby."

Abel appears on the upper landing. He's chasing down a boy, waving a card at him. I frown. "What's he doing?"

Victor turns, trying to get a look at the commotion. "He's trying to get Jacob Moor to sign your dance card."

Jacob is running from Abel like one would run from a demon, not a dance card. Abel is admirably persistent.

Victor sees me frowning. "Oh, don't take it personally. They're not running from you. They're afraid of Prior."

I note that the scarab doesn't flutter. "Why?"

"He's staked claim on you," Victor says. "He's been speaking of your eventual marriage since we were twelve. He threatens anyone who shows interest in you."

Who's shown interest. My curiosity rises at the idea that anyone has shown interest before being chased away.

I take a steadying breath. "His audacity astounds me."

"Oh, the tips of your ears get red when you're angry. You're like my sister," Victor says, his smile wavering. "You didn't know Prior had claimed you?"

"Do you believe men can claim women without their consent, Hornsby?" I stop dead, and the couple behind us crash into Victor, making their apologies. I say nothing and I refuse to move, so they're forced to go around us. We become a large rock parting the stream of dancers.

"Of course not," Victor says, trying to lead me back into the dance again.

I feel the heat in my cheeks. I say, "Then why did you dance with me?"

"He's my cousin. And he's not even here yet. He's late."

I arch a brow.

"Should we find you someone else to be engaged to? Whoever it is would have to beat Prior in a duel, which would be a challenge, but I think..." Victor searches the room. "Finnegan Massey could do it."

The scowling block of a boy with a mop of red hair leans against one marble pillar. He's holding a whole tray of appetizers and is shoveling them one after another into his large mouth.

"I'll duel Prior myself," I say. "Unless you're suggesting I need a man to fight my battles for me."

"Of course not." Victor's face blazes red. He looks truly hurt. "I didn't mean it like that. Look, it's obvious to everyone you aren't interested. You come from an old and powerful family. I imagine there is a great deal of expectation heaped on you, like all the girls around here, but that doesn't mean you have to marry who they want you to."

Something in my chest loosens, even though I know Hornsby must have his own motives for being kind.

He sees me relax and flashes a nervous smile. "You're every bit as fearsome as one expects a Bishop to be. I just thought you might want someone to take on Prior *with* you."

"Stop flirting with me, Hornsby. Or I'll tell your fiancée."

At last, his smile comes easy again. His stiff shoulders soften. His formal tone falls away. "She isn't worried. She knows she's had me wrapped around her finger since our first tea party when we were four."

I imagine Victor, with his height and broad shoulders, at a tiny table drinking from a teacup. I can't help but laugh.

"Amelia Bishop, the greatest demon hunter of an age, *laughs*."

My amusement tightens. The warmth fades.

Whenever someone is nice to me, I can't help but wonder why. One day, Victor may need something—magic, or a hunting partner, a political ally—and he'll come to me for help. I'll remember this ball and how he was nice and made me laugh. And he knows I'll remember. Would he work as hard to cheer up girls from families with less magic?

I can't help but feel like this is a calculated investment, like everything in our world.

And I hate it. Alex is the only one I've never questioned. Him and the aunts.

The dance ends and Victor places a kiss on the back of my hand. "Try to have a good evening, Lady Bishop. Who knows how many we have left."

The hairs on my arms prickle at his ominous words. Before I can regain my composure, he's replaced by Nicolas Roanoke, a knobby-kneed boy with sandy-blond hair and an enormous, hooked nose. It seems Victor is right. Every boy approaches me as if approaching the gallows. When they take my hand, they're either shaking or so stiff that it's like dancing with a plank of wood. One boy, Harold Joornell, darts away the second the song ends and runs right into a waiter with a food tray. Spinach pinwheels sail across the room like disk-shaped confetti.

But in all honesty, this nervousness is working to my advantage. The boys can't look away from the main doors long enough to consider the motive behind my questions. And for all Perdita's faults, this lineup of suitors is actually helpful. They're from the families most connected— connected to the Priests themselves. They're full of gossip and intrigue, painting a perfect picture of the speculations surrounding the attack.

Did the Priests have a feud with anyone?

Had they been hunting recently? Could anything have followed them home?

Any hexed objects in the house?

Any family curses come due?

The eldest daughter was rumored to be engaged. Any jealous suiters?

I ask every question I can think of. Sometimes the scarab flutters, letting me know when I'm on the right track. I make mental notes of what to tell the aunts when I get home.

The general consensus is one of three theories: the Priests made a mistake and blew themselves up. Or the attack was coordinated by a high-ranking demon seeking revenge against the demon-hunting family. Or a family of witches as powerful as the Priests murdered them for some unknown political reason.

"It's the only logical explanation," Damien Isidare says. He's a squat boy two inches shorter than me, with a crooked front tooth and a smattering of freckles across his cheeks. Every other word from his mouth whistles a little at the end. "No one else is strong enough to bring down a First Family but another First Family."

"If you really believed that," I say, looking down at him, "I wonder why you came to Perdita's party or danced with me. You're telling me everyone here is *fine* with the idea that we're a bunch of murderers?"

"It's not like you'll kill us. We don't have much magic," he says, frowning. "I'm glad about it too, because my mother says too much magic warps the mind."

"For some, I'm sure that's true," I say. "For him, *certainly*."

I nod toward the grand staircase. Prior stands on the landing, searching the crowd.

Damien bows stiffly and sprints away.

Is that what they believe? That the Bishops, the Hatts, or the Priors murdered the Priests?

Prior's eyes lock on mine. He looks surprised. Shamelessly, he lets his eyes roll over my figure in the enormous dress, not even hiding the languid pause at my exposed chest.

If Prior insists on a confrontation, then I'll strike first.

I lift my skirts and march toward him. He meets me halfway on the dance floor, extending his hand. I seize it and crush it in my grip. He flinches but doesn't pull away. Instead, he slips his other hand around my waist and pulls me into the rush of shuffling feet.

His grip is harder to break than I'd like to admit.

"I suspected you liked it rough," he whispers in my ear on the first turn. "But I think you'll enjoy my hands much more if they're unbroken."

"If you say another word about hands or enjoyment, I'm going to cut out your tongue with my athame," I say, matching his grin. "I hear you've been threatening people to stay away from me."

He snorts. "It clearly isn't working as well as I'd like."

Magic rolls along my skin. The couples around us react immediately. Several heads turn toward us. The closest dancers step back, putting some distance between us. No one wants to get caught in the crossfire of my explosion. I don't blame them. I wouldn't want chunks of Dean Prior in my hair either.

"I can appreciate your fiery temper, Amelia. I'd never want you if you were weak," Prior says coolly, keeping his voice low. His hand tightens on my hip, almost like a dare. "But you need to learn the difference between a friend and an enemy. I'm no threat to you."

Scarab wings twitch in my pocket.

"Is that so?" I ask. "You'd never hurt me?"

"Not unless you liked it." He flashes too many perfect white teeth.

Scarab wings flutter again, and stronger this time.

"What do you think happened to the Priests?" I ask, almost all my concentration focused on my left pocket.

"I think they were fools who messed around with something they were too stupid to understand."

January's words surface again. *Take the book. I want it out of the house. I think Melody has been messing with something she shouldn't be.*

"Demons?"

"Obviously."

Nothing. The scarab remains still.

Prior keeps talking, seemingly unaware of my divided attention. "I heard that Mr. Priest visited that kooky shopkeeper. Has he said anything to you?"

"Mr. Priest is dead. Of course he hasn't said anything."

Prior huffs. "No, Ibis. You're always there. Honestly, I don't know why. I hate the smell of the place. Come on. Tell me. Has the traitor said anything to you?"

I love the smell of The Shop, the old books, incense, and herbs. If Prior doesn't think that smell is heavenly, that's one more reason to despise him.

"Yes, well, Ibis made me an offer of marriage," I say. This is a complete and utter lie, but I want to see Prior's reaction. "I suppose you'll duel him for that?"

The splotchy red on Prior's face intensifies. Then he forces a nervous smile. "You're joking."

"Of course I'm joking." But in doing so I also saw the truth. Prior is afraid of Ibis. I suppose he isn't the only one. Most people I know speak of him in much the same way. Part wary reverence, part fear. They view the mysterious owner of The Shop on 42nd Street as an uncomfortable necessity.

"What's so special about him?" Prior asks. His eyes sparkle in the candlelight as we turn around the room again. I find myself grateful for Perdita's stupidly large gown. It keeps Prior at a distance. I might not be able to rid myself of his hands, but at least he can't press himself against me.

I list Ibis's many lovely traits. "He's knowledgeable. Educated. Cultured. He *reads*. I think owning a shop like that is an amazing accomplishment."

"Honestly, Amelia. Are you being dense on purpose? I'm talking about your loyal dog. Laveau."

I stop dancing. "Are you trying to lose an eye?"

He tries to reinitiate the dance, but I don't move a muscle. I become the rock in the flow of dancers again, but the problem is, unlike Victor, Prior won't let go of my hand.

He pulls himself up to his full height. "He's the only one you let close. You smile for him. You laugh for him. He's not half as powerful as I am and yet you—"

I cast my thoughts out, searching my mindscape for Alex. I think I sense him upstairs in a far corner of the Hatts' grand house. *Where are you? If we don't leave now I'm going to murder Prior.*

"—I mean just look at them." Prior gestures to the couples twirling around us. "Every one of them, just pathetic. These low-born families have just enough magic to attract demons, but not enough to fight them. They *need* us, Amelia. Without us they'd lose their entrails to the first half-breed to cross their paths."

I hear the Priest children screaming in my ears. My stomach turns. "Do you ever get tired of listening to yourself speak, Prior?"

"What do I have to say to make you understand?" Prior pitches his voice low. He's backed me against a wall, out of the flow of dancers at least. "*I* want to be the one at your side. Together we could be the most powerful witches who ever walked this earth. Do you understand that? There's nothing I wouldn't do for us."

Apart from the disgusting outpour of his suffocating feelings, I note the scarab's stillness. Goddess help me. This idiot really believes what he's saying.

Alex appears on the landing, hair mussed and shirt untucked. His already full lips look swollen. His concern is clear as he searches the crowd for me. He finds me while still frantically trying to tuck his shirt back in.

Prior sees me staring and turns, his gaze fixing on Alex. He leans in and whispers into my ear, "Your aunt married her keeper and look how that ended."

He's talking about Demi. And he's right. She and Charles had over twenty years together before the demons inside him consumed him and she was forced to take his life.

"Don't be stupid," I say. "Alex is family. I love him like a brother, not that it's any of your business."

"And you'd do anything for your family, wouldn't you?"

"Yes," I say, without thinking of the consequences such an admission might provoke.

Prior steps back, his sneer sharp. "I guess we'll see if that's true."

CHAPTER 10
THE TIES THAT BIND

I lie on my bed, leafing through my mother's old journals.

Alex is beside me, his right side pressed to mine, head to foot. Every so often he tries to put his socked toes in my ears, and I repay him by trying to stick mine up his nose.

"Listen to this," he says, sitting up on an elbow. "Use this enchantment to induce automatic sleep. Render someone unconscious to avoid physical altercation."

"I could've used that last night," I say, my blood still boiling at the thought of Prior's threats. I don't know what I'm going to do about him yet. The aunts will expect me to find a diplomatic resolution rather than outright murder, but I know beyond a shadow of a doubt there will be a fight eventually. It feels inevitable.

"She has spells for everything," Alex says, turning the page in his journal, a sage-colored notebook with ginkgo leaves fanning the cover. "It looks like your mother took hunting very seriously."

It wasn't enough to save her life, I think. But he's right. My mother was prolific, to say the least. There *are* spells for everything, and the spells change with her age. The oldest journals were started when she was even younger than me. She has incantations for vanishing pimples and changing one's hair color, minor glamours that Perdita Hatt probably memorized ages ago.

By the time she's eighteen, there are notes about how to form mental connections with animals for every purpose imaginable—espionage to thievery to simple delivery. She seemed particularly interested in how to establish a magical connection to non-familiar animals. Her familiar was a raccoon named Scooner. He died the night she died, in the same bloody battle. Demi once told us that when they went to retrieve my mother's body, they found Scooner curled up on my mother's chest, his snout nestled in the crook of her cold neck.

They buried them beneath the sacred tree together.

"What the *hellebore* is that?"

I lower the journal at the sound of Arty's voice. She's in the doorway, pointing the head of her carved cane at the mound of cream tulle lying on my floor.

"Perdita charmed my outfit, and I don't know how to undo it. But I better figure it out because my leather jacket is in there. Somewhere."

"Where's the scarab?"

I pat my front pocket. "Safe and sound. Just the jacket is lost to me."

Arty arches an eyebrow. "Ask Demivere to help you. I've never been adept at glamour. What did you learn tonight?"

I snort at Arty's use of Demi's full name.

"Half the witches think *we* killed the Priests," I say, tucking a pressed flower into the journal to hold my place. I return it to the pile. "The other half thinks they were messing with magic they shouldn't have and blew themselves up."

Arty's eyebrows arch higher. "You're joking."

I fill her in on what I learned, about the theories regarding who—or what—could or couldn't have killed the Priests.

"The only one I didn't properly interrogate was Prior."

"Amelia," Arty moans. "I doubt he has the capacity or the gall for such an act. He couldn't have taken January in a fight, let alone the entire Priest family. What little evidence we've collected from their house isn't conclusive, but nothing points to him."

"Because of the fire," I finish. Too much was lost in the fire, which I suppose was the idea. Whoever set the blaze likely knew what they were doing.

Aunt Demi appears in the doorway. "They're here."

Arty's eyes flick to Alex stretched out in my bed trying to stick his toe in my ear. "It's time to go home, Alexander."

Alex's outstretched foot falls, but we both know he isn't in trouble for that. "Ouch, Arty. What's with the tone?"

"Go on, now." She does sound kinder, or at least as kind as Arty gets. Something is up.

"What's happened?" I ask. "Where's Melody?"

"Resting in her room." Arty nods toward the closet door. "Send him on his way."

I use the skeleton key to send Alex home. When the door to the closet is closed again, Arty says, "We have a binding. Put on your citrine and meet us downstairs."

I should have known. There's only one thing they would send Alex away for. They don't want him to watch another demonkeeper's execution.

I cross to the desk, preparing to search for the large citrine pendant the size of my palm. But my desk isn't the cluttered war zone it was yesterday. I'm surprised by this until I remember the hearthstone's magical intervention.

The citrine is lying neatly in plain view on top of a leather book, *Cursed Objects of Ancient Egypt*. The large orange stone is held in place by an ornate Celtic setting made with sterling silver. I pick it up by its long chain and clasp it around my throat. It's heavy, tugging on my neck.

At the last minute, I grab my athame too.

Just in case.

It's chilly when we step out into the yard. My breath puffs white in front of my face. We stand in a clear stretch of land not far from the forest's edge. Our guests have formed a circle: three demonkeepers and a witch, Kaliha Yzi, stand opposite my aunts and me. I'm ashamed that I don't know all the keepers' names. They're much older than me. The man sitting in the center of a circle of stones is maybe sixty.

A fourth demonkeeper steps into the light. When his St. Bruno pendant sparkles, I recognize Arty's keeper, Monsieur Lambert, immediately. Alex's dad is like an older version of Alex himself—dark skin and a bright smile—but with a lovely French accent to boot.

The demonkeeper who is about to be executed is on his knees in the middle of our circle. A demon trap. He is naked from the waist up. His arms and torso show signs of a struggle. Cuts and wounds of varying severity crisscross his skin.

His smile is so soft and sweet that I return it. Someone should smile at him before he dies.

"Forgive me for not standing, Lady Bishop," he says,

and gestures to the demon trap around him. "It lets me have my body one last time." I nod, not bothering to tell him I know this. Maybe he thinks I'm too young to understand how the bindings work, but I do. The aunts have never protected me from this dark knowing.

"Tran," Demi says, the sadness in her voice grating against my skin. "I'm so sorry."

"Is there anything you want to confess before we proceed?" Arty says. "You know better than to think we will judge you."

Tran hangs his head. It's enough to make my own throat tight. "Murder. Rape. In the hours I lost myself, they used my body to commit many sins, Madam Bishop."

"What happened?" I ask. I want to know the trigger. I'll take any knowledge I can, any at all, if it means keeping Alex safe.

"I was overtaken."

"By what?" I press. "What kind of demon was it?" *Tell me what to keep Alex away from.*

"Why does it matter?" the witch Kaliha hisses, her grieving face red and tear-stained.

"Kaliha, she's a girl," Tran says. Kaliha turns away from me.

Her shoulders shake. I know she's crying even if she has hidden her face.

Will this be our fate, Alex and me? Am I destined to see him here one day, on his knees in a demon trap, begging for my forgiveness for whatever the demons made him do before I could stop him?

Here, beside this house where we played as children. *Kill him* as if he isn't family. As if I haven't loved him all my life.

"How many do you hold inside you?" Arty asks. "I don't want any surprises when I get in there."

"Seventy-nine," he replies.

"Do you have any requests?" Demi asks. I notice that she leaves out the word *last*.

How can she do it? Doesn't this bring back memories of the night she lost Charles? I can't bring myself to ask her.

Tran pulls some small trinket from around his neck and offers it to Kaliha.

"Give this to Frida." Then he slides a ring off his finger. "And give this to Carlos."

Carlos, I know. He's eleven or twelve, and already being trained as a keeper. Alex works with the kid and says he's one of the spunkier ones. How does this man feel knowing that someday his son will be on his knees in a demon trap? Killed by the very people who are supposed to love him most?

"Are you ready?" Demi asks Kaliha.

How can you ask her that? You know. You know—

Kaliha straightens her spine, turning back toward us. Her wet cheeks shine.

"We give you the honor of expelling seventy-nine demons from this world," Arty says. "We see your strength and your bravery, Tran."

Arty and Demi shift their stances and the power hits like a crashing wave.

Monsieur Lambert and the other two keepers simply shift their weight, as if bracing themselves against the force of it. To me it feels like electric fire in my veins. It's like my blood is running backward. Tran shivers as if he is freezing to death.

The aunts unfold him like a flower, tearing off each petal. He has layers and layers of demons crowded inside him. I can't see them exactly since they are little more than shadows crouching inside Tran's mindscape, but I can feel what the aunts are doing. They find a demon and bind it to the circle.

Tran starts bleeding from his nose.

About seventy demons have been marked when something changes. We are down to the last few, the most powerful, those smart enough to hide deep inside the keeper.

The change is very subtle at first, and I can tell that the aunts are so busy with the binding that they don't feel what I feel. Their attention doesn't waver.

But a cold tremor of power taints the air. A shiver of malevolence.

My eyes open and immediately connect with a keeper's. Not Tran or Monsieur Lambert, but one of the standbys here to absorb a troublesome demon if the need arises.

I know immediately I'm not looking into the eyes of a keeper. I am looking at a demon, one which has surfaced and taken over the man housing him.

Arty's head snaps up in that instant and she makes a startled sound beside me. I don't even have time to react to her surprise, because the possessed keeper tackles me before I fully understand what's happening.

I hit the ground with the flat of my back and the air leaves me. My ears ring and the stars above me spin before his snarling face comes into clear view.

"You are well disguised, little *witch*." He says the last word like a joke, and he wraps his large hands around my throat and squeezes. "But I was *there*, on those golden battlefields. I know your stench!"

The keeper is struck from behind and his body is thrown off me.

"Hellebore," I curse, and sit up.

"Run!" Demi yells. *Through the woods and don't stop until we call for you.*

"I'll fight!"

"No!" Arty hisses. She flings a hand out at the other three keepers, Monsieur Lambert included, who are kneeling and clutching their talismans. "You're calling their demons. Get away from them!"

I'm calling their demons? *I'm* making all the keepers lose control? And if I don't leave now, not one but all the keepers will have to be killed.

Alex's father will have to be killed.

"Run!" Demi screams. The first edge of real panic in her voice sends a sharp pang of terror echoing through me. The man-demon who choked me a moment ago is on his feet and charging after me. Arty's power shoots like lightning from her hands and makes a deafening crack as it slams against him.

I bolt for the forest. I could have gone into the house, used the skeleton key to go far away, but I don't want to leave my aunts. I refuse to abandon them in the middle of a fight. I'll take my magic out of range so that the keepers have a chance to regain the upper hand. But if they can't, I want to be here to help. I can't do that if I jump blind, halfway across the world.

"Oh my!" Phelia says, appearing at my side as I run through the trees. I duck under a branch then leap over a fallen log. I'm off the path. I don't care. I keep moving. "Are you playing hide and seek with Alex again? Is he winning? He always wins."

"No games, Phelia. It's demons," I huff, my breath heavy.

"Demons!" she squeaks. "It's your chance, Amelia! *Die! Please die*—"

"Not now!" I run until my lungs are on fire. The tree line breaks open and I am overlooking a cliff on the edge of the mountain. Nothing but wilderness and a large ominous moon hangs in front of me.

And the steep drop below.

A flash of silver moves in the periphery of my vision, and I whirl, athame pointing.

Ciel steps out of the forest, looking very much like the warrior from my dream, except without a helmet. His shining face is bare, eyes shimmering with starlight. I only saw him in the cemetery for a moment, but his face is so much more familiar now. The small upward tilt of his nose, the plane where his throat meets his shoulder and chest.

Phelia takes one look at him and disappears with a squeak.

I realize I'm staring and he's letting me. My cheeks flush.

"I sensed the demons," he says. "Are you all right?"

He steps closer and I lift the athame higher.

"You still do not know me?" he asks. His tone and face give nothing away.

"You're Ciel."

"Yes."

"You're the lieutenant to the queen."

"Yes," he says, the fur along his collar ruffling in the mountain breeze. "But these are facts, not knowing."

He steps toward me, and I hold up a hand. "Stop. I don't want you to kiss me again."

The scarab flitters in my pocket. He looks down as if he heard it. Can he? He must be from another world then, if he has hearing that good.

It's impossible for my face to burn any hotter.

His full lips quirk to one side. "Are you lying?"

"I don't know where you come from, *Ciel*, but here no *means* no. It doesn't matter what I'm thinking. It matters what I say." I jab the athame at him. "And I say *no*."

He stops. And I realize he never made a sound. No twigs snapping. No crush of grass. He isn't that far away, yet I can't hear his breath.

Too fast for me to see, Ciel encloses me in his arms. For a moment, I'm struck dumb by the press of his body against mine. I'm aware of every place our bodies touch. At the thigh, at the wrist, at the chest. I'm softening against him, some part of me deep in my gut loosening, giving over.

One touch and I'm surrendering in a way I've never done. Not once in all my life.

The smell of flowers—of a whole field of flowers—makes my head reel.

No, a voice says. A hard, cold voice. *Snap out of it.*

I open my eyes, expecting to meet his starry gaze, but I'm confronted by a long braid instead. He's turned his back on me, taking a step away.

A cruel, raspy voice rises from the darkness. "You thought you were clever, Lord Ciel, but he knows. He *knows* what you did."

The blood in my veins ices. What a haunting voice.

I step around Ciel, but he puts an arm out, stopping me. A keeper stands in front of us, his brow damp with sweat. His eyes flick to mine. He laughs. A deep, bone-rattling laugh that makes my skin crawl.

Now I understand why the voice sounds the way it does, with so many demons fighting for control of those vocal cords. The voice is one of many. Tonalities rise, fall, and collapse on themselves. They speak over one another, passing the voice around between all those inside. How many are in there? Forty? Fifty?

The demon cackles, a sound that feels like sandpaper on the back of my neck. "We'll drag her to Hell, to our master, before you can even—"

His words are cut off by a raging snarl as Ciel lifts his sword high over the keeper's head.

"No!" I scream, but it's too late.

In one swift movement, Ciel brings his sword down and beheads the keeper. The head hits the soft mountain grass and doesn't roll.

"Why!" I yell, furious. "Why did you do that?"

"You're in danger."

"You killed an innocent man and he died for nothing! We'll have to catch all those demons again."

"They're dead," he says, sheathing his sword.

"Ugh, *no*." How do I explain demonkeeping to this creature?

"Come with me," he says, stepping over the dead body of the fallen keeper as if that isn't someone's lover. Someone's precious friend. "You're no longer safe here. Until you fully awaken, you're too vulnerable."

"I'm wide awake. Look at me."

He reaches for me, palm outstretched. "I cannot leave you here."

I step back. "I'm not leaving."

"You're not safe here."

"I'm pretty sure running off into the night with a guy who beheads innocent people isn't very *safe* either."

The air crackles and a white flash of power cuts through the night. Ciel deflects the blow without even taking his eyes off my face. It isn't until the snap-crack of Demi's power pings off Ciel's arm that I notice what it struck:

metal cuffs, ornate and stretching from wrist to elbow. I feel like I saw this piece of armor in the dream, too.

Demi steps out of the trees, chest heaving. Her hair is down and wild around her face.

At the sight of Ciel, she freezes on the spot.

"Amelia, are you all right?" She won't even look at me. She's staring at Ciel, but she doesn't attack him again.

Why? She would never hesitate if she thought him a demon.

Does she know what he is? What he's capable of? Until now, my education has been focused on demons—learning their breeds, habits, and weaknesses. I thought I was being practical by specializing my education. Now I realize I've made myself blind. There is so much I don't know.

"He killed—" My voice falters. Shame floods me. I don't even know his name. This keeper was just murdered, and I don't even know his name.

"Hector's dead?" Demi spares the briefest glance at the beheaded body before fixing her gaze on Ciel.

"It's time," Ciel says. He isn't speaking to me. He's returning Demi's intense gaze over the dead man's body.

"You can't take her," Demi pleads. "We need her now more than ever."

"You have fulfilled your bargain. You owe us nothing."

"It isn't about the bargain," Demi insists. She turns and searches my face. "We love her."

"She's not safe here."

"We've always protected her." Tears sting the corners of her eyes, silver in the moonlight. "Please, we need—we just need more time."

Ciel turns those starlit eyes on me and my heart stumbles. "I will not take you against your will, but you will come with me."

"Like hellfire I will," I manage to say, and the scarab doesn't flutter.

His shoulders slump with obvious disappointment. For a long moment, he only looks at me. Then he says, "Call and I will come."

He disappears into the woods, leaving me in the pine-musk clearing with my slack-jawed aunt and a dead body. I stare into the trees after him, but there's nothing but darkness. Not a single sign. No proof he was there at all except Hector's body at our feet.

I face Demi. "What the *hellebore*?"

"I—"

"You *knew* him."

She turns and hurries back toward the house, her head down in intense thought. I dog her every step with questions.

"Demi!"

"I met him before. Yes. A long time ago."

"Where?"

She doesn't answer. I see the house appearing through the dense woods and my questions intensify.

"He kissed me. He said I need to wake up and that I'm not safe here. What the hell is going on?"

Demi stops, searching my face. "He kissed you? On the mouth?"

I throw up my hands. "Certainly not anywhere *else*."

Demi swears and her steps quicken.

I won't let up. "What did he—?"

"Amelia, please. Stop asking." Demi seizes my hands. She's trembling all over, her cold hands shaking in mine. "I recognize that you are confused and likely scared, but I need to speak to Artemis first."

"But—"

"Do I have *suspicions*? Yes." She squeezes my hands really hard. I try not to yelp. "Does his appearance have a great many implications? *Yes*. But this is serious. I shouldn't say anything until I'm sure I know what's going on. I might make things worse."

"A binding went to hell and a demonkeeper was beheaded. This can't get any worse."

But I'm wrong.

We emerge from the trees to a ghastly scene. Monsieur Lambert and the two other keepers are heaving Tran's body onto a blazing pyre. Kaliha, who'd been crying openly over the flames, sees me and lets out a shriek. She storms toward me, eyes blazing with firelight. I feel her magic rising. Reflexively I raise the athame, preparing to recite a shielding charm.

"What are you playing at?" she hisses. She looks like she wants to strike me.

"I know you're not insinuating that my niece is to blame for this." Arty hobbles to my side.

"It was her magic. I felt it!"

Monsieur Lambert is at my shoulder in a few easy strides of his long legs. "She's not to blame, Yzi. I know what the demons thought and felt better than you. They wanted to capture her and take her to someone."

"Who?" Arty hisses. Demi reaches out and places her pale hand on top of Arty's at the head of the cane. Arty's eyes unfocus. Then she swears. "*My Goddess.*"

"I want an explanation," Kaliha demands. "Because of her, Tran had an unclean death!"

"That's not true," Monsieur Lambert says, touching the pendant at his throat. "His soul passed unharmed. I assure you. If you hadn't panicked and broken the connection, you'd know this for yourself."

I'm so relieved to see Alex's dad is okay and in control of himself. He spares me a small smile.

Kaliha's nostrils flare. "You can't know for sure! It happened so fast!"

She waves a hand over the yard as if to signify all that passed. The other two keepers are standing vigil over Tran's body as it burns on the makeshift pyre. But that's not all they are doing. They're also casting nervous glances my way. A mixture of disbelief, curiosity, and horror plays across their faces in the dancing firelight. What did the demons tell them?

Would they tell me if I asked?

"I'm sorry. Whatever happened," I say to Kaliha, "whatever that was, it was an accident."

I'm apologizing to thin air. Kaliha has already stormed away.

"You're not to blame," Demi says, but her voice lacks its usual kindness. It's a perfunctory condolence at best. "She's suffered a great loss tonight. She won't be in her right mind for a while."

A great loss. Like the one Demi herself suffered.

But even as I try to be compassionate for Kaliha, I'm angry too. Why didn't she work harder to protect him if she loved him so much? Isn't she also to blame for what's happened? If something happened to my keeper, I would have only myself to blame.

"Hector?" Monsieur Lambert asks with a hopeful face.

"Dead," Demi says. "I'm sorry, Guillaume."

A dark shape shifts in front of a second-floor window, and I turn, lured by the movement.

It's Melody, standing in the stairwell and looking down on us from the landing. She watches us without moving. Her stillness makes my flesh crawl.

I recall Arty's words. *The skeleton key kept taking me to the vault.*

You're a demon, I think, looking at the girl in the window. A demon who slaughtered her whole family, and she's squatting in our house.

Before she turns away, a ghost of a smile tugs at her lips.

"What will we tell the coven about Hector?" Demi whispers, low enough that only Arty, Monsieur Lambert, and I can hear.

"Amelia was attacked by a keeper who lost control and you beheaded him," Monsieur Lambert says simply. "I will agree to this."

"It isn't right!" I say, trying to keep my voice low. "You can't place the blame on him."

Arty laughs, but it's a cruel, hard sound. "Do you think he gives a damsel seed about his honor now? Come off it."

My insides boil.

"I need to speak to you in the library," Demi says to Arty. Then she turns to Monsieur Lambert before he can return to the keepers, and adds, "Guillaume, you'd better join us too. Please."

He nods over his shoulder. "Let me leave instructions for Hector's retrieval."

As soon as he walks toward the other keepers and exchanges words, Demi squeezes my hand. "I want you to go up to bed now. It's late."

"You can't just send me to bed. I'm not a child."

"We'll be the first to give you answers once we have them," Demi says.

"Why can't you discuss it in front of me? Why can't—"

Demi reaches up and taps my face, three times. An overwhelming exhaustion consumes me. As soon as she's done it, I know it for what it is. My mother's knockout spell—or is it Demi's spell, stolen by her younger sister?

No matter. The result is the same.

My knees give and I fall back into sleep as if I have complete faith someone will catch me.

Witches.

Can't trust a one.

CHAPTER 11

THE SHOP ON 42ND STREET

Sunlight streams into my eyes. I squint, trying to sit up. I'm in my bed, still wearing the clothes I wore last night, the large citrine pendant heavy against my chest. The only thing that's been removed are my shoes.

I'm disoriented, trying to remember how I got here. The last thing I remember is standing in the yard with Alex's dad and my aunts and—

She knocked me out. Demi used the knockout spell, pushing me into a sleep so deep I didn't even dream.

I leap from bed, run down the stairs. I check every room. I throw open the door to the library. The desk is empty. The fireplace cold.

Phelia stands near a bookcase. The sunlight makes her pale, little more than a wisp. She sighs longingly at the titles.

"Everyone is gone?" I ask. "Even Melody?"

"Who's Melody?" Phelia asks.

Maybe Arty took her to the vault after all.

"And you're not dead," Phelia whines.

"I'll try harder next time." I rub my forehead. "Did they say anything before they left?"

"Oh yes. They were talking a great deal. And they looked terrible. They're so *old*."

"They aren't old."

"They look old. Maybe *they'll* die soon," she adds hopefully.

"Phelia, focus, please. Where did the aunts go?"

"You can't follow. They warded themselves against you."

My heart thumps in my chest. "Why would they do that?"

"So you wouldn't follow with the key. They don't want you to know where they've gone."

"Which is...?"

"The border."

"Mexico? Canada?" Weird.

"Open Gluck for me, please. The one about the flowers."

"Not unless you tell me about the border."

"Open the book and I'll tell you," she says, lifting a stubborn chin, as stubborn as a chin can look without a body.

I cross to the shelf and comb the spines for the thin book of poems she wants. I find it sandwiched between Wislawa Szymborska's *Here* and T. S. Eliot's *The Waste Land*.

"The first poem, please," Phelia coos as she slides into the window seat, bouncing with anticipation.

"If I open this book you'll stop paying attention." I hold the book against my chest. "I want you to answer my questions. And *then* I'll let you read."

"I want a poem for every question," she says.

My head is about to explode. "Phelia."

"I've already answered four questions. You owe me four poems. Deal or no deal?"

If only ghosts could have their ears twisted or noses flicked.

"Come on, Amelia. You get to go to parties and kiss boys, and all I have is this." She bats her ghostly eyelashes.

"Perdita's party was horrible. And I haven't been kissing anyone."

The scarab twitches in my pocket, startling me.

"I *saw* you," Phelia insists. "You let him put his tongue in your mouth. In a *cemetery*."

"I didn't *let*—" My face blazes with heat. "Look. Can we just focus? Where did the aunts go?"

"I told you. The border."

"*What* border?"

"The Elysium border."

Goosebumps rise on my arms. "Elysium."

And I would be King Vinae, Husband of The Living Queen, Sephone of Elysium.

"It's a real place?" I ask, and realize my hands have begun to shake. But why am I surprised that Elysium is a real place? Ciel is real, isn't he? Why not Elysium?

"Yes."

"What's—what's there?" I ask.

"The fey. The fey rule Elysium."

The world tilts and I drop the book of poems in favor of a good grip on the window seat. The room is spinning around me.

Ciel is fey. Ciel is fey. I've been kissed by a fey.

And that is what terrifies me more than anything. The fey are usually depicted as kind rulers who taught witches magic. They gave us the power to protect ourselves from the demons. But the fey also take witches as wives. Bewitch them. Enslave them.

What had he said? I desperately rack my memory for his exact words.

I will not take you against your will, but you will come with me.

You will come with me—a fey.

We've had stories about enchanted kisses from the very beginning. And hadn't Ciel said something about waking up? But waking from *what*? I'm not asleep. There is no castle and prince here. None of that damsel nonsense.

"They went to the border to talk to Ciel about not taking me," I say, more to myself than to Phelia. "Wait, did they take Melody to the border?"

Phelia shrugs.

"Rowan," I call out. "Is *she* still here?"

The house doesn't answer, but for some reason I am suddenly aware of a dark presence somewhere. It's coming from the direction of Phelia's room.

But I looked in there before coming to the library. The room was empty. Is she hiding from me?

I pull at my face and groan. "What is going *on*? Why can't they just talk to me?"

"They never even *look* at me," Phelia says with a huff. "Come on, Amelia, why can't they see me?"

I think of Arty's careless *I hate ghosts* and frown sympathetically. "Do you want Aunt Arty to cast you out?"

I don't mean to frighten her, but her lip trembles all the same. "No."

My chest hurts. I want to make Phelia happy. I really do. I want to give her the life that was taken from her. She just wants to be part of this family. To share her days with me and the aunts here in Rowan House. To be seen, spoken to, loved. But Arty is so scared of ghosts I know she'll banish her the second they realize she's still around. And I can't tell

Demi because she can't keep a secret from her sister to save her life.

But I haven't given up the hope that one day I'll find a way to make Phelia's dream come true.

"Let's read some poems," I say, and begin turning the pages for her.

But my mind wanders. I'm searching everything Arty said, Demi said, even Monsieur Lambert's words—anything for some hint to the truth.

"Next," Phelia calls out when she wants me to flip the page.

Is this about the demon attack? Is something larger and worse than I imagined happening here? A brilliant flash of the armored fey and clawed demons burns in my mind. Is it a war?

"Next."

Did war spill from their world into ours and it cost the Priests their lives? It wouldn't be the first time war took innocent lives. And it won't be the last.

But what is Ciel doing here? What does it have to do with *me*?

"Next."

Ciel. It unnerves me how easily I've taken to his name. Since first hearing it, I've used it without reserve, despite the power in names. Is it the magic that's making the name seem familiar? Or have I really heard it somewhere before?

"Next."

A sharp screech echoes through the top of the house followed by a tapping on the library door. When I get up to answer it, Phelia shrieks, "Hey! I'm reading that."

I toss the book at her knowing it will go right through her and land on the window seat.

"Rude," she says, arms crossing.

I open the door and Dragon swoops in on blue-gray wings spread wide. He lands on the desk, his claws digging into the leather spine of a book for balance. At first, I'm terrified that he's injured. His flying is awkward.

But then he drops a circular object onto the desk. It skitters across the wood.

The breath leaves me.

Phelia shrieks. "Is that...is that...?"

"A bloodstone," I say. My mouth goes dry. I dash forward and grab the stone as if it's going to disappear. The blood-red rock is about half the size of my hand. The magic echoes through my bones as I touch it.

Hear me hear me hear me.

It's warm in my hand.

Hear me hear me hear me.

My heart pounds in my ears.

"This came from the Priests?" I ask, and realize I'm shaking. I barely register Dragon's excited whirls and chirps.

Hear me hear me hear me.

"Let me—" Phelia whispers over my shoulder. I turn around and meet glowing twin red flames where her black-water eyes should be. "Let me see it."

Hellebore.

I hold the stone tighter as I slip my free hand under my collar, groping for the skeleton key.

"Phelia," I say with a low warning growl. "Stay where you are."

"Please." Her voice is darker than I've ever heard it. "I need to hear it. I need to hear her words." Her little hands stretch out in front of her, reaching for the stone.

"No."

Phelia shrieks. Her sweet, childlike form transforms

into a wraith-like creature. Her outstretched fingers curl into claws. The pools reflecting a pulsing stone burn brighter.

She lunges for me.

"Now!" I command Dragon.

His wings spread wide as he launches himself from the desk. His screeches drown out Phelia's as the blue jay dives toward her face, wings flapping. She falls back, howling.

I run. I dash for the library door. But instead of throwing it wide and running up toward my blood-sealed room, I slip the skeleton key into the keyhole beneath the library's door handle. The bone warms in my hand, twitching with magic, and the light under the door shifts. I cast one last look over my shoulder to see Dragon swooping and diving at Phelia. She's batting at her head wildly, trying to knock him away.

He squawks, claws tangling up in her ghost hair.

I dart through the library door. Her howling is cut short as I slam it shut. The wood rattles in the frame with the force of it.

"Ibis! Ibis!" I cry.

I've run to the place I always run to when I want answers the aunts won't give me.

A chair groans. A cabinet slams shut. A string of grumbled curses followed by quick steps and then suddenly a tall man is in front of me. He looks down his long straight nose at me. Ibis's thick black hair falls into his eyes. His lips seem permanently pressed into a thin line, as if he is always refraining from saying something he really, *really* wants to say.

For a second he just stares, eyes wide. Then he blinks rapidly and speaks as if forcing himself to do it.

"H-hello, Lady Bishop." His voice is stilted as he takes

me in. "Might I ask what in the hellebore has happened to you?"

"A lot."

"I see that," he says, his brows rising. "Care to share?"

A gold chain runs from the breast pocket of his heather-gray vest out of sight beneath a suit jacket. He always dresses that way. I once asked the aunts if it was an English thing and they said no, it's just Ibis. I'd caught enough commentary from the aunts to understand that something had happened in London and he was banished for it. Now Ibis is confined to his shop, under a sort of probation. Or would it be considered house arrest?

"Is the shop warded?" I ask, my chest heaving from my escape.

"Of course," he says, his gaze still heavy. "Warding isn't something I take down for maintenance."

"*Ghost* warded?" I press. "Because I've got a ghost who is feeling a little wrathful today."

He shifts his weight from one leg to the other. "What's happened?"

Ibis is the only person who knows about Phelia, apart from Alex and me. I'd asked him for advice when Phelia first returned, for tricks that can help keep her hidden from the aunts. I was only ten at the time and I was afraid they might see her and cast a spell that would separate us again. He gave me the sigil that would keep the aunts' spirit blind and showed me how to carve it into the undersides of their beds with my blessed athame when they weren't looking.

It's for that very reason that now, with complete trust, I show him the bloodstone, holding it up in a beam of sunlight cutting through a dusty stack of books.

"Ah yes, that will do it." His long, slender fingers pluck

the stone from my hand. "Truth be told, this would enrage any spirit, even our dear, sweet Phelia."

"I thought I could calm her. Clearly, I'm an idiot." I'm talking too fast, as if trying to outpace the heart rabbiting in my chest.

"No, not an idiot. Just inexperienced," he says, still grave. "All ghosts are obedient to the call of a bloodstone. It's no indication of the strength of your relationship with her."

"Why are they called?"

"It's an ancient magic. One of the few magics that have existed since the beginning of time." He pats the gold time-piece in his pocket as if that's where he keeps all the time in the world. "The dead must honor the dead. If someone went through the trouble of creating a bloodstone with their last breath, the dead must honor the request hidden therein. If a ghost hears the message, they will stop at nothing to fulfill it. You were smart to hide this from her. Who knows what dark task she would have been charged with."

"It came from the Priests' house," I say, looking up into the sky-blue eyes hidden behind the frames.

Ibis stills. "Did it now?"

"Dragon brought it to me."

He's staring at me. Staring as if he hasn't quite seen me before.

"What?" I demand.

He starts. "Nothing. It's just interesting."

He turns away from me and holds the bloodstone up to the light again. "It's good that you stopped Phelia all the same. If the Last is a request for revenge, it would have been nearly impossible to stop her from tormenting someone until they took their own life. She doesn't need that on her little conscience."

"Then why did the killer leave the stone behind? Why not take the most damning piece of evidence with them?"

"Even if they were to spot the stone in the rubble, they probably couldn't touch it."

My brow furrows. "Couldn't touch it?"

But Dragon had been permitted to touch it. Is the stone really able to tell the difference between friend and foe?

Ibis seems to read my thoughts. "The stone wants to be opened. Its only mission is to be found by an ally and unlocked. But the same magic protects it from the named enemy. When we unlock this stone, I imagine we will discover which Priest cast their Last. That person will name their enemy, the person they believe betrayed them. And *that's* the target of revenge, whoever is named in the Last."

"We need to crack the stone to find out who killed the Priests?"

"To find out who the Priests *think* killed the Priests," he corrects. "But yes. The sooner the better. Do you know how to open a stone?"

"No," I admit. "That's why I brought it to you."

He nods as if he suspected as much, and there's something about it that makes me feel bad. Is this what Ibis has come to expect of me? I always turn up here when I need something and I always get straight to the demands? I never say, *Hello, Ibis. How are you today, Ibis?*

"Do you miss London?" I ask, unsure of how to fill the silence but feeling like I should nonetheless.

"Sometimes," he says simply.

And that's the end of that. What a lovely conversationalist I am.

I'm left looking around the grand store. An open atrium

stretches up six stories. I've never asked, but I suspect the top floor is Ibis's living quarters. Grand bookcases seem to reach all the way up. The ceiling looks like a cathedral, with an enormous fresco of floral fields and a woman with long hair walking through the flowers. Animals of all sorts are blended into the painting, and I can't help but feel there must be a thousand details that I can't see because it's so high above.

This place is part bookshop, part warehouse, part supply store. Anything a witch may need is here, and if it isn't, Ibis is the man who will get it for a price.

The Shop on 42nd Street.

Something crashes in another chamber.

I try to peer around Ibis, who only says, "I have other customers, Lady Bishop. None who are as graceful as you."

A second box falls from an unseen shelf and hits the floor. A cat screeches.

Ibis sighs. "I should check on him. Excuse me."

He takes only three steps before turning on his heels and whirling back to me. He's staring again. Seriously? Is there something on my face or what?

He says, "I have some powdered cacao in the herbs. For your sister." When I only blink at him, he adds, "It's like catnip for the wraithed. Blow it into her face and she'll purr like a kitten again."

I mutter my thanks and head to the herb section. While I swipe at my face with my sleeve, just in case I do have something horrible stuck to me, I pass shelves of crystals in all shapes, sizes, and colors. Black onyx, rose quartz, hematite, amethyst, citrine, amber, and heliotrope—all of which I recognize on sight. But some others are harder to distinguish, jasper from agate, sodalite from lapis.

The gates from my dream flash in my mind. The stone

wall interrupted only by those massive bird sculptures guarding the presumed door. What had they been made of? The Southern Gate, the one destroyed by the warring king, had looked like black tourmaline. I'm sure that's what the vultures had been carved from.

This part of the store reeks of incense. A whole display is given to sticks and cones in every scent imaginable. Gold thuribles hang from a hook overhead. Soapstone incense burners line a shelf.

I don't know much about the uses of incense. The Bishops don't specialize in ceremonial magic, so I should admit my education has been lacking in this area.

I finally find a cluster of stone barrels with labeled cards. These barrels must weigh hundreds of pounds. No offense to Ibis, but I doubt the shopkeeper in spectacles lifted these alone. He used magic or had help. And what an odd choice to hold herbs in. But each barrel is full: lavender, marjoram, rosemary, sage, sweetgrass, copal, willow bark, and so many others. I slip my fingers into a bin of caraway seeds, feeling the cool grains tumble off my fingertips.

An encompassing, heady scent of the earthy plants makes my head swim. I close my eyes. I feel like I could roll around in it.

"Caraway," Ibis says.

I blink my eyes open and wonder how much time has passed. He stands beside me in the shadowy aisle. I'm still elbow deep in the barrel. I pull my hand out slowly, as if I've been caught doing something I shouldn't have. I spot the powdered cacao in one of the smaller containers.

"The fey love caraway. Are you having problems with fairies as well as wraith sisters?"

I freeze mid-scoop.

A bright image of Ciel's kiss blasts through my mind. I

could ask Ibis about it. It would be embarrassing and more than a little weird, talking to him about kissing, but he might understand the implications. He wouldn't brush me off the way my aunts had.

"What do you know about the borderlands?" I ask, and start filling a small plastic bag with cacao powder.

He lifts his chin a little higher as his hands slip into his pockets. "There's a great deal of written history on the borderlands, Lady Bishop."

"*Amelia.*"

"Lady Amelia."

I sigh and pinch the top of the cacao bag closed, and slide the stone lid back onto the container.

"I have a good book on the subject, if you're interested."

I'm not surprised. Ibis always has a book. He loves books. If the stacks with musty bindings stretching skyward are any indication, books are Ibis's favorite thing.

"Though I must admit that your own library should have a copy."

"Why do you say that?" I ask.

"It was written by your ancestor," Ibis says, a little pedantically. "Mara Bishop, sister of Rowan, daughter of Isolde."

Mara Bishop. The first witch of *the* First Family. Supposedly, she was the one who struck a bargain with the fey for our magic. She formed the alliance that allowed a handful of trusted families to lead a war against the demons and protect our world.

I didn't know she wrote a book.

Why didn't I know she wrote a book?

"Your aunts didn't tell you Mara Lightbringer was an author as well as our savior?" He's grinning in that mischievous way of his. "How *interesting.*"

To Ibis, everything is *interesting*.

"How interesting?" I ask.

"They say the sister queens of Elysium *only* trusted Mara Bishop. The rest of us they deemed questionable."

"That is interesting. Can I borrow this book?" I ask. Because I know I couldn't possibly afford it with the few crumpled dollars I have in my pocket. And yes, we have a house account here, but buying an ancient book is no doubt expensive. And an expensive book will *not* go unnoticed when it's time for the aunts to settle the bill at the end of the month. I would buy it just to spite them for keeping me in the dark about Ciel and whatever is going on, but I don't want them searching me, not while I'm still in possession of a bleeding, demonic grimoire.

He looks at my face for a long moment, considering me. I try not to squirm or look suspicious.

"No," he drawls at last. "I cannot let you take the book. I don't know if that would be wise."

"But—"

"I'll let you read it," he adds before I can fully protest. "While I examine the bloodstone for you. But it should stay here."

My shoulders relax. "Fine."

"Go sit by the hearth. I'll send Athena to keep you company."

The hearth in The Shop on 42nd Street is cut from snowflake obsidian. But it's much smaller than the hearth we have at Rowan House. Or at least, it seems dwarfed beneath the high ceilings.

But it's still cozy, because the surrounding shelves create makeshift walls.

I settle into an oversized chair the color of honey and pull my legs into the seat. A clink of porcelain makes me look up to find a gilded pot, teacup, and saucer on the wood table beside my chair. Two silver containers—one with sugar cubes and the other with milk—appear beside the pot too. I reach for them, but they scoot away.

I sigh, resigned. Ibis still doesn't trust Americans to make their own tea.

I let the teapot serve me. Watch the spout fill my cup with fragrant black tea. Watch as a splash of milk and two sugar cubes are added, as a small gold spoon swirls clockwise four times. When I'm finally allowed to take the cup, I drink deeply, enjoying the sweet warmth and rich scent. It's delicious.

Something catches my eye. A large tawny cat with pointy ears slinks my way. Black tufts of fur wave from those ear tips as Athena, Ibis's familiar, a Eurasian lynx, approaches with a rather large book clamped between her massive jaws. I set my teacup down.

"Thank you," I say, and wait for her to remove her teeth from the red leather binding. I don't want to know what she'll do if I'm rude enough to pull the book from her jaws.

She inclines her head to me before moving closer to the fire. She stretches, and disturbingly sharp claws protrude from her paws before she settles down on the old Tapiz rug and closes her large amber eyes. A nice nap in front of the crackling fire on a rainy day, not a terrible idea at all.

I open the book and find a page marked with a strip of leather. I'm grateful. This book weighs a ton. There is no way I could have finished it cover to cover in one afternoon. Knowing where to start will save me a lot of time. I rub the aged paper between my fingers.

A Comprehensive History of the Borderlands

1945 edition, translated from Classical Irish to Modern English by Sir Ruddy O'Malley at the behest of The Academy of Itinerant Scholars

Translator's Note
   In the alliance forged between Mara Bishop and Queen Naja of Elysium, we were rewarded with the greatest gift: knowledge. Queen Naja bestowed this wisdom upon Lady Bishop, sometimes known as Mara Lightbringer, in hopes of solidifying peace between the realms. Lady Bishop dutifully transcribed the wisdom as it was told unto her, and I, Ruddy O'Malley, have tried to remain utterly faithful to that transcription. Regardless of errors contained within, let it be forever known that the fey are our friends and allies, and may this compendium serve as a sign of our open trust and unified faith in this alliance.
   Three worlds intersect on this plane: Elysium, Hell, and Septem Terras—the Elysian name for our Earth. Collectively, they are known as the borderlands. Each of these worlds has their own history, as we have ours. What follows is the chronicle of The First War between mortals and the demons, but also the histories of Elysium and Hell as told to Mara Lightbringer by Queen Naja.

The rest of the page is blank. For a second I think I'm going to have to read the whole book after all, but then I find a second leather strip deeper into the volume. My fingers spiderwalk across the pages. I pry the book apart, remove the leather strip serving as the bookmark. I sip my steaming tea and read.

Chapter 22
Rule and Governance of Elysium

Elysium is ruled by two queens, Queen Sephone and Queen Naja, but never at the same time.

My heart pounds at the mention of Sephone. Queen Sephone. The fey queen of my dreams.

I wet my lips and keep reading:

Once their mother left them, the sister queens divided their reign. One remains awake to govern the realm of Elysium and is known as The Living Queen. The other queen rests in stasis[136], renewing her magic. In this state she is known as The Dreaming Queen. Queen Naja was The Living Queen during the time of The First War.[137]

In Elysium, The Living Queen reigns for an era. [138] As she nears the end of her reign, The Dreaming Queen's soul is cut from her sleeping body using a moonblade[139] and the sleeping queen is reborn as an elfin child. The elder queen sister bestows three gifts to her reborn sister, unique to that reign: powers which the elder believes the new queen will need most in order to protect the realm and their people during her forthcoming reign.

Once the new queen reaches maturity and is prepared to serve Elysium as The Living Queen, the elder queen enters her own dormant stasis and sleeps, henceforth becoming The Dreaming Queen once again. The Dreaming Queen rests in stasis in The Temple of the Moon, a great stone structure at the center of Elysia. [140]

As The Living Queen nears the end of her reign, she will feel the stasis coming upon her and will awaken her slumbering sister with the moonblade, initiating the reincarnation process anew.

Whether living or asleep, each queen is served by her chevaliers. [141]

Depending upon the queen's status, the role of her chevalier will change. When she is The Living Queen, he is her mate and adviser. When she experiences dormancy as The Dreaming Queen, he is her guard, watching over her body until she has regained the strength to reign again. He is a vessel for her magic and her sacrifice in war, absorbing damage so she may conserve her power and strength.

The queens' power cycles mimic the cycles of our own world: a summer of full power, the fall of approaching stasis, a winter of dreams, and the spring of rebirth, which she lives as an elfin child, rediscovering her gifts and power once again.

---

[136] Though immortal by our standards, the queens have a distinct life cycle unique to their species. While their core consciousness remains intact, their physical form deteriorates with time. Stasis is a chief component of this life cycle. Near the end of her reign, the queen's magic wanes, signaling her approaching stasis. To rejuvenate, she will enter a stage of suspended sleep and recuperate her lost power. It is said that with each incarnation, a queen grows more powerful.

[137] Recorded demon attacks stretch back as far as 800 BCE. However, 1059–1063 CE are the accepted dates known as The First War. It is marked by The Burning of 1059 and Queen Naja's sworn allegiance to the Bishop family in 1063.

[138] Naja herself suggested her reign spanned roughly 1,000 human years, but this has not been confirmed.

[139]A metal that is unknown on Septem Terras, forged with an alchemy we seem unable to replicate.

[140] The principle city of Elysium. To learn more about Elysia, please see Chapter 23. To learn more about the geography and cartography of Elysium, please see Chapter 20. Specific references to The Temple of the Moon can be found in Chapters 23, 25, and 26.

[141]Lady Lightbringer makes distinct note of the queen's reluctance to share information about her own chevalier. She did not give his name, and Mara makes no mention of a male companion present with the queen during The First War. Due to this secrecy, the Itinerant Scholars have drawn the conclusion that the queen did not view the union worthy of mention. It is concluded that the chevalier is little more than a loyal servant in the fey social class.

And where did the lieutenants fit in, I wonder. In my dreams Ciel is the queen's lieutenant. I have the impression that Ciel and Queen Sephone are—*together*. But she didn't use the word *chevalier* for him. Is the lieutenant the same as a chevalier? Or was Ciel something else? Or maybe this queen has more than one partner? But it hadn't felt that way, when I was in her mind, dreaming about the war. Ciel was all that mattered to her, apart from protecting her people and her realm.

But if they're together, why would he kiss me?

Maybe it was just a magic thing so that I could have her memories. The book says they keep their magic.

Is Sephone The Living Queen now? Did she send Ciel to retrieve me? Does Sephone need a Bishop to help with the war she's fighting? The fey came when we needed help against the demons. Maybe it's our turn to repay the favor?

You've fulfilled your bargain, he'd said to Demi.

This book mentions Mara's bargain. Did the queen and my ancestor strike a deal? I'll give you the power you need to destroy your enemy, and then in exchange, I'll steal one of your daughters later when I need her?

I feel like I could read this enormous book and all of its two thousand pages and still not understand everything.

Ayck!

A sharp cry echoes through the atrium. I look up and see blue-gray feathers darting beneath the ceiling's elaborate fresco, like a momentary flash of the painting come to life. Dragon swoops, dives, and comes to perch on Ibis's shoulder.

Ibis pulls a peanut from his pocket and offers it to my jay.

I can't help but utter my surprise. "You too? He never comes to me first anymore."

How long has he been standing there watching me puzzle over this book?

"Might I suggest peanuts?" Ibis asks.

"*I'm* not supposed to buy his love," I say. "*He* chose *me*."

"Don't take it personally, Lady Bishop. Blue jays are notoriously opportunistic."

"Amelia."

"Lady Amelia."

I scowl up at Ibis as Dragon flutters to the adjacent shelf with his prize. It's Ibis's turn to look affronted as the jay begins shredding the shell, raining bits of its papery exterior onto one of his immaculate displays. Athena raises her head, giving Dragon a predatory stare. My jay freezes, returning the cold gaze. After a daring shriek at Athena, he flutters up to a higher shelf.

"Find anything interesting?" Ibis asks, nodding toward the book.

"I haven't gotten very far," I tell him. "Footnotes always slow me down."

Ibis slips his hands in his pockets. "Ah, yes, Sir O'Malley was very fond of those, even if his *colorful* assessments did cost him the position of Official Scribe and First Translator at the Academy."

"He was fired?"

Ibis snorts. "Oh, yes. And this edition of *A Comprehensive History of the Borderlands* was banned. That's why it's best you not leave this shop with it."

"Banned? You gave me a *banned* book?"

He clucks his tongue. "I gave you the best book there is on the subject. I don't hand out second-rate resources, Lady Bishop. I have my pride to consider."

I look at the red leather monstrosity in my hands and frown. *Banned.* Sir O'Malley must've done something truly offensive to have his book banned. Witches love books. We prize knowledge above everything—even magic. It is better to be wise than possess magic, for more power lies in wisdom, an ancient saying I've heard all my life.

"Can I come back and read it?" I ask him, sensing he's about to kick me out.

"Of course. If you can be quiet that I am in possession of it."

"In possession of what?" I ask.

He grins, looking as sly as Athena. "Thank you."

"What about the stone?"

He gives me an apologetic shrug. "I need more time to work on it. I would continue now, but I have a private appointment. A consultation."

What option do I have? I don't know the first thing

about opening bloodstones and decoding the last words of the witches preserved within.

I close the book. "Will you call me when it's done?"

He nods, and I move to pick up the teacup, but he waves me away.

"I'll clean up. Give the book back to Athena. She knows where to put it. And she is better at reaching the higher stacks than I am."

With a great deal of reluctance, I close the book and offer it to Athena. My heart skips several beats as she opens those enormous jaws to clamp down on the cover, her fierce teeth gripping the leather less than an inch from my fingers.

"Gently, Athena," Ibis says with a click of his tongue. Athena rolls her yellow eyes to meet his reproachfully.

Having relinquished the book, I motion to Dragon that it's time to go. He chirps. I already have the skeleton key out of my shirt when I realize there might be something else I need from the shopkeeper's extensive stores. Besides, there isn't a more knowledgeable person in the world. That's the rumor anyway. That even the British Coven that banished him hadn't the heart to actually harm Ibis. He was too valuable a resource to simply kill.

I pause, key in hand, and ask, "Ibis, do you have anything that will kill a demon? *Actually* kill it? All the books claim it can't be done with magic, but maybe you know about a cursed object that could do the job."

Ibis's eyes twinkle with curiosity, then grow heavy as he considers me. "Up to new tricks, Lady Bishop?"

I ignore the taunt. "Or even if killing them is impossible, maybe you have something else that might be useful. I'll take anything. Even if it only knocks them out."

Hands in his pockets, he looks the part of a perfect

English gentleman again. I wonder if he's trying to find a way to politely tell me I'm an idiot—a fool for thinking he's got some great secret hidden that will just happen to answer all our troubles. After all, if a demon-killer did exist, wouldn't every hunter know about it already?

My shoulders slump. "Thanks anyway."

I'm almost to the grand door when he says, "Actually, I may have something for you."

I stop and turn back.

"Mind you, other hunters have tried to use this trinket and have failed."

Ibis's grin turns wicked. Devilish.

"But none of those souls had an inkling of your power, now did they? A daughter from a long, distinguished line."

His flattery makes me nervous. I raise an eyebrow. "What's the catch?"

"A small caveat, really," he says, looking down at his shoes. "You can't tell your aunts I gave it to you."

"Why?"

"They'll be angry," he says, his eyes flicking up to meet mine.

"Why would they be angry that you gave me a trinket?"

Because it's not a mere trinket, a cold voice whispers in my head. *Because it must be very dangerous.*

"*All* magic carries risk. You're old enough to understand that," he says. He's staring again, looking me over.

I don't answer. I pretend to consider the deal thoughtfully, so that I don't seem too eager. Too desperate. But let's be honest. There is no risk I wouldn't take for Alex's life. I'll wager anything and everything if it means giving my one true friend the long, happy life he deserves.

Ibis nudges me. "I will give you the trinket to aid in your

experiment, and you won't tell the aunts I aided you. Do we have a deal?"

I extend my hand. He takes it with a smile as his magic skitters up my arm. "Deal."

It's a long time before I realize he used the word *experiment* even though I never told him—or anyone—what I've been up to.

The skeleton key warms in the lock. The world moves to accommodate my desires, realigning its many points in time and space.

The door swings open on the demon vault created so long ago. Was it Mara Bishop who built it? Did Queen Naja advise her on its construction? It seems strange to me that I never thought to ask. I close the door behind me as each candle ignites itself. Spilled sea salt still glitters on the floor.

Despite all the bizarre flattery Ibis laid on me regarding my powers, I have doubts that this trinket can actually kill a demon, but maybe I should look at it before I make judgments. I haven't even seen what's inside the flannel-wrapped bundle he gave me.

Fishing the soft fabric out of my pack in the candlelight, I inspect his gift.

It's a jagged piece of steel.

No, not steel. But not stone either. I'm not sure exactly what it's made of. It looks like a broken athame. One end is jagged, the other shaped into a partial hook.

I hold it up to the light, turning it over, noting the odd

glow. The surface doesn't catch and reflect the candlelight like ordinary blades might. The glow seems to come from within.

Ibis gifted me a broken blade to stab the demons with?

I hold it up to the light, trying to make out the shapes and patterns, but again, this strange metal doesn't collect and reflect the light like ordinary silver. It really does radiate its own glow.

I sit on the floor, a broken blade in one fist. I came to practice on the ghoul. Came to see if I could work another one of Asmodeus's spells and get that much closer to the answers I'm looking for.

But now all I can think about is the scrap of text I read about Elysium and the blade Ibis has given me. It's a message. And I'm flattered he thinks I'm smart enough to figure it out.

What does this have to do with the fey and Elysium? Does Ibis know about Ciel? Mara's bargain? Was there something he wasn't telling me?

Now I'm just being paranoid.

I was the one who asked about the borderlands.

And yet..., a little voice cautions. Hell, Earth, and Elysium are all borderlands. Why hadn't he marked the pages about Hell? I'm a demon hunter. It would make more sense to tell me about Hell and its demons, wouldn't it? Ibis is very practical that way. And yet, he'd pointed out the fey chapter.

Why?

The sounds of feet drag me out of my thoughts.

Lights appear at the edge of the supply closet door, and I recognize the familiar click of the handle turning.

I have only enough time to shove the blade and scrap of flannel into my pack, zip it up, and sling it over my shoulder before the door pops open. I shove my back into the nearest corner as if I could call the shadows to hide me. I can't. All they need to do is look over here, but that doesn't stop me from pressing my shoulder blades hard against the cold stone.

The aunts step across the threshold, a brilliant stream of sunlight flooding in behind them. Between them they drag an unconscious man—floating him, rather. Not Monsieur Lambert, I realize with relief.

I'm frozen in place with my hammering heart blotting out all sound. I haven't moved a muscle. I'm not even sure I've taken a breath.

My aunts drop the unconscious man into the center of the trap with a great sigh.

"Hopefully we'll get further with this one," Arty says with a groan as she straightens.

Demi turns on me suddenly, raising her hands as if she plans to blast me.

"It's me!" I blurt. She must have felt my emotions. Fear and panic are hard to hide. But she would be smart to blast first and ask questions later. If a demon had somehow escaped a bell jar, it wouldn't wait to pounce on her. "It's just me."

"Hellebore!" Arty hisses, tapping her cane furiously on the stone floor. "Is she here with you?"

This surprises me. Surely they don't mean Phelia. "Who?"

"Melody," Demi says. "We've searched Rowan House high and low and can't find her."

My heart takes off like a shot. "What do you mean you can't find her? So she could be out there killing another family right now?"

"Well, no," Demi says, her voice strained.

I look from one aunt to the other. "No?"

"After we spoke I blood-sealed Rowan House. She can't leave."

"So she's trapped in Rowan House."

"Yes," Demi says. "Unless you brought her into the vault. We thought maybe you did."

"No," I say cautiously. "I didn't."

Though it's not a bad idea. I'm sorry I didn't think of it. And she didn't follow me in here either, because I would have certainly noticed her and all her creepy demonic glory.

"Then what are you doing here?" Arty asks.

What am I doing here?

An excellent question for which I have no answer. None that I want to give, anyway. Instead I say, "I needed some moon water. What are you doing with him?"

Yes, redirect the conversation. Not obvious at all, *Amelia*. I'd slap myself on the forehead if it wasn't a dead giveaway.

Arty hobbles toward me, leaning heavily onto her cane. She must really be aching. My hip hurts just watching her.

Please don't open my pack. Please don't open my pack.

I don't want to imagine what the hellebore will go down if they find a bleeding book in my bag.

"You're lying," she says, and in one swift movement she snatches up my pack.

"That's mine!" I follow her into the center of the room. My magic rises as if called. The air crackles with it. Both aunts go perfectly still, the pack dangling in Arty's grip. "Give it back."

Arty's own chest is heaving. "Why did you lie?"

"Because what I'm doing is none of your business!"

"And what we are doing is none of yours!" Arty fires back.

"Who's lying now?" I hiss, stepping toward her. My power churns, flaring around me.

"Amelia," Demi says softly. I feel her cool power brush against mine, its back arching like a cat's. She's trying to soothe me before I mass-eject magic on them both. "Breathe, Amelia."

I realize I'm trembling. "Give it back."

Arty doesn't move.

"Artemis," Demi says, her cool power shifting. My poor aunt, forever the mediator between two of the most ill-tempered witches. "Be reasonable."

Arty throws my bag at me and it hits me square in the chest. Hard. She has a mighty arm for a crone.

"I don't need to look inside to know what's in there," Arty says, her voice dangerously low.

My heart flops in my chest.

Right. I should've known I'd lost the upper hand the second she took the bag away from me. She needed only to hold it. The smoky quartz at my throat can hide me and my choices—but it isn't going to shield a bag in someone else's grip.

Stupid. I'm *so* stupid.

She leans into her cane. "Why do you have a demon spell book and a broken moonblade in your bag?"

Demi gasps.

I'm not sure I'm hiding my shock well either. *Moonblade?* Ibis gave me a moonblade, a fey weapon. So it wasn't my imagination that he is drawing some connection between me and the fey. Is the blade to help protect me from Ciel?

I can't possibly tell the aunts where I got it or why. Not only because I promised Ibis I wouldn't, but because they don't trust him like I do. Just the way they wrinkle their noses when they say his name, *Ibis*, is enough to make their sentiments clear.

And why should it matter if I went to Ibis for help? That's what he's there for. And they aren't helping me, are they? They can't keep me in the dark and expect me to just sit back and accept it.

Finally, my anger eclipses my fear. I like it better when I'm angry. Anger is productive. I know how to use anger. "I should think it was obvious what I'm trying to do. I'm trying to kill demons."

"They can't be killed," Demi says, her hand toying with the tiger's eye pendant hanging at the hollow of her throat.

"I don't believe that," I say, my voice still hard, sharp at the edges. "I've never believed that."

Arty measures me with that hard gaze.

The possessed man in the demon trap stirs. He groans. Some distant part of me registers the puppeteer and wonders what they want him for.

"So your mission is to kill demons?" Arty asks, and it's strange how she says it. "That's what you came here for?"

What I came here for? She must mean why I came to the vault. But I feel like we aren't talking about the vault.

"Yes. And your mission is to keep me in the dark, apparently. Neither of you seems willing to tell me what's going on."

"Artemis, stop," Demi says. "You're confusing her. She doesn't understand that part of it any more than we do."

That part of it.

"Which part?" There are so many parts now. The Priests' murder part. The Ciel part. The binding gone wrong part. And now this new part—*why* did Ibis give me the blade?

"Have you had any further contact with the fey?" Arty asks, her voice cold and flat.

"No."

"Since he kissed you—"

"Artemis—"

"—have you felt different, started seeing things?"

"Dreams," I say. "And two old witches acting crazy and secretive."

"We aren't crazy," Demi says, her hands on her hips, bangles jangling.

"Just secretive then."

"We haven't been any more secretive than you," Arty counters, the bottom of her cane scraping the floor. "Coming and going at all hours. Casting strange spells. Visiting shopkeepers of questionable repute."

She has me there. And I haven't told them about the bloodstone. About Phelia. About what I'm trying to do for Alex.

"Like I said, I'm trying to kill demons," I say, raising my chin. "That's what I'm trying to do."

They both consider me again. Arty, immovable with her palms gripping the top of her cane. Demi fumbling with the tiger's eye almost frantically.

"Your turn," I say. "What are you doing?"

"Interrogating demons to find out the truth."

"Truth about the Priests or about the fey?"

They go perfectly still.

"Fine." I throw my bag against the ground. "I guess we'll just keep lying to each other. But I think you *do* know. Maybe not what happened to the Priests or what went wrong with the binding—but with Ciel and my stupid dreams? I think you know exactly what's going on with *that*."

"We don't want to say the wrong thing and make it worse," Demi pleads. "Please be patient with us."

"Make *what* worse?"

Arty waves my concerns away. "You have more immediate problems."

I almost laugh in her face, except her words strike a new chord of terror in me.

She doesn't wait for me to synthesize a retort. "Dean Prior is going to make Alex an offer."

The world tilts. I feel like a demon has leapt up from the earth and torn out my heart. I manage a faint, "What?"

"Prior is going to make Alex an offer. To be his chevalier."

"No," I say. I'm looking at Demi as if she's going to let me in on the joke, but her face is grave. "*No.* You're trying to distract me from what's really going on. You thought up the worst thing you could think of and—"

"This is not a joke," Arty says, and some of the softness has returned to her voice. "I saw it."

Instinctively, my hand goes up to the quartz around my throat.

"Calm your aster. I didn't see you," she says. "I saw Ysabel's boy."

"When?" I could've just as easily asked, *How much time do I have?*

"Tomorrow night. The coven wants an update on our progress. We are reconvening tomorrow in the grove. After we present our findings—"

Demi huffs as if to say, *What findings?*

"—he'll make his offer."

"He can't!" I yell.

"He *can*," Arty insists. "He can and he will before the entire assembly unless you make an offer first. Or a counteroffer. Either way, you'll likely have to duel him, though I didn't see it."

I laugh. A cold, hard sound that's just a hairbreadth from sobbing.

"Make Alex an offer or watch Prior take first rights."

I turn away. I tug a rough hand through my hair. I pace a circle on the floor as the demon captive groans again, louder this time.

No, no, no.

I can't bond with Alex.

Fight Prior? With pleasure.

But binding Alex to me starts the clock. He'll start absorbing demons—*any* demon we fight.

I scream and kick the bag.

"Do you really think you should kick a book that bleeds?" Arty says.

"It bleeds?" Demi places a hand over her throat.

I can't even think about Arty using her vision to look into my bag. My thoughts are consumed with Dean Prior.

I knew provoking him was stupid. I knew he would find a way to hurt me, twist my arm until he got what he wanted from me.

"I'm not marrying him." I pace, back and forth, in front of the demon trap.

"Good!" Arty croons. "Because these Machiavellian Molotovs likely wouldn't cease once you were married."

My pacing quickens. "He thinks he can manipulate me into being his toy, but he's wrong."

"That's the spirit," Arty says. "Now get out."

I stop pacing.

"You need to plan a duel, and Demi and I have a lot of work to do."

"What about Ciel?" I ask.

"Forget the fairy!" Arty says. "Focus on keeping your eyes open and your guard up. If you haven't noticed, there are a lot of demons about."

She is not safe here.

We will protect her.

What had Ciel been trying to warn them about?

"Is that what you're trying to protect me from? The demons?"

"From everything!" Arty hisses as she hobbles toward the shelves in the back of the vault, her cane echoing loudly with each tap-scrape against the floor.

Demi comes forward, covering my hands with her own. "I know you're confused, but please understand we're not intentionally keeping you in the dark, dear. We're trying our best to figure this out."

Bright tears stand in her eyes, catching and reflecting the candlelight of the dark chamber.

From deep in the shadows, Arty calls, "Stop coddling her! She's a warrior, not a worm."

Demi squeezes my hands. "Once we understand what's going on, you'll be the first to know."

I can't bear the tears sliding down her cheeks.

"Let's put her in diapers while we're at it!" Arty cries.

"*Please*, be patient with us."

"Mash her peas and carrots!"

I groan and pull away. "I'm leaving."

"Don't be mad at us," Demi says, that tremor in her voice. "And keep an eye out for Melody. It's obvious she isn't what she seems."

"You think?"

"Amelia," Demi begs. "Amelia, please—"

It would be my luck that Demi would die suddenly and her last thought would be about how I was mad at her. And

I've never been good at being mad at Aunt Demi. Arty, oh, Arty and I can hate each other in stubborn silence for a week before reconciliation—but it's different with Demi.

We love her, she'd said to Ciel. And she'd said it so tenderly.

"I'm not mad." I flick my eyes in Arty's direction. "At *you*."

I pull away from my aunt and slip the skeleton key over my head and into the door. I wait for it to warm in my hand.

But Prior—I'm going to *murder* him.

I don't sleep at all. I stay up until three in the morning searching every book I can think of, looking for a loophole that will let me out of my Prior problem. But the rules are absolutely clear on this.

Any unmatched hunter can make an offer to the keeper of their choice. They must state their offer before the entire coven so that anyone who may want to contest the claim can do so. If two witches want the same keeper, this is where it gets tricky. If the dispute is between a low-born witch and a high-born witch, the First Family witch usually wins because the witch with lesser magic will defer to the stronger one, but if the dispute is between two First Family witches, then it is settled by duel—and the winner of the duel wins first rights to the keeper.

Yes, Alex can say he would rather be bound to me and refuse Dean's offer outright, but that is considered an insult and Prior might counter by challenging Alex to a duel as well. And as much as I love Alex, he would not win against Dean in a magical duel. In a fist fight—absolutely. If it were only blades and strength, Alex would clean the floor with him. But physical contact is forbidden in a duel, and Alex simply doesn't have the offensive magic needed to win.

I throw the book I'm reading, and it rebounds off the wall.

I collapse on the brown leather chaise angled against a bookcase. I'm so mad I can't think straight. In fact, I'm so mad I start crying.

This—I realize—is why Arty warned me.

She isn't worried about me losing to Prior. He couldn't take me in a fight, no matter if we're using magic, blades, or fists. She's worried that I'll be too upset and make a fatal error. I'll overlook some important rule at a time when only the rules matter. Prior is probably hoping he will win by default, simply because I make one of the thousand missteps that could forfeit my win.

Because duels aren't simple. They're the archaic remnants of a long-ago society that cared way too much about pomp and circumstance. And here, I'm ashamed to admit, Prior is better versed than I am. I could never care as much about pompous displays of power as he does.

Once I clear away the rage tears, I drag myself to the desk again and open *A Lady's Rules and Manners of Dueling*.

I begin to read.

And I must doze off because I wake at the sound of a floorboard creaking. My head snaps up. The library is empty, the fire at my back only embers now. The room has that smoky, wood-burnt smell that I love.

Shadows move beneath the door.

I call up my magic instantly, feeling the hairs on my arms rise. The person on the other side of the door pauses. In a random fit of boldness, I storm forward and throw the door wide.

There's no one. No one in the hallway.

I step forward into the atrium and look up at the higher landing in time to see Phelia's door close.

Not-Melody had stood at the library door and listened to me sleep. She was close. Too close.

My skin crawls. At least we know she's still in the house.

Something slams into me from behind. I tumble to the floor, sprawled in the atrium. My cheek connects with the wood, sending a ringing shot through my ears. I curse and roll onto my back in time to see Phelia.

She's a second from pouncing again when a burst of wind tears from my abdomen and slams into her, pushing her back. She sails through the wall without stopping. I use the few seconds this buys me to shove my hand in my pocket for the cacao powder. My fingers brush stiff, spindly legs and I shudder. Not cacao powder. The beetle.

I toss the scarab away and dig for the cacao again.

Phelia's screaming. No, *howling*. "Give me the stone!"

My fingers brush the small plastic bag and I yank it free. She's inches from my face when I dump the powder into my hand and blow.

A puff of brown blooms between our faces. The scent is mostly sweet, with an afternote of bitter chocolate.

Phelia stiffens, her incorporeal form going suddenly rigid. The cacao hangs in the air. By the time it clears, Phelia is just standing there, eyes wide as if dazed.

I take a step back. "Phelia?"

Nothing.

"Phelia? Are you okay?"

She blinks those ectoplasmic lashes. "Amelia?"

"How do you feel?" I ask. I'm not about to take a step toward her.

"Good," she says, only it doesn't sound right. "*Oh.* I feel *sooo good.*"

"Uhhh..."

"Oh, *Amelia.* What was that?"

"Chocolate. Basically."

She runs her hands down the length of her body. "I feel like I'm—I feel like I'm *alive.*"

A peal of laughter erupts from her little throat, and she moans. Then she's running through the house, wailing with delight.

I stand there in the atrium, holding the emptied plastic bag in my hand and thinking, *Ibis, what the hellebore.*

I catch a glimpse of Phelia's bedroom door on the landing above and see it's cracked. Just a little. When I move to get a better look, the door snaps shut. Did not-Melody see Phelia? Has she been watching us?

If you've come to kill us, what are you waiting for? I wonder.

I creep back into the library.

And find Phelia turning circles and skipping from one end of the room to the other.

I take one look at my screeching, deliriously happy ghost of a sister and turn on my heels. I drag my sore, exhausted body to my bedroom, my eyes never leaving Phelia's closed door. Once I cross the threshold, I slam my door shut and collapse onto the bed to the sound of a little girl giggling.

Phelia is spinning circles in the middle of my bedroom and laughing like a pirate.

"I'm going to kill him," I groan, thinking of the shop-keeper. "This better wear off soon."

Of course, I don't know why I'm really complaining. A dead sister high on cacao is better than a wraithed one, right? Except it's hard to appreciate the improvement when I've been up all night and dawn is fast approaching.

I look at the red cat-shaped clock on my desk. It's almost four and the aunts still aren't home.

Are they still looking for answers about Elysium? About the Priests' murders? Both?

"Argh!" Phelia cries, and jabs her imaginary sword at me. "On guard, you scallywag!"

I blink at her. She flicks her eyes to the plastic sword I brought from our room. When I don't move to pick it up, she nods her head toward it again, more emphatically than before.

Because I know this isn't going to end, I pick up the plastic sword and wave it at her. She feints left and right, pretending to parry blows that I don't have the heart to deliver. I cover my face with my elbow and keep waving the sword at her.

"Argh, you think you can beat me with yer eyes closed, do ye, scallywag?"

I wiggle the sword half-heartedly.

She makes a sound, almost like choking. It's so reminiscent of the final sounds she made in the river that my eyes fly open. I turn to find she's impaled herself on the plastic sword. She's stepped forward so that it appears to be sticking right through her back.

And now she's dying. Again.

But smiling about it.

At least I'm nice enough to hold the sword in place until she finishes her performance. She takes a very long time to die.

Finally, she pops up, grinning bigger than I've seen her grin in a long time. She climbs onto my bed and crosses her legs, bouncing a little.

"Now what do *you* want to play?"

"Sleeping Beauty. I'll do the sleeping."

A lazy meow wakes me. I find Jinx, Demi's familiar, on a mound of pillows and blankets at the foot of my bed. He's blinking his green eyes at me. The aunts must be home. As soon as I think it, I hear them: pans clanking and the rattle of dishes, voices murmuring from downstairs. Without taking his eyes off me, Jinx commences giving himself a bath.

"I'll give you some privacy," I say to that aggressive stare.

Demi is standing over the stove, her back to me, when I enter the open kitchen.

"What time is it?" I ask.

"Almost dinner time."

She's alone in the kitchen.

"Who were you talking to?" I ask.

"Orion," she says, and points upward toward the rafters. I lean my head back and see the speckled screech owl. Arty's familiar.

Shriek.

"Good evening," I reply.

She ruffles her feathers as if to make herself look bigger, though I've no idea who she's trying to impress.

When Demi turns around, a bruise the color of crushed plums is visible on her cheek. It's still swollen, a lump of flesh pressing her left eye partially shut.

I hiss through clenched teeth. "What happened? Was it Melody?"

"No, she's still hiding."

"Then what was it?"

"Demon," Demi says, looking more embarrassed than hurt. "I wasn't paying attention."

It looks fresh. Did it happen this morning? After pulling an all-nighter, her reflexes or magic couldn't have been in top shape. And she looks exhausted, though of course I'd never say that to another woman.

"Are you just getting home?"

"We got in around noon, but we didn't want to wake you. Artemis is still sleeping."

"Why aren't you?"

"I can't sleep when I have so much on my mind." She gives me a faint smile. "What about you? Have you seen..."

Her voice falls away, but I know she's talking about Ciel.

"No," I say. "He only shows up when I'm in trouble."

"Do you think he'll come tonight then?" She looks alarmed by the idea that Ciel might storm into the coven meeting, sword drawn just because I've been challenged to a duel.

"I hadn't thought of that."

Her frown intensifies. "Does Alex know what's about to happen? Have you told him?"

Alex.

My heart clenches in my chest as if a demon is squeezing it. I should tell him. I should warn him. But I can't. How will he react? Will he be angry that Prior is threatening him? No doubt. Will he be happy I'm finally bonding with him? Maybe. Unless he gets mad that I'm only doing it because I've been forced to.

Demi keeps watching me, stirring the pot.

I can smell the garlic and peppers. Then I see the box of dry pasta by a second pot waiting to boil.

No elaborate feasts for the Bishop women. Not with all this going on.

"No, he doesn't know." I put my face in my hands. "I don't think I can tell him either."

"He's going to be there, Amelia."

Good point.

"Alex will know. As soon as we're bonded, he'll know exactly why I did it." Because there'll be no hiding anything from him then. The little wisps of telepathy we share now will seem as primitive as shouting through tin cups when compared to the bond a fivefold kiss will create. He'll know I only agreed to bind my magic to his to protect him from Prior. It's hardly flattering.

"I keep hoping Prior will change his mind," I say, rubbing my face.

"Has Arty ever been wrong?" Demi asks. Her brows try to lift but they're not working quite right due to the swelling.

"No." It's one of the reasons Arty comes across so smug. She's rarely wrong. "But I live to see the day."

"You're a smart girl, Amelia," my aunt says. She reaches up and cups my cheek across the island counter. "You'll do what is best."

I place a hand over hers. "You need to put mugwort on that eye. And keep your eyes open for Melody. I saw her creeping around earlier, though she ran from me before I could get a good look at her."

"Don't confront her. We told you to be safe." She hands me a plate of steaming noodles, covered in sauce. The drawer rattles open and a fork appears. "Eat up. You have a long night ahead of you."

It's hard to eat when my stomach is churning so badly. I feel like I've eaten a quart of worms, and they're just wriggling inside me, desperate to escape. But under Demi's unrelenting gaze, I choke the noodles down and keep them there. Somehow I clear my plate.

"Last light," she sighs, her eyes filled with the orange sunlight pouring through the high windows. "I better wake Artemis."

I return to the library and find all the books I dragged out earlier have been put away, save one. It lies open on a page. It's a spell, one near the end of the book, further than I'd had time to read before caving to exhaustion.

I read the spell and smile.

It's perfect for opening a duel.

"Thank you," I say, not sure if I'm thanking Arty or if I'm thanking Rowan House. It's hard to know where help comes from sometimes.

I'm still smiling when the library door opens and there's Alex, a clean shirt the color of sunrise clinging to his muscles. He's washed his hair and it's still wet at the tips, darker than the rest of his curls.

"Good evening," he says with the air of a gentleman. "I just want everyone to know that my boyfriend has forgiven me, and we just spent *three* hours—What's wrong?"

Of course he knows. One look at me and he knows I'm upset.

I go to him, stopping just short of him. I can't look him in the eye so I settle for staring at his cheek. "Listen, I need to tell you something before we leave."

His lips thin and brow furrows.

"Stay close to me tonight," I say. "Even if Lance bats his pretty eyes at you and wants you to sneak off to some dark corner, *stay* with me."

Alex's frown deepens. "Seriously, what's going on?"

"Arty warned me—She saw—" I break off. I can't bring myself to say it.

He shifts his weight. "Warned you what? What's going to happen?"

I try again but I still can't speak. I can't force my mouth to form the words.

"Just stay with me tonight, okay? Stay close to me."

"Here's a radical idea." His annoyance is on full display. "You could just tell me what's going to happen."

"Sorry, Laveau." I give him a lopsided smile. "Seer's Law."

It's a pathetic excuse and he probably knows it, but Seer's Law states that only a clairvoyant can reveal her visions and only to whom she chooses. If he wants to know what's coming he has to ask Arty himself. Of course, he wouldn't dare, and I'm using that to my advantage now.

"Amelia, it's time!" Demi calls out. "Head on over and Arty and I will meet you there."

I give Alex's shoulder a squeeze and pull him toward the closet. "Let's go to the hollow."

I pull my skeleton key off my neck and use it on the library's door. It warms in my hands.

When I open the door, the night blooms in full view, the moon high in the sky above.

I close the library door tight behind him just in case that devious hellspawn squatter of ours gets any ideas.

The stone amphitheater slopes downward toward a grassy knoll in the center of a grove, the trees circling it on all sides. At least ten or twelve rows of stone benches are filling quickly with the arriving witches.

Alex follows me dutifully through the cool night as we maneuver around the crush of bodies.

Gossip is leaking around us as badly as a sprung ship.

"—demons ate every scrap of skin before—"

"—wouldn't throw myself right into the fireplace. I would have—"

"—heard the Priest girl hasn't said a single word—"

"—I didn't see her—"

"—took her so she wouldn't tell—wouldn't be surprised if she's a prisoner in that house—"

I barely acknowledge the gossip. I couldn't care less what these people think. Let the aunts and brown-nosers like Prior obsess over public opinion.

I plop onto a stone step serving as a seat at the very bottom of the amphitheater. Alex sits beside me, his splayed knees brushing mine. He's taking my request to stay close seriously. Good. Especially if there's going to be so many people. It'd be difficult to find him in a crowd so large.

A shriek pulls my gaze up to the starry sky. A swarm of birds flit back and forth across the moon. Familiars are filling the branches of the tall pines encompassing the amphitheater, just as eager to watch the meeting as the witches they accompany. A darting creature breaks from the pack and dives toward me. It's moving so fast that I only have a second to register that it's Dragon before his blue-gray wings snap open inches from my face.

His claws clamp on to the fabric of my jeans as he uses his wings to balance himself. I reach up and scratch the crest on the top of his head and he nips my finger, a little too hard. "Okay, okay."

I scratch his white chest instead.

Alex runs a dark finger down his spine.

"Mind the crest," I say. "Apparently."

Dragon shrieks again and I pull a handful of peanuts from my jacket pocket. I spread them on the stone between

Alex and me, and he hops down to inspect them. He seems pleased that I've caught on to his expectations.

"You stay close too," I tell him. *In case I need you to peck out Prior's eyes.*

Dragon caws, a rally cry.

"Look what we have here." Prior's voice is like a slug on the back of my neck.

Snickers chorus around us.

Speak of the devil.

I turn to see Prior on the landing above us with three other witches. They look away when our eyes meet.

Alex stiffens for only a second before he leans back onto his hands, adopting the pose of nonchalance.

Prior descends the amphitheater steps, coming around to stand in front of us on the grass. He sneers, looking from me to Alex and back again. "Really, Amelia, why do you keep resisting the inevitable?"

Dragon shrieks at him. His crest rises and his wings flap open in a direct challenge.

Prior snorts. "Of course, your taste in company has always been questionable."

"Oops." One of Prior's cronies hops down to the landing where we're seated. "Sorry, keeper."

I glance over my shoulder to see one of the boys standing on Alex's hand. I shove the jerk hard in the back of his knee and he falls over, the other boys laughing.

"I said I was sorry!" the crony says.

"Oh, you do Laveau a disservice, Hamilton," Prior says. "This one isn't even a proper keeper yet. You're a little old to still be *training*, aren't you?"

Prior looks at his friends over his shoulder. "Maybe I should make him an offer."

My insides ice. It takes everything I have not to scream

no. Not to jump up and punch Prior hard in his mouth until I see his blood spread across my knuckles.

Prior leans down into Alex's face. "Would you like that? You and me bound together? Maybe then Amelia would finally come to her senses and do what's expected of her. For once."

Dragon shoots up between us in a flurry of blue-gray feathers, shrieking, talons out.

"No!" I command. But I'm too late. Dragon's talons dig into the side of Prior's face in one vicious swipe, drawing blood from that pale cheek.

Am I surprised? No. As if my jay has ever taken an order in his life. His wings beat Prior about the face. He snips at least three times at Prior's nose.

Prior yells. His badger, the ruthless four-legged garbage disposal, comes bounding across the darkening field toward us.

Up! Up to the trees! I cry silently.

At least now he listens. Dragon flies straight up to the pines above, disappearing into the dark. My heart is pounding ruthlessly in my chest. The disappointed badger smacks his lips.

Several witches have turned our way and they're watching us.

Prior himself straightens slowly, gingerly touching his face. Tears stand in the corners of his eyes.

Somehow, I manage to steady my voice before speaking. "Honestly, Prior, if you're going to harass my jay like that, I'm going to have to file a complaint with the coven."

Prior reaches into his pocket and pulls out a white handkerchief. He dabs at his cheek. "My sincerest apologies, Lady Bishop."

The witches closest to us look away, eager to return to

their own hurried conversations. A knot in my chest loosens despite my pounding heart.

"Attention! Witches! Please! Your attention!" It's Arty's voice thundering over the crowd.

I become fully aware of my surroundings again, of the massive crowd that's filled the amphitheater and surrounding grove while our little melodrama with Prior played out. Thousands are here, I realize. Maybe even all the covens of North America.

Prior's cronies are already shuffling away, searching for seats among their other friends several rows to my left. Prior hesitates before leaning close and putting his mouth near my ear.

I could thrust my fist up into his throat at this angle. It would be fast and would wind him completely.

Oh, the *temptation*.

"Mark my words, Amelia," he whispers, his vile breath hot on my ear. "Soon, *very* soon, you'll be in no position to bargain. You'll be groveling at my feet in front of everyone, desperate for me to take you. You'll be lucky if I accept you, as imperfect as you are."

"And just when I thought I'd seen the extent of your delusions, you surprise me," I say, meeting his gaze. I let my power rise beneath my skin, let him feel it. I know he does because his smirk twitches, goes tight.

As grateful as I am for my magic, it would be so much more fulfilling to hurt him with my own hands. I could lift my knee and hit him square in the groin.

I imagine doing it. I imagine the way his soft flesh will cave on impact. The way the tears will spring to his eyes.

Please, I beg silently. *Please lay a finger on me. Give me a reason, any reason—*

His dangerous smile returns as he looks from me to Alex, as if he's sharing a joke all to himself.

Soon, he mouths. He mimes begging with his palms pressed together and an exaggerated quiver of his lower lip, before he turns away to join his friends.

A breath whooshes out of Alex beside me. I realize he's been holding it this whole time. "What the hell, Amelia. *Seriously*. That wasn't his usual petulance, that was—"

"How's your hand?" I interrupt him. "If that jerk broke so much as your fingernail, I'll black his eye."

He ignores my attempt at distraction. "Is Prior about to do something? Is that what Arty warned you about? Is—"

His words are stamped out by the rap of Arty's cane.

"Please!" Arty claps her hands again to settle the crowd, her cane propped against her side. She comes to stand ten feet away from me, Demi in her long skirts trailing beside her. "Please, everyone, take your seats."

I catch sight of Orion's white wings flittering overhead as she swoops up to perch in the pine branches behind my aunt. No sign of Dragon, but I hear him chattering away in the trees, bullying some other familiar no doubt.

"Everybody settle down. We don't have all night."

A wave of calm washes over me. I recognize the touch of Demi's power immediately even before people start to settle onto the stone seats and quiet themselves. I wonder if they'd be angry if they knew how often my aunt swayed them like this.

"We have several things to report on the progress of the Priest case," Arty says to the now silent crowd. "First and foremost, no, we have not apprehended who is responsible."

A soft murmur builds, and Demi's power crashes against us again. The voices die away.

"Secondly, we have determined that it was a demon attack, but that the demon did *not* work alone. At least one witch was involved."

A sharp uproar. Even Demi's power can't dampen it completely.

"What are you saying?" a man snaps from the right. I can't see his face clearly in the darkening night, nor do I recognize his voice outright. Thick purple twilight has fallen on all of us.

"We're *saying*," Arty says, "we found traces of blood magic. The residue makes it clear that the Priests were murdered by a demon because of the damage done to the b-bodies—" Her voice falters. "But the demon was not acting alone."

"What spell?" a shrill woman calls, another faceless voice from the dark. "Which spell was it?"

"Someone cast a Faustian Pact."

Gasps. Then everyone begins talking at once.

"Impossible."

"Heresy."

"Who in their right mind?"

"You can't undo it."

"—sold their soul—"

"A fool."

I turn the words over in my mind: *a Faustian Pact.*

It's the name we have for a deal struck between a demon and a witch. Some high-ranking demons—knights, lieutenants, or kings—possess and control magic just like the fey do. They can bestow or teach magic too—again, just like the fey.

And some witches—an insane few—who want more power than what they were born with have sought out these high-ranking demons, willing to pay anything, sacrifice anything, for this power.

A man stands slightly to my right. "Someone in *this* coven has cast a Faustian Pact?"

It's Mr. Holt, leader of the Midwestern clan and fellow coven member. He looks sick, ghastly pale in the low light.

"To be fair, Mr. Holt," Demi says, "we don't know it was a member of our own coven. We've received the names of several rogue witches who could be in the area from the international covens, and two of these rogues even had bad blood with the Priests. Therefore, we're investigating the possibility that an outsider may be responsible."

"The Priests did a great deal of international business," someone chimes in. A squeaky, feminine voice somewhere over my right shoulder. "It could be someone they knew from abroad."

A wildfire of mumbling agreement.

Yes, I think sourly. Better to blame an outsider than to think we've any terrible people right here.

"We are exploring every possibility," Demi says. "We assure you."

"How do we know it wasn't *you*?" a slurred voice calls. This one I know. Mulgrave, the resident drunk.

"Sit down, Mulgrave!" someone calls.

"Fool."

"Bloody drunk."

"—the strongest witches here—what would they need a pact for—"

"—power-hungrier than the rest—"

"No!" Mulgrave cries. He staggers to standing and points—*points*—at my aunts. No one in their right mind would point at a witch. "I want a declaration of truth! I want it from all of you!"

Mulgrave and Mr. Priest were cousins, so I'm not shocked by this level of belligerent grief.

Nor are my aunts, which is probably why Arty places her hand to her throat to speak the declaration of truth without much resistance.

She opens her hand and conjures the green flame of truth. It burns in her palm as she speaks. "We, the Bishops, did not wish harm on the Priests. We did not take their lives, nor have we harmed the girl Melody. Not one of us three had any part in their deaths. They were our friends. Our allies. And they remain so still."

A rare tenderness compresses the end of Arty's words, and I can't help but look at her. But whatever emotion her voice betrayed, her face is as stoic as ever.

The crowd waits. No one moves a muscle or looks away. All eyes are fixed on the glowing green flame.

But it doesn't turn red.

"Grandmistress speaks true," someone says. "The Bishops are innocent."

Mulgrave's face crumples and he sinks back to his seat, crying. Those closest try to offer reassurances. Several others look from me to the aunts with shame on their faces. At least they know we're innocent now. Arty would not have been able to conceal a lie while the flame of truth is burning.

Others look angry rather than sad or relieved. Perhaps they resent us for ruining the gossip.

Arty closes her fist and the green flame disappears.

"Please, everybody," Demi begs, palms out in surrender. "We're almost finished."

The aunts outline the final details about the curfew and hunting ban still in effect. I listen, ever the dutiful niece, until I feel intense eyes boring into the side of my head.

I look up to find Prior staring at me.

Some are just power-hungrier than the rest.

I'm looking at the most power-hungry person I know. But I don't think Prior has the gall to stare down a demon lord, a knight, or general. Demons that powerful are terrifying. Not to mention that such a pact requires that the witch give the demon a pound of their own flesh.

In no world would Prior be willing to feed even an inch of himself to a demon.

Alex nudges my knee and I turn back. He flicks his eyes up toward the aunts, panic washing over me as I realize I've missed something.

What I've missed is Arty trying to get my attention.

Both of my aunts are looking at me now. They're prattling on about nominations for a new coven leader, to be elected by the Northwest clan. They're listing desirable traits in such a leader, how we must respect and honor the Priests but also maintain a proper order. They're repeating themselves, circling the end of the conversation.

And suddenly I realize why.

Alex thought I was getting the hard stares from my aunts for not paying attention. He didn't realize they are waiting for me to make a move.

Recognition dawns and Arty must see it in my face.

"Try not to smile," I whisper to Alex.

"What? Why?"

Arty turns her back on me and calls loudly over the crowd, "Does anyone else have any other bus—"

I'm on my feet before she finishes her sentence.

Out of the corner of my eye I see that Prior has also stood up, but it doesn't matter. I'm a First Daughter. I will pull rank and exploit my privileges if I have to.

Prior slides back onto his stone seat.

"Yes, Amelia?" Arty says, and if I'm not mistaken, she's trying to keep a smile off her face. "Have you business with the coven?"

"Yes."

"Speak up!" Arty growls. "Some of us are older than this amphitheater."

Demi offers quiet laughter for my benefit. She's trying to ease my cold panic. But I'm shaking and suddenly grateful that no one can see me clearly in the moonlight.

"Yes," I call loudly, hearing my voice echo off the stone and trees, reverberating against the sky. "I have business with the coven."

"State your business," Arty prompts.

I lick my lips. I try to take a deep breath but manage only a shallow pant. A black hole has opened in my chest and I'm collapsing into it.

Steel spine, girl.

I force the air out of my lungs, over my tongue, and through my teeth. "I am Amelia Bishop, Daughter of Jocelyn Bishop." I'm surprised, pleasantly surprised, that my voice is clear and strong. It doesn't betray an ounce of the solid fear riding me like a demon. "Tonight, before my coven and my family, I make an offer to Alexander Desmond Lambert-Laveau."

I turn and look at Alex, see the shock painted across his face.

"Laveau, will you do me the honor of becoming my chevalier?"

CHAPTER 14
THE FIVEFOLD KISS

Alex is perfectly still beside me. I'm worried he's too shocked to speak.

I'm unsure of what to do in the face of that silence when I see a slow, amused grin spread across Arty's face. It makes me nervous that someone might suspect the scheming. But then why wouldn't she smile? Her niece finally chose a keeper. And it's the son of her own keeper. At least, I hope that's what everyone is thinking.

"Would you like to add something, Lord Prior?" Demi says. I follow Demi's gaze and find Prior standing again. He's looking from Arty to me as if he knows I've been warned.

I arch an eyebrow at him, *daring* him to challenge me.

"We're getting cold," Arty barks at him. "Stir the cauldron or leave the pot!"

Laughter ripples through the crowd again.

It's all the push Prior needs. "As the son of Ysabel Prior, I would like to make a counteroffer to Alexander. It would be my honor if he were *my* chevalier."

Alex's leg twitches, his knee knocking against mine. I don't dare turn back and look at him.

A soft murmur of disbelief rumbles through the crowd. The aunts have the decency to raise their eyebrows and look as surprised as everyone else. Though if you ask me, Demi is overselling it. She's clutching her throat and the *O* of her mouth is too round.

"Very well. We will settle this in the Lady's way," Arty says. "In a simple, three-spell duel. Amelia, since you are the one being challenged, you will have first spell. Name your second."

Name my second.

Foxglove. I'd forgotten about that. And it can't be Alex. I can't second the aunts because of the role they play in the coven. My eyes sweep the crowd, hoping a friend will just magically appear. But I don't even see Phelia—not that a ghost is a suitable second either.

What a horrible time to discover the repercussions of my loner personality.

My eyes are drawn to movement in the middle of the third row. Perdita Hatt practically bounces in her seat. She's waving at me. Abel White is beside her, pointing a finger at his quivering fiancée for emphasis, as if he wants to make sure I've seen Hatt—as if I could miss her.

Why in the world would she volunteer to be my second? Does she imagine us standing in the middle of this amphitheater like Arty and Demi one day, row upon row of listening ears trained on us? I should probably make the time to discover her motives.

Scheming aside, I'm not sure Perdita is a suitable choice as my second. She's a decent fighter, on the few occasions I've seen her and Lance fight demons. But dueling is a different beast.

I hesitate, and this only seems to encourage her desperate waving. Abel goes so far as to stand up, jabbing his fingers downward at Perdita.

Oh, just pick her, for witch's sake, Arty whispers in my mind. *You won't need her anyway.*

True. The second only casts on my behalf if Prior renders me unconscious or maims me before I've thrown all three spells. I suppose at that point I've lost anyway. Rather reluctantly, I say, "I name Lady Perdita Hatt as my second."

Perdita squeals, *squeals*, as she jumps up from her stone seat and descends the amphitheater steps.

Abel is clapping loudly, seemingly unaware that he's the only one doing so. "Excellent selection," he calls out. "A very fine choice."

Hatt doesn't stop squealing even after she reaches my side.

She seizes my hand and shakes it rather emphatically. Her blond curls tremble.

"Your second!" She beams, shaking me harder. "Oh, Amelia, I'm so honored that you think so highly of me. First you come to my engagement ball, *dance* with me, and now you name me your *second*. Goddess above! This is the best week of my life."

"Please be quiet," I say to her.

"Oh, yes. You must be *very* nervous. Don't worry about a thing. I am very knowledgeable on the rules of dignified combat."

Alex's leg is bouncing against the back of mine, a nervous tick he's had since we were children. I nudge him and he stops.

"Lord Prior," Demi says, turning her black raven eyes on him. "Name your second."

Without hesitation he says, "I name Lord Victor Hornsby."

Victor flashes a tight, pained smile and stands from where he was sitting with Hannah Livermore. I note the fact it's far from where Prior and his cronies sit. The cronies don't seem surprised by the duel or the choice of Hornsby as second. Did he brag about this beforehand?

Of course, if I were Prior, I would have chosen Hornsby too. He is the better spellcaster and he's family. If Phelia had been alive, I would have chosen her. I wish I *could've* chosen her, to be here with me for my first public duel.

A dull ache throbs in my chest.

Arty taps her cane against the nearest stone bench. "Five minutes to prepare and then we'll begin. Clear the ring!"

Everyone from the lowest rows of seats rises and moves higher.

"Amelia!" Perdita says. "Your weapons! You have to take them off or you'll be disqualified for the use of magical objects. You'll lose by default."

Damsel seed. She's right. I look across the field connecting the two ends of the amphitheater and see that Prior has pulled off his cloak. Then he removes a long splint of bone from his ear before handing the earring over to Hornsby.

I pull the skeleton key and quartz off my neck and hand them to Alex. Perdita doesn't insist I give them to her, thankfully. Then I pass over my athame and its hip holster to him too. I reach up my sleeve and pull the small knife out of its forearm sheath and hand that over as well.

"Amelia," he whispers, and I see real fear in his face.

"It's going to be okay," I tell him, and squeeze his trembling knee. "I'll slit his throat in front of everyone before I let him bind you."

"Two minutes!" Aunt Arty gives the stone bench closest to her a final tap.

I squeeze Alex again and turn away.

Both Demi and Arty step up onto the ledge themselves before Arty murmurs an incantation that I can't hear from where I stand at the opposite end of the amphitheater. But I see her lips move and a shimmering barrier emerges from the dark green earth, rising twelve feet into the air on each side. The magic meets overhead, sealing the four of us completely inside. The magical barrier goes up between us, and now that it's only me and Perdita on this end of the amphitheater, I can't hide my panic.

"What am I doing?"

"Don't worry," Perdita coos. "Dueling is easy."

"Have you done it?" I ask.

"Oh no. But I read all about it before I made my offer to Lance."

"Twenty seconds!" Arty calls.

Alex's eyes are still burning a hole in the back of my head, but I don't look back at him.

If I do he'll know how afraid I am of screwing this up— afraid for him. I couldn't care less what happens to me. But Alex...a lot of terrible things could happen to Alex if he becomes magically bound to Dean Prior.

"Haven't you trained with your aunt?" Perdita asks.

"Why would my aunts train me to duel?"

"Oh, well, Grandmistress Artemis holds the perfect record for dueling. Thirty-seven wins. Mother says that's the exact number of fools that we have in the North American coven. They wanted her position as head, of course.

When it was clear no one could best her, everyone else wised up and the challenges stopped."

I didn't know that. I knew there had been challenges but I hadn't known how many.

I watch a witch press against the magical barrier and pull her hand back, laughing.

"Why do we need a shield?" I ask, not expecting an answer. I'm honestly just trying to fill the space around my panic.

"To protect the spectators," Perdita says, looking over the crowd. "And Lance. If I'm hurt we don't want the magic to transfer to him, do we?"

I open my mouth to ask what she means—transfer what? What would transfer? But she's already talking again.

"I hear that Dean has pain in his left knee." Perdita puts her hands on her hips. "From the demon attack last June. You could shatter it? A bone blast may do nicely."

I can't hide my shock.

"What?" She grins, tilting her head coquettishly. "We're here to win, aren't we?"

Note to self, never cross Perdita Hatt. There's some menace under all those ribbons and lace and it's not all reserved for demons apparently.

"The first rule of combat is to remove your opponents' weapons," she goes on. "Your first spell could be to remove his voice. Of course, but then you'll be dueling Hornsby, and he's rather good at it."

"I already have my first spell picked out," I say.

"Oh," she says. She looks pleased, maybe even a little relieved. Maybe she thinks I wasn't expecting the duel. Why would I be expecting it? "Let's see it then."

Arty taps her cane against the nearest stone bench like a

gavel to quiet the murmuring crowd. "Amelia, first spell, please."

I try to clear my mind over my pounding heart. But it's hard. I'm not afraid of Prior or what he might do to me. I'm not even afraid of a good fight. I'm terrified of that little voice in my mind whispering, *You're going to lose. You're going to lose and he'll take Alex away from you. Hurt him, to hurt you.*

I hold my hand up in front of me. I'm grateful it doesn't shake.

The swirl of magic alights on my palm, a soft pink glow dancing. Prior tenses, Hornsby takes a step back. But the glow recaptures my attention, drawing me like a moth to flame.

A brilliant memory of the lieutenant's soul, Ciel's soul, dancing in the palm of the demon king's hand overwhelms me. I stumble as if kicked.

"Amelia?" Perdita whispers. "Are you all right?"

I feel disconnected from my body, as though I'm in the dream again, pushing and fighting to be freed of dark waters.

"Amelia?"

"I'm fine," I whisper, my voice hoarse. I will myself back to this moment. *This* time and place.

Don't ruin this, I command myself. *Think of Alex. Think of Alex.*

I renew my focus on the magic forming in my palm. It builds and builds until my skin is itching, ready to leap off my bones. Still I hold on until I can't any longer. Then I place my hand over my heart, feel the magic stab through me, covering me head to toe in a ripple of power. I seal the spell with a whispered command.

For a long moment, no one moves or speaks.

Prior snorts. Then his snort becomes full laughter. "Is that *it*? *That's* your first spell, Bishop? I expected you to at least try to take my eye or something."

The crowd laughs—*everyone* laughs but Alex and my aunts. Perdita seems torn between panic and amusement.

I say, "First spell complete."

This only makes Prior laugh harder.

Perdita mumbles, "This is no time to show off, Amelia. I know you're powerful, but you don't need to waste an entire spell to prove it. You only get *three*."

"I didn't waste a spell," I say.

"But—"

"Hatt, please be quiet. I'm concentrating."

Arty's face is unreadable as she pivots on her cane. "Mr. Prior, your first spell, please."

Prior's lips quirk. I have a feeling he chose his first spell ages ago and his practiced movements only solidify this theory. He throws his arms up in a dramatic, sweeping arc.

An explosion of fire leaps across the amphitheater. A ball of red-orange flames hurtles toward me. Perdita yelps and jumps back, bumping into the barrier, which shimmers and repels her, knocking her to the side.

I don't move and the fire keeps coming.

Alex stands behind me as the flames grow larger and larger. When it looks almost certain they're going to slam into me, incinerate my skull and body, the flames bend. They warp around me as they connect with an invisible shield.

I can feel the heat, intense and all-encompassing, but it doesn't connect. It can't because of the rebound spell I cast. *Rubber and glue, rubber and glue.* A rhyme hiding old magic.

The fireball rebounds, sailing back across the amphitheater toward Prior. He curses and ducks beneath the flames as they slam into the barrier behind him. Hornsby also rolls out of the way at the last moment. When the fire fails to hit me a second and third time, it splits into a dozen smaller ones. These zip faster from shield to shield, gaining speed with each rebound. The four of us are trapped in a blazing pinball game.

Flame grazes Perdita's shoulder. Without thinking, I dive over her, knowing I'll block the next one that zips by. I yank away the charred fabric, and she cries out. I lift a hand to cast a minor healing charm, and she seizes it with more strength than I thought the walking cupcake had in her.

"No!" she says, crushing my fingers together. Tears stain her bright, pretty eyes. "It'll count as your second spell. You have to hurt or disable him or it's a draw."

My hand hovers over her charred flesh as two more shooting flames hiss by.

"I'm fine," she insists, but the tears are collecting in her long lashes, silvery in the moonlight. "Don't waste your spell on me. Amelia, *please*."

Someone cries out.

I search the dark field and spot Hornsby writhing in pain. He isn't faring much better than Perdita. He's got scorch marks in three places along his torso and one under the left side of his throat. The moment I see the blackened skin, I smell his singed hair from here.

They're taking too much damage.

The seconds can't even cast to protect themselves. They can only cast if their firsts falter.

If I don't counter Prior's spell, Hornsby and Hatt will be dodging hits until this is over. If they survive that long. But if I do cast a spell to counter his fire, that leaves me with only one spell. One spell that is terrible enough to render him unconscious or somehow unable to counter it—I see my mistake now. By making an offer to Alex first, I've robbed myself of the chance to cast the last spell.

Perdita screams beside me. Her beautiful hand is now blistered from wrist to tip. Her delicate knuckles, blackened. Prior sidesteps a fireball but his sleeve catches. Lightning quick, he tears off the flaming fabric and throws it on the ground.

Yeah, didn't think this one through, did you, idiot.

"Amelia!" Arty calls over the roaring flames. "Second spell!"

I curse and lift my hands, palms out.

A blast of cold air explodes from my hands. The grass beneath me frosts, crystalizing white as ice stretches the length of the amphitheater. The racing flames caught in my arctic blast crackle and die.

But I don't stop with neutralizing the fire balls. I focus that magic on Prior, slamming into him with it.

He rocks back, his shoulders pinned against the shield by the force of my cold wind. He bares his teeth at me, refusing to cry out. The shield ripples and bends behind him but doesn't give. I want to crush him, squish the brains out of his ears. I want to see his eyes crystallize milky white in their sockets.

The magic shifts. The arctic air abruptly changes direction before hurtling back toward me.

"Countercharm!" Perdita hisses the second before the arctic air slams into my rebound field.

I cease my second spell, chest heaving. Sweat trickles from my temple down my jaw.

"I believe that counts as your second spell, Lord Prior," Arty says, twisting her cane in her grip.

Prior glares at her through the shimmering shield but

doesn't protest. He doesn't want to lose by default any more than I do.

"Third spell, Amelia," Demi says. *Make it count.*

A third spell. A third spell that will render Prior incapable of going on. Something he can't neutralize, leaving us in a draw.

"Third spell." Prior smirks. "While I'm still young and beautiful, Bishop."

His cronies laugh on cue, but no one else is laughing.

Many of the spectators are leaning forward, barely balanced on the lips of their stone seats, mouths agape.

Incapable of going on...unable to cast the third spell... can't be countered...because if I don't manage it, I'll find myself in a draw. Draws are unpredictable and almost always roll in favor of the counter claimer. Tiebreakers don't have the rules that duels have. They're full of opportunities to cheat and Prior is the biggest cheater I know. End it now or risk losing Alex.

The way I lost Phelia.

Her small, beautiful body rolling beneath the river's current. The way she screamed, desperate to be saved. The way she slipped from my arms and tumbled over the edge of the waterfall's cliff. The way I felt when my own body tipped forward in the current, ready to spill over that limestone lip before Alex caught me and hauled me to safety.

I fix my gaze on Prior. My loss wells like dark water within me. Wind whispers through the trees. A cloud moves across the moon. In the excited chatter of a hundred birds, I hear Dragon's shrill jay call.

When it feels like my heart is breaking, raw with what was taken from me, I whisper, "Inber."

Prior's smirk tenses on his face. His eyes widen, bigger and bigger until I can see the whites completely. He clutches his throat as the first bit of water bubbles over his lips.

River water.

He opens his mouth to try and speak but only that same dark water spills out, before turning silver in the moonlight. It splashes down the front of his nice dress shirt, soaking the fabric.

He tries to speak again but chokes. His nostrils flare as he tries to suck in a breath but chokes again. A ragged cough takes him to his knees, pale hands seizing the frosted grass beneath him.

He coughs again and again, spitting water onto the ground. *Inber...inber...inber...* The spell whispers through my mind.

I'm drowning him. Drowning him the way Phelia drowned, filling his lungs and nose with unrelenting water. The world blurs. Starlight and moonbeams merge spectral. I swallow against the hard lump in my throat as wave after wave of regret crashes against me. When my chest burns out of breath, I gasp and blink against the tears clouding my lashes.

Hornsby goes down on his knees beside Prior, trying to help hold him up.

Prior raises his hand, waves it. He's glaring at me, hate flaming in his eyes. He's trying to cast with his hands. Trying to cast with his mind.

He can't do it. He's not strong enough.

Mr. Prior, Dean's father, stands suddenly from where he sits, wringing his long fingers. He licks his lips and waits and waits.

When he can't take it anymore, Mr. Prior cries out, "Concede!"

Several others encourage Dean to do the same.

Prior *will* die if he doesn't concede. He will drown, and maybe a keeper can pull the fluid from his lungs, or maybe they can't if the damage is too bad.

I know I should feel something. Compassion. Maybe concern. Deep in my mind, I acknowledge this, but the emotions don't come just because I *should* feel them. For the first time in my waking hours, I feel like the fey queen from my dream. In my armor, on the battlefield with slayed demons all around me.

With a cold, unmoving heart in the face of my enemy.

A cold, unmoving heart for anyone or anything who threatens what I hold dear.

A ruthless heart that says, *I will destroy you and not think twice about it.*

Hornsby is holding him up by the chest as water continues to bubble out of Prior's mouth, over his wobbling chin. Hornsby's eyes meet mine. I don't know what he sees. I can't possibly be that intimidating while I stand at one end of the field with a tear-stained and stony face.

But his eyes widen all the same. With a hissing breath, Hornsby yells, "We concede! We concede the duel!"

The stands erupt in applause as the shield falls. Perdita is whooping, squeezing my hand with her uninjured one.

Alex is on me in a heartbeat, grabbing me in a giant bear hug and lifting me off the ground so my feet can't touch. I exhale a breath I'd been holding into the nape of his dark neck.

He releases me just as Lance vaults into the amphitheater and seizes Perdita's wounded hands. I feel his keeper magic rise, warm and welcoming around us as he works to heal her wounds.

Alex sets me on my feet again, planting a kiss on my

forehead. "What just happened? What in the *hellebore* just happened, Amelia?"

The sound of a heavy limp approaching makes me turn. Arty and Demi are hurrying across the amphitheater.

Arty waves me closer with her cane and I meet them halfway. "What's wrong?"

"You need to cross the folds," Demi says, breathless.

"Perform the kiss. *Now,*" Arty adds. "Before Prior realizes he can contest the results."

"He can do that?" I ask.

"Yes," my aunts say in unison.

"Hornsby conceded instead of casting the final spell. Prior can dispute that and declare a misduel. He will the second he catches his breath."

I glance over Arty's shoulder and see Hornsby still hovering over the choking Prior. Someone has stopped the water flowing but he's still wheezing, still breathless.

Damsel seed.

Hornsby conceded instead of fighting me.

As Prior's second, he could have easily neutralized the attack, or even cast a spell that would have disabled me and given Prior the victory. But he conceded.

Hornsby locks eyes with mine and gives the faintest of nods. So he didn't make an ignorant mistake. He did me an intentional favor.

Demi glances over at Prior, who is trying to stand. "Amelia."

Exhaustion and fear wash over me. I thought I'd have more time. Thought that by winning the duel I would save Alex without actually having to seal his fate. We lock eyes.

He's smiling.

"We'll clear the amphitheater and seal you in again.

Just get through the first fold and then Prior can't stop you," Arty says.

I barely register the aunts hurrying away, calling out orders. My eyes are fixed on the other end of the field. On Hornsby, who is hauling Prior to the first ledge even as Prior tries to push him away. Prior's father finally reaches him, waving his own keeper over, forming a makeshift triage team around his son.

Alex crosses the grass to meet me in the middle of the moonlit amphitheater. He hands me my athame. I grip the cold steel and let out a shaky breath.

Before I can lose my nerve, I use the blade to draw a diagonal cut across my left palm. Then I hand the blade to Alex, who does the same.

No, no, no. My mind starts pulling back.

But he's already slipping his warm hand into mind. Our blood mingles between the crush of our clasped palms.

"I, First Daughter Amelia Bishop, bind myself to you, Alexander Laveau. I offer you my loyalty, my love, and my magic." I can't hide the wavering in my voice, the tremble in my lips.

Betrayal. I'm supposed to love you but I'm betraying you.

"I, Alexander Desmond Lambert-Laveau, accept this bond. I am your chevalier from now until the moment of my death. My strength is your strength. My power is your power," he says. His immense and overwhelming happiness slams into me even as tears prick my eyes. It draws a sharp, surprised breath from me.

And just like that, we've cleared the first fold of the five-fold kiss—the open declarations and the sealed promise of shared blood.

The pounding in my head is joined with a second, stronger beat. Alex's heart. First they echo each other. Then each drum settles into a new rhythm that is neither mine nor his alone. They merge and mingle until a common song emerges. Together they sing, *Our blood. Our blood. Our blood.*

"The blood is shared, the first fold complete," Demi says, and I see her pinched features even out. Beside her, Arty's shoulders lower. They're relieved. They really thought Prior would challenge me.

They may be relieved but I'm dying. My chest burns. My throat is on fire. All strength has left my arms. I feel like I'll fall over and combust at any second. Any second my knees will give and—

Stay with me, Alex whispers through my mind. He squeezes my hand gently to get me to look at him. *Begin the second fold.*

After binding ourselves through flesh, we must bind ourselves through spirit.

Please, Amelia.

But what if I run, I wonder. What if I break through the barrier and run off into the night? Will it bring this whole terrible thing to a halt?

Then Alex would be bound to Prior by default. And if Alex refuses, there would be a second duel between Alex and Dean, which Alex would surely lose, and unlike you, Dean would complete the fivefold kiss without hesitation, a dark voice says. *So don't be a coward now.*

I call up my magic. I let it rise up within me, creating an enormous cloud of need and power. This desperate need washes over us. Alex's eyes pinch close in euphoria, taking a moment to enjoy the feel of the magic I offer.

Then he calls his own power. It's cool water to my hot flame. It's starlight to my moonlight. It's the perfect balance to all that I am.

The magics blend and merge, acknowledging one another. But it's an old familiarity. Is this because we've been friends our whole lives? Is it because we grew up together? Have loved each other from the start, even when we pulled each other's hair or called each other names? When we lost his mother, then my mother, who treated him like her own son. When we lost Phelia…

I don't know.

Whatever the reason, our magics embrace the way one embraces an old friend.

"The magic is shared. The second fold is complete," Demi calls, but her voice is very far away.

Something in my mind opens, like a keyhole, bending and stretching to become a doorway. Alex's emotions strike me hard and fast. I reel back from the power of it, but he has hold of my hand. He keeps us upright so that I don't fall.

His thoughts crash over me.

Wanted this forever. Wanted this forever. Fight beside you. Protect you. Family. Family.

Tears stream down my cheeks.

How can you want this? How can you possibly?

Even as my sadness threatens to tear me apart, his happiness beams through, bright and unrelenting through the cracks. His happiness hurts. It burns my lungs and constricts my chest.

He pulls on my hand, tugging me forward until my head rests against his chest.

His mind feels open in a way that I've never known before. His thoughts. His feelings. His memories. His dreams.

I see a thousand memories in a second. Shared memories of our childhood, of our families. Other memories were new. Memories of Alex's mother. Running along Haitian beaches at sunset, trailing her laughter. How bright her eyes were.

Private moments.

Of the first time Alex and Lance kissed.

Of the first time they did more than kiss. Naked in the dark. Hard bodies pressed against each other. Of the soft sounds Lance made in the hollow of Alex's throat as he fisted Alex's hair.

Alex tenses beside me and I have just a second to worry what he's seen of me—because this must be a two-way street. What secrets am I giving up now, without knowing it?

"The mind is shared. The third fold is complete," a distant voice intones.

Because my eyes are still pinched shut, Alex places a finger under my chin and tilts it up so that our lips are aligned. I part my lips. Then he inhales, sucking the air out of my mouth into his. I feel that soft transfer of power skittering across my teeth.

Once the breath ends, I take another, this time pulling the power from him into myself.

"The breath is shared. The fourth fold is complete."

And here we are, already at the end of it.

I can't do this. I can't do this to you.

The brilliant, panicked image of the keeper's body burning on the pyre flashes bright in my mind.

I can't be your executioner.

Alex crushes me against him.

"Trust me like I trust you," Alex whispers. *Trust me not to fold. Trust me to never give up on you, just like I trust you never to give up on me.*

He pushes his own bright and brilliant image across the

wide-open mind link we now share. A loving image of his father, Monsieur Lambert, and Arty together. They were on the porch of Rowan House. Arty's cheek was bleeding from two fresh claw marks. Monsieur Lambert had a large, nasty bruise forming over one eye and a split lip. But in this moment of recovery, they looked over at one another and burst out laughing. *Arty* gracing him with one of her rare smiles and honest laughs.

His father and my aunt have fought side by side for decades. They've outlived so many, including our mothers, and suffered so much.

They're both strong, but together they're stronger.

Unstoppable.

I want that for us, Alex tells me without words.

The lifetime of friendship. The unbreakable bond.

"We're stronger together," he says. *I'll never quit on you, Amelia. I swear I'll never quit.*

Tears spill over my cheeks—even as I direct our combined magics into the earth, commencing the fifth fold.

Alex reaches up and rubs a thumb across my cheek to wipe away the tears.

"The bond is consecrated by the earth," the distant voice says. "This life is shared."

I'm standing here, consumed by the hum of our magic and struck by the irony of it all.

Alex thinks this is the best way to protect *me*. It's Alex who wants to protect me the way I want to protect him.

I'm over here running through cemeteries and chasing ghouls and searching demonic spell books to save him, but he thinks it's *me* who needs saving. I've never considered myself as someone in need of saving. But I've never seen myself the way Alex sees me now.

To him, I'm always the first into the fray. The first to

stare down a demon and draw a blade. He has a mental inventory of every wound, every scar on my body, and the blows I took to receive them. He thinks this life will kill me. That I'll be just another demon hunter who will die young and bloody—like our mothers.

But I can save you, he thinks.

But I can save you, I think.

"The fivefold kiss is complete." Demi's voice is loud and clear again.

The audience erupts into cheerful applause. Alex turns and beams at the rabid crowd. I should be happy, but the sadness pulls me down into darker waters.

I try to let Alex enjoy his moment of induction into our world, the glory of becoming a full keeper for whatever it's worth, and I scan the crowd for Prior, expecting him to hurl a knife at my head.

But I don't see him among the bright, happy faces calling their congratulations. Several of my aunts' closer friends, other coven members or clan officiants, come forward to shake our hands. They're congratulating Arty and Monsieur Lambert as if this is their victory.

Lance and Alex lock eyes over Hatt's shoulder. I feel Alex's desire to grab the back of Lance's neck and kiss him.

"Hellebore," I curse. My cheeks flush hot. "Easy, Laveau."

"We'll have practice shielding like Lance and Perdita do." He barks a bright, cheery laugh. Then he whispers, "And you have a lot to explain—bleeding books and that guy in the cemetery? My aster. I see what you mean about the lavender eyes though."

My face burns at the first mention of Ciel, but he isn't looking at me. He's smiling at Lance. Whatever he saw in that moment of wide-open connection, it hasn't dampened his spirits. He's too happy. He's finally gotten what he wanted at long last. He sees the rest of my mess as a temporary problem to be dealt with in time.

I catch another glimpse of Lance's bare chest in my mind. "Alexander!"

"Sorry!" he laughs.

A tap of a cane against my backside makes me turn. Demi embraces me before I can see anything, but I know her bergamot scent and those coarse raven curls. Arty stands behind her, her expression neutral.

"Head back, both of you," Arty commands, presumably talking to me and Alex instead of me and Demi. "You'll need a couple days to get used to the power fluxes between you. Don't do *anything* until we have a chance to walk you through it. You don't want to blow each other apart, now do you?"

"And enjoy it, my love," Demi says as she holds me at arm's length. "It's a bond worth cherishing."

She has tears in her eyes, and I can't help but think of her keeper again, long dead. The love of her life gone. Of course Charles is on her mind tonight. Her bittersweet smile says it all.

Alex squeezes my shoulder affectionately, letting me know he's ready to leave when I am.

But we don't have time to bask in our newfound connection, or even a chance for me to wallow in what I've done to someone I'm supposed to love.

Because before we can do anything, the screaming starts.

CHAPTER 15
HUNTER, HUNTER, BURNING BRIGHT

"**D**emons!" someone screams, the voice high and quavering.

"Keys out! Everyone!" Arty cries over the explosion of panic and rabid fear. "Go!"

Hundreds of birds erupt from the trees, screaming, shrieking, flying in all directions. At least a dozen howling cats sprint across the damp amphitheater, the frost from my second spell already melting.

It's complete and utter chaos, and for a moment, all I can do is stand there, staring up into the sky with a dumbfounded and panicked look on my face, mesmerized by the swooping screech of countless birds.

A rough cord scrapes my cheek, breaking the spell. Alex is tugging the skeleton key and crystal back over my head. The weight of the polished bone on my chest snaps me back to the reality of the moment.

A woman screams, emitting an unmistakable wail of pain.

A witch, no older than thirty, is pinned beneath a demon. A snarling Hate has its hands pressed into the stone seat as it sits astride the witch. The witch screams as it roars into her face.

I jolt forward without thinking.

I only get two steps in before a sharp chunk of wood hits the back of my knees, knocking me down. I catch myself with my hands, rolling without thinking. If it's a demon, I need to get on my feet as quickly as possible.

But it isn't a demon.

It's Arty, the butt of her cane shoved sharply into my solar plexus.

"No!" she barks. "To Rowan House. Now!"

"You're crazy!" Because I'm a hunter. Hunters *fight*.

"He isn't ready!" she snaps. She waves her carved jaguar head at Alex. "Would you sacrifice him already?"

I roll over, getting to my feet in time to see Alex's magic whirl fiercely around him. His gaze is fixed on the Hate closest to him as his fists open and close. He's itching to get into the fray as badly as I am.

"*Foxglove!* Listen to me!" Arty hisses again. "There are things about your bond you don't understand. You can't possibly understand. Take him home!"

Did Arty see something? Or is this just friendly advice from an elder to a young witch who's never even had a keeper before? I don't have time to find out.

"But what about everyone else?" This isn't a stupid question. People will die here tonight if the hunters don't protect them.

"We'll handle it." Arty gestures in Demi's direction, and I see that my second aunt has cast an enormous shield. She's using it to protect the exits, forcing the demons further and further back so that more people can escape.

"I may have done this before!" Arty snaps at me.

Hellebore.

I grab Alex by the arm. "Come on."

He doesn't budge, so I yank him harder.

"Laveau! *Move.*"

We run at full speed, taking the stone landings one at a time as we push through the screaming throngs of witches bolting for safety.

Everyone runs toward the circle of cabins a hundred meters away, trying to get past the shield Demi maintains, Artemis and Monsieur Lambert guarding her back.

I pause to look behind me, making sure I haven't lost Alex.

I'm here, he says, his magic brushing mine. *Don't stop.*

The one-story cabins grow larger and larger. I've *just* passed the shield, no more than thirty paces from finding an exit to Rowan House, when I hear a snarl and snap behind me. I *feel* Alex's body slammed into the ground rather than see him. I skid to a stop, slipping out of the stream of screaming people rushing for the cabin doors.

Cursing, I dive through the bodies, colliding with elbows and shoulders before making it through to the other side.

Alex is on his back, grunting, as a kappa demon clambers on top of him, trying to dig its long talons into his throat. Its fangs snarl and snap inches from Alex's face. He's pulled a blade and has buried it in the beast's shoulder. It screams, but Alex is struggling to shift his position and get out from under it.

Without thinking, I throw my magic in a great lashing arc. I don't even know what spell I cast. But I see it crack like a giant whip across the back of the kappa demon.

It snarls, rearing up. It bares its long vampire fangs at me. But it's off Alex and that's all that matters.

I lash it again and again, the magic crackling against its

back. It takes six strikes before the kappa runs off into the night.

Alex reaches up and takes my extended arm, letting me haul him up. He has an ugly scratch down his right forearm, but it's already healing.

"Are you okay?" My voice is too high and tight. I don't sound like a warrior at all. I sound like a scared little girl.

"I'm fine. It just surprised me." He hisses, fingering the cut.

Alex looks past me, over my right shoulder. I turn in time to see Perdita and Lance rush across the threshold of the cabin's door and out of sight.

"He's okay," I assure him. *And we'll be okay too.* As soon as we figure out what the hellebore is happening. How did the demons even find us? It's almost impossible to get a sense of how many there are, and who they're attacking and why. Is this how they descended on the Priests' house?

Another scream raises the hair on the back of my neck. My gut sinks like a stone. Ten feet from the cabin, Victor Hornsby is pulling Hannah out of the arms of an Envy. She's crying, tears streaming down her doll-like face. A giant tear in her dress reveals her gashed and bloody leg.

Hornsby casts four or five spells in rapid fire, knocking the Envy back, but it just keeps coming.

Alex is already moving toward them, but I grab his wounded arm. "No."

"We don't run!" Alex screams over the commotion. *We've never run and we won't start now.*

He isn't ready. Arty's words echo hauntingly through the hollow of my mind. If it's between keeping Alex safe and saving Hornsby and Hannah, I'm sorry. There's no question for me.

But Alex has capitalized on my hesitation and is already tearing across the moonlit night to them.

"Hellebore!" I pull the athame from its hip sheath and chase after him.

I rapid-cast several spells. Then I jump, throwing all my weight into the demon's body. We roll, tumbling over one another, end over end.

When we both exit the roll, it's screeching like an alley cat. My athame is buried in its back. Damsel seed. I want it back.

The Envy's green eyes look like emeralds, mesmerizing in the dark. I pull my little four-inch blade from my forearm sheath and lunge.

The Envy dodges me this time, ready for the attack. It casts its own spell, and I brace for the impact.

I don't feel anything. Is it possible it missed? Demons have fantastic aim. The demon looks as surprised as I do, and I take that moment to reclaim my athame, wrenching it from its back.

It screams.

And Alex drops to his knees in my peripheral vision. A bright bloom of blood pours from his chest.

I freeze, terrified. Nothing touched him.

Nothing touched him—*How*—

The Envy strikes me with his magic again, and I *feel* the magic connect, warping around me. But instead of splitting my own skin, causing wounds to my own body as it has in every demon fight since I became a hunter, the magic ripples down our bond and slams into Alex.

I barely have enough time to dodge the third strike, my mind reeling with shock. I dive and drag my blade across its throat. It skitters away. It doesn't make it very far. Hornsby is on his feet just in time to land the killing blow, taking its head.

I'm on my knees beside Alex, watching the blood pour from his chest.

"I—I—" My Goddess. Words fail me.

"He's your chevalier," Hornsby says, in a painfully gentle way.

"What?"

"He's your sacrifice," Hornsby says, running a hand through his dark hair.

I rip off my shirt, not caring who sees me in my bra, and compress the wound. "English, Hornsby!"

"That's his gift as your chevalier. He can transfer all magical blows to his body through your connection. He absorbs them. His body is easier to heal than yours, so he transferred the blows to his own body so you can keep fighting."

"Idiot!" I hiss into his face, but Alex doesn't even hear me. His eyes are closed.

A demon gallops past me. A djinn.

I do a double take.

A djinn?

I've never seen one in real life, only in books. All around me, I see demons—rare demons. Hates and Envies are a dime a dozen. But kappas? Djinn? I even spot a feline bajang and a long-tongued aswang. These can't even be found in North America.

Did a hell mouth open or something? Where are they coming from?

Were the demons drawn to the amphitheater because of our magic? This certainly has been the largest gathering of witches in some time, but the grove should have provided protection. Hidden the stench of our magic. Did someone summon them? It's possible, but why would they do that? And why would they summon so many? Demons don't coordinate well. They're loners, like me. It would take a really *big bad* to wrangle them and force them in line.

Who could do that? *What* could do that?

Wherever they came from, they're returning. All the attacking demons have stopped trying to tear people apart and have begun to run in all directions, scattering like seeds in the wind.

"They're running from something," Hornsby whispers beside me as I continue compressing Alex's wound.

"Let's hope it isn't a bigger demon," I say, my hands still on Alex's chest.

Heal yourself, I whisper through the bond. *Hurry up and heal yourself.*

It's not a bigger demon.

I know it because I feel him before I see him. His presence is a lick of fresh mountain air on the back of my neck. I instinctively know just where to look. Through the trees our eyes meet.

Ciel's gaze catches and holds my own. I'm not even sure anyone else can see him through the play of shadows, but I recognize that gleaming sword the second he brings it down across the neck of the bajang who was stupid enough to cross his path.

You, I think, my heart speeding up at the sight of the fey. *The demons are running from you.*

Maybe Ciel is the *big bad*.

The tap-scratch of a cane breaks my concentration. Arty's haggard face appears through the flood of bodies, the crowd considerably thinner now.

As soon as she sees me, she curses. "I told you to leave!"

"I'm glad they didn't," Hornsby says, vouching for me

immediately, despite the fact that he's defying his elder and senior coven leader. "I don't know how Hannah and I would have survived if they hadn't helped us."

Demi's hand is already lifting Hannah's skirt, inspecting the wound, cooing as Hannah starts to cry. I see her pitifully tear-stained cheeks and think some people are too sweet for this world.

"I told you he wasn't ready," Arty snaps. "You berserker! You're going to get him killed fighting like a hellcat."

The words sting like a slap.

Monsieur Lambert appears beside me, frowning down at his unconscious son.

"Please." That's all he says. I move out of the way so he can lift the bloodied shirt I'm crushing against Alex's wound.

Slowly, he peels back the cloth. It looks *awful*.

"I had no idea an Envy could cause so much damage," I say.

"Not to you, it doesn't!" Arty stamps her cane against the earth. "But you aren't fighting with your body anymore, and you'll do well to remember that!"

"Artemis," Demi whispers in a low warning.

I try to recall every wound I've ever received. An Envy has never landed a blow this serious before, and I don't think it's because I have some kind of battle savvy.

What is Artemis saying?

In truth, she doesn't look like she's trying to say anything. She looks ready to beat me with her stick.

Monsieur Lambert says, "I've used my powers, but he will heal faster if you stay with him. He'll draw from the bond."

"Take him home and *stay* with him," Arty commands.

Defeated, I drag myself to my feet. Hornsby holds Alex

upright as I slip his other arm around my shoulder. Demi carries Hannah in her arms. Monsieur Lambert hands me the bloodied shirt and says nothing. That makes me feel even worse. Anger I can handle. Outrage even.

But he looks disappointed. Utterly disappointed that his son is a chevalier to a witch like me.

A lump forms in my throat as Hornsby and I synchronize our steps, maneuvering Alex to the exit.

I catch sight of the fey lieutenant through the trees. He's crushing the limp body of a demon in one grip, the sword pointed at the earth.

Protect them, I whisper, wondering if he can hear my thoughts the way Alex and the aunts can. I project images of my aunts, and the other witches still left behind, trying to flee to safer ground.

Please, protect them.

Ciel raises his sword, bright with blood. He says nothing.

CHAPTER 16

THE FAMILY SECRET

I am back in the dream. I know almost immediately, even as my dream-self sits on a cold stone slab. Above our heads, the moon shines through the opening in the temple's ceiling. Ciel's eyes are full of tears as he removes the thick armor protecting my chest. He says nothing as he undresses me. Then I'm bare in the night air, and a delicious chill sweeps over my moonlit skin.

"You're a fool," he says as he inspects my wounds tenderly.

"You have always made me a fool." I cup Ciel's cheeks in my hands. He's so beautiful it hurts to look at him. Devastatingly beautiful, and I might not look on this face ever again. "I've accepted the name. I cannot undo it."

He turns away from me.

The exhaustion, the crushing exhaustion of my oncoming stasis, weighs on me. How ill-timed this war is. I should not have been the one to lead it, as weak as I am. It's a marvel that Vinae did not take us sooner.

Vinae. My husband.

My stomach turns.

Ciel watches me with the same hurt expression. "You cannot leave with him."

But I will. For Ciel's life. For Naja's safety. For the freedom of Elysium, and all those who trust me as their queen—I will do anything.

"He came now for a reason," Ciel insists. "He knows you're weak. You might be able to fight him for a while, but with your stasis—"

"Hush," I say. I can imagine the coming horrors without his assistance. I extend my hands toward him. "Come here."

He looks ready to refuse me. But he moves forward, stepping between my parted legs where I sit on the stone slab. I reach up and unclasp the first buckle on his armor. Then the other. He shrugs his breastplate away. My fingers slip under the linen of his shirt and lift, revealing the smooth planes of his scarred chest. I run a thumb over the moon tattoo on his bicep, feeling the raised, scarred flesh beneath.

He breathes my name. "Sephone, please."

I start to count all the things I'll miss about him.

The look of his smile in the moonlight, or the way his eyes sparkle in the sunlight, a blue so deep they look like lavender. The smell of him—water and cassia—and the weight of him above me.

The way a room warms when he enters it.

I think of the first day he woke me from my last great dreaming. It was a day spent in a field of narcissus that stretched as far as the eye could see. I was a child. I asked countless questions, as children do, and he answered each, patiently, as bright yellow blooms swayed in the breeze around us.

Much later, when I was no longer a child, this was also the field where we first made love. We lay down amongst purple, fragrant flowers. Grape hyacinth. Vicia cracca, Wild Iris, and, of course, the narcissus.

I'm locking these memories up, wrapping them in a shroud that will survive my passage to Hell.

Ciel runs a cool hand down my back, pulling me from my thoughts. "I cannot let him take you."

"There is only one way out of this bargain." I kiss his throat. I'll never kiss him enough, hold him enough, smell or taste him enough. "You know I speak the truth."

He stills under my lips.

"Until I die, I will bear the name he gave me. I am his wife."

"You will bed him?"

"Jealousy does not suit you."

"Surrender does not suit *you*," he snaps. Such pain in those beautiful eyes. "I will fight for you even if you will not."

"No," I say, an order. "You will stay in Elysium. You will serve Naja alongside Bast. You will protect them until I find a way to return to you. That is my command."

Protect them. The first hint of reality echoes through the dream. *Please protect them.*

"You can't be serious." He's pleading now. He's crushing my hands in his. "With your stasis that's a thousand years. At least a thousand years and—"

The dream skips ahead.

I glimpse an elfin child. She has brilliant ice-blue eyes far older than her form suggests and is held closely by her own chevalier. "Serve her well, Bast."

He dips his head, his dark eyes forever unreadable.

The beautiful child is crying. I let her kiss my cheeks and squeeze my neck for the hundredth time.

"But if I were bigger—" she weeps.

"No," I tell her. I cannot let her blame herself for this. "Not even if you were bigger."

"I will walk you to the gate," Ciel says. He stands in full armor beside me. I shield my eyes and look up at The Temple of the Moon, a slanted pyramid of stone against the sky. Birds circle its pinnacle, shadows darting against the otherwise clear sky.

I don't object to his company as we mount two horses —mine a dappled gray—and ride from Elysia through the fields south of the city. We stop at the edge of the wood to make love—a fierce, frenzied sort of passion, the kind of act that precedes *goodbye*.

After, we lie on the earth, tangled in each other's arms. He picks grass blades from my hair and says nothing. I try to reach into his mind, but it's still closed to me. He's been closed to me for days. I don't know if it's my waning power, the approach of my stasis, or if he is punishing me for conceding to Vinae.

It hardly matters now as we linger until the sun dips beneath the trees and the earth turns gold with its diffused light.

My heart is full of terror when the Southern Gate appears, the two stone vultures unmoving, ever watchful.

King Vinae steps forward, separating himself from the shadows. I dismount my horse.

"I thought I was going to have to come in and retrieve you," Vinae calls, unable to hide his greed. "Shall I do so now? Carry you over the threshold as befitting a bride?"

"No," I say. "I will walk on my own two feet."

Several demons snicker, but Vinae doesn't seem to mind. His spirits are too high to be deterred by a bit of insolence.

Ciel commands the horses to stay as he joins me at my

side. He matches me step for step as I approach the gate, and whatever dark fate he has in store for me.

"He's not coming," Vinae says.

"No," I say. "He belongs here."

Vinae relaxes at that.

Forgive me. Ciel's voice and power flow through our bond and strike me.

My steps falter. I turn in time to see Ciel plunge a blade into my chest, white fire erupting inside me. I seize his hand only to realize it's a moonblade.

A moonblade. And its magic is slicing me in two.

I collapse into his arms. Blood pours from my chest onto the earth as the demons burst into roars. But I can't see their attack. I can't see anything but the stricken face of my lieutenant as he lowers my dying body to the ground.

What have you done? I ask the encroaching darkness. *Ciel, what have you done?*

I jolt awake, a scream bubbling in my throat.

I'm drenched in sweat and shaking as the ghost ache of a buried blade throbs in my chest. For a long moment, I don't know where I am—who I am. The betrayal. The fear. The shock—all of it rides me like a demon. I'm panting, trying to draw enough air to still the spinning room.

It feels like forever before shadows recede. My bed comes into focus first. Alex lies beside me, his chest rising and falling in the deep, steady rhythm of a healing sleep.

Then I remember who I am and what's happened. The fivefold kiss. Alex's wounding. Arty's harsh words. *You berserker! You're going to get him killed!*

And there's still a demon lurking in this house.

These are my problems. Not some fey war. Not a knife

to the heart from a man I love more than Heaven and Earth. Nor crushing weight of that betrayal.

I pull at my face.

I collapse onto my back, staring at the ceiling. I lie there for a long time. When it's clear sleep isn't coming, I roll over and pluck my mother's journal off the top of the pile.

After reading two pages on the medicinal uses of comfrey, I toss this one aside and grab a second, a third—I lose count of how many journals I leaf through. Eventually I come across the most diverse volume yet, a mixture of spells, personal thoughts, sketches, and observations.

I turn the page and note a drawn line separating two entries: one about birds native to the Smoky Mountains and another dated March 4, 2000—six days after Phelia and I were born.

I sit up on my elbow, angling the book to better illuminate the pages with bright clear moonlight.

My heart kicks against my ribs.

March 4, 2000

I have to write this down before the encounter becomes nothing more than a dream in my mind. In the morning light, I'll surely think it was a hallucination or a waking nightmare brought on by too many sleepless nights.

Tonight, I was almost asleep in our warm bed when I heard Phelia cry. It was a strange cry, one that shot right through me. The magic in my veins trembled awake at the sound of it, and before I was even fully aware of what I was doing, I was out of bed and running down the stairs to her room.

I found Phelia in the nursery.

In the arms of a man. If I can call him a man. Human-like and androgynous, with skin as white as the moon's.

He stood beside Phelia's cradle. He held my baby in his arms. She was so still and so quiet that I was certain she was dead. Only then did I realize another child, a second baby which looked just like Phelia, was lying in the crib, pink and healthy— looking more vibrant than Phelia ever had with the pneumonia drowning her since birth.

Slowly, as if the Goddess herself had whispered the wisdom into my ear, I knew what was happening.

A fey was here to carry off my dead daughter, and in her place, he had left a changeling.

A changeling. Dear Goddess, a fey child!

I fell to my knees before the fey and begged. I don't even remember what all I promised if only Phelia could be spared. I used every excuse I could think of.

I explained how hard I tried to conceive her. How I used magic and potions and knew the danger of conceiving a life using magic rather than a man. I explained how Phelia herself was a gift from the Goddess. Phelia was alive, despite the odds, and even still in spite of the fluid in her lungs.

But even as I begged, I knew she was dead. I knew she had not survived the pneumonia. This whole time she hadn't made a single sound in his arms. She hadn't stirred. Her tiny body had remained motionless and ashen in the pale light.

But I begged. And begged. In my heart, I believed Artemis's prediction that my child would live past infancy. Suddenly, I believed with a delusional intensity that Phelia would live if I just said the right thing, promised the right thing to this creature here and now. That her survival came down to this very moment.

Artemis had shared that vision with great reluctance—and now I suspect I know why.

The fey didn't speak once as I cried and pleaded for my daughter's life. He remained silent, watching me with cold eyes. When I had nothing left to promise, nothing else to offer, he simply said, "I cannot undo her fate."

"More time," I begged. "I just want more time."

"Mara made a bargain and you will honor it."

I agreed—though I've no idea what such a bargain entailed —and promised I would do anything as long as he put Phelia back into her crib, alive.

In the smallest gesture, the fey lifted Phelia to his lips in what looked like a kiss. A small sound was made like water spinning down a drain and light sparked between them. As soon as he laid her in the crib beside the second child, Phelia began to cry.

I've never been so happy to hear my daughter cry!

The fey made me promise I would look after the changeling as if she were my own, made me promise I would protect her and show her only kindness. He said she was loved, and if I did not treat her kindly, he would destroy the Bishop clan and burn Rowan House to the ground.

I believed every word.

So I promised. I promised to do everything he asked and more before placing my head in my hands and weeping a lifetime's worth of gratitude.

When I finally pulled myself together, he was gone.

All that's left to prove he wasn't a dream is the child. The child! A beautiful, healthy girl who looks exactly like my own Phelia.

Two daughters. From childlessness to two daughters. I haven't the slightest clue what this must mean for us, what this child must mean—but for now I am only grateful. I feel so incredibly blessed.

• • •

I reread my mother's entry over and over again. I search the whole book cover to cover for something else that might tell me more about that night in our nursery. Nothing. There's nothing else about the fey or changelings. Then I go through the other journals.

Nothing.

Not a word.

My heart is thundering so loudly that all I can hear is the rush of blood pumping in my ears. I stand, spin a circle in my room as if I'm unsure which way to go, because all of me is going everywhere at once.

Alex stirs, his brow pinching in his sleep.

I'm a second from shaking him awake until I see the bloodstained bandages across his chest. Arty's words bite into me again.

Instead of waking Alex, I creep from the room. As soon as the door is shut behind me, I'm running as quietly as one can run, down the hall to my aunts' rooms. I throw the door open on one dark bedroom, then the other. Both queen beds are empty. Their shared master bath, also empty.

I check Phelia's room, bracing myself to find a *thing* pretending to be a girl. But this room is empty too. The bed is made, untouched, not a wrinkle in the covers.

"Where the hell are you, demon?" I whisper.

A chill runs through me. I'm itching for a fight. I want to take this frustration and pain out on something.

But the kitchen, den, library, pantry, greenhouse, and surrounding yard—all are dark. It's 3:16 in the morning and the demon won't come out. And the aunts aren't home to interrogate.

All I'm left with is this anger making my limbs weak. Or rather a mixture of anger, anxiety, and disbelief.

A changeling.

A changeling.

I stand in the moonlit yard, shivering in the early April morning. My socks are soaked through with dew, my feet so cold I can barely feel them. I note all this distantly with some part of my brain meant to track my physical well-being.

But the rest of me, the rest of me is still in the bedroom, still trying to make sense of the words.

Changeling.

Changeling.

If my mother—my *mother*?—hadn't written down Phelia's name, I'd assume I was her child and Phelia the changeling. But I wasn't the one named in the journal because I hadn't had a name.

I wasn't born to Jocelyn Bishop. I'm not the twin of Ophelia Rowan Bishop or the niece of Artemis and Demi Bishop.

I'm not a witch.

And at the thought, clues begin to surface. The wild and often overblown way my magic presents itself. The trust my aunts showed in my power and ability even at a young age. They would warn Phelia off stunts or magics deemed too dangerous. When I said I wanted to be a hunter at thirteen, they hadn't protested, despite the fact that hunters usually join as late as twenty.

Arty's words surface from my dark panic.

It doesn't hurt you! And you aren't fighting with your body anymore and you'll do well to remember that!

Alex. Oh Goddess, what have I done to Alex? What does it mean to be a chevalier to the fey? Is it even worse? Even more dangerous than being one to a demon-hunting witch?

How will I know? I don't know the first thing about the

fey. A week ago, I thought they were just a story. But then in the cemetery—

Ciel.

Ciel had come to me. He'd kissed *me*. He'd said, *We cannot wait any longer.*

The aunts said they didn't know what was going on— and maybe it's true. Maybe they never really understood what I was or why they'd been forced to take me.

You've fulfilled your bargain. You owe us nothing.

Ciel must know. He must know who I am and why I'm here.

I'm running full tilt through the woods before I realize where I'm heading. Twigs and sharp underbrush stab at my feet, but they're nearly numb from the cold. My socks are soaked through. I don't stop. I heft myself over fallen logs and duck beneath branches until a stitch in my ribs aches.

Ciel promised to stay close, to be reachable. *Call and I will come.*

I reach the edge of the cliff, where the trees break open suddenly to reveal sloping mountains as far as the eye can see. The mountaintops hidden by thick fog seem to glow in the ethereal moonlight.

A quarter moon.

"Ciel?" I call out. My voice is high, very near hysterical.

My voice echoes out over the peaks.

Ciel! Please come. Please.

I stand shivering in the mountain breeze. My teeth chatter. My skin is covered in goose flesh.

I wait long enough that I start to worry he can't hear me. Or maybe something awful happened at the amphitheater. Maybe that's the real reason why the aunts aren't home.

The aunts.

Not *my* aunts.

A sharp pain cuts through me.

I'm not a Bishop.

I cup my face in my hands and try to breathe. I can't stop shaking.

A twig snaps and I stand, pulling my athame in one fluid movement. I press it against a pale throat as iridescent eyes stare down into mine.

He doesn't flinch at the blade. He doesn't try to disarm me. Ciel only stands before me, waiting.

"I'm fey," I blurt, feeling tears prick my eyes. Ridiculous. I'm being absolutely ridiculous. "You brought me here twenty-two years ago. You left me here. Why?"

"To protect you." Those eyes hold my gaze. "To hide you."

"From what?"

"The demons."

I laugh, but there's no humor in it. "You picked the wrong family then. We're neck deep in demons."

"It's not the half-breeds I fear. They could never hurt you the way he can."

"Who?" I ask, lowering the athame. I note the red line where the blade pressed his throat. I didn't break skin, but I pressed hard.

Ciel doesn't seem to mind. He doesn't rub his neck. "King Vinae."

King Vinae. I recognize the name from the dreams.

"Why would King Vinae give a damsel seed about me?"

"You still don't remember who you are." It's not a question.

My heart knocks wildly against my ribs. I'm standing on the edge of the cliff. I know if I ask this next question, I'll tumble over into the dark, and there will be no climbing out again. There will be no escaping the rocks below, the rocks surely about to bash apart the ignorance I've relied on.

But I've never been one to turn back.

"Who am I, Ciel?" I ask.

"You are my queen," he says. "Queen Sephone of Elysium."

CHAPTER 17
CIEL'S SACRIFICE

The world tilts. Or rather, I'm tilting. I'm shaking all over. *Queen Sephone. Queen Sephone.*

Not Amelia Bishop.

Queen Sephone. Not just some random fey brought to Earth.

A large fur coat falls over my shoulders. Ciel pulls me against him, trying to warm me with the coat and his body heat. It's too cold to be out here shoeless, coatless. Or I'm shaking for other reasons.

"They weren't dreams," I say through chattering teeth. "They're my memories. But how? I'm human."

"For now," he says. "I hid your soul in a human body, but you are immortal. Your vessel changes but you live on."

"What about magic? Don't the demons know I'm fey?"

"I suppressed and bound most of it. I didn't want you to be discovered when you were a child. I broke the binding when I kissed you."

The kiss.

"As you awaken, your memories and powers will return to you."

A scrap of memory surfaces. I'm standing at the Southern Gate, Vinae's yellow eyes roving over my body in anticipation, then the sharp jab of a blade through my chest.

Ciel stabbed me.

Ciel *killed* me.

I throw off the cloak and grab the athame again. I press it hard against his throat, and this time blood blooms under the blade. "You killed me!"

He says nothing.

"You stabbed me in the heart!"

"You bound yourself to Vinae. The only way to end that bond was to end the life sworn to him, and to rename you. The Bishop name is a strong one. It's served its purpose."

"But you killed me." I can feel the blade, that burning cold metal, even now.

"I cut your soul from your body using the moonblade," he says quietly. "I did this without your permission. I did it prematurely, before you could enter stasis and regenerate yourself. I betrayed you. But it was either betray you or allow you...allow you to..." His eyes pinch shut. "I could not. I *still* cannot."

He opens his eyes to reveal shining tears collecting in his long silvery lashes.

"You made me into a changeling."

"I don't know that word. You are blade born."

"What?"

"I did not change you. You were reborn of the blade. And I do not regret it." He says this as if I've accused him of something. He raises his chin. "It cost me, but I would pay any price to free you from him."

"What did it cost you?" I ask, my voice little more than a whisper.

"I was punished."

"By whom?"

"Your sister. Queen Naja." He flicks his eyes up to meet mine. In this light they're more silver than lavender. "I'm not sure how much you remember."

I remember the fierce ice-blue eyes set in an elfin child's face from my dream. I remember hair as black as crow feathers. I remember the footnotes from Ibis's book. Sister queens. The Living and The Dreaming. If I'm here, Naja must be The Living Queen of Elysium now. "How did she punish you?"

"It doesn't matter." He looks away. "She was too lenient."

I search his face, looking for deception or trickery. I see only the lieutenant from my dreams—my memories. The loving and faithful companion. He has the same soft face, the same tender voice.

"How could you lose me if you knew where I was?" I ask. Part of me sees a stranger. Another wants to move closer.

I lower the blade but leave two feet between us, the athame's handle cold in my grip.

He motions with the cloak, and I nod. I let him wrap me in it again. His hot breath warms my cheek as he drapes his arms around me. For the moment, he's so close.

"You must be careful, my queen. This body is fragile."

"How did you lose me?" I ask again, afraid he didn't hear me or will refuse to answer.

"We were—" His jaw flexes. He searches my face as if the words he needs are written there. "Important to each other."

A bright memory of our bodies entwined as we lay

among the flowers, that last frantic release before facing Vinae. My face heats.

"I remember a little of that," I say. I quickly add, "Not much."

Pain, bright and clear, flashes across his face. "You don't understand what was lost."

"I'm sorry." I don't really know what I'm apologizing for, but it's clear I've hurt him somehow. The pain is so easy to read in those pretty features. "Can you explain it to me?"

He turns away from me. The muscular planes of his back remain tight. I watch it rise and fall with his breathing. He speaks without looking at me, still giving me his back.

"You're no longer bound to me," he says softly. "I don't know your mind. I don't know your heart. I can find you by sensing your magic. I can hear you if you call, but any fey of Elysium can do that. You are the queen. You've forgotten every time I stood beside you on the battlefield, every time we bled side by side. Every night we slept side by side. Every time I've taken you into my arms. Every kiss, every—"

"Okay," I interrupt, lest my face catch fire. "We have a history. Got it. A long one, if the queens really do live for thousands of years."

"Our hearts no longer beat as one," he says.

I think of that shared thrumming between me and Alex. What had begun as two rhythms merging into one. Is that what Ciel means?

What that must be like, to love someone and they don't even know you. A fist of sadness squeezes my heart. "I'm sorry, Ciel. I'm sorry I don't remember."

His eyes flick up to mine. "You gave your freedom for

my life. I sacrificed our bond to regain that freedom. You owe me nothing."

A pang of shame turns my stomach sour. I feel frozen between the urge to hug him, console him, and that part of my mind saying, *Stranger, he's a stranger.*

I remain frozen on the spot.

"I will win your affection again," he says, staring at my lips as if he's waiting for them to do something. "If it takes a hundred years, a thousand. The moon can fall from the sky. The comets can burn out their light—and I will be here, loving you."

I'm struggling to draw a breath. I'm starting to think this cloak is secretly some kind of bone-crushing corset.

He tilts my chin up and waits. He's waiting for me to stop him. His eyes are full of inquisitive longing. He's asking permission.

"Will it help me remember?" I ask him. I don't recognize my own voice. It's low, husky.

"If you want to remember."

I close my eyes, leaving my mouth tilted upward.

A soft brush of lips causes my breath to hitch in my throat. Muscles low in my stomach tighten. The light touch deepens. He opens his mouth slightly, parting my lips.

My legs start to shake. It isn't just the wonderful kiss.

It's the magic. That same heady wave of power I first encountered in the cemetery rolls over me. The pulsing warmth is replaced by undeniable dizziness. I reach out and seize the thing closest to me, which happens to be Ciel. His arms slip under mine, pressing my body fully against his. This makes it worse. I sag in his embrace. He's drowning me in power. His chin works against mine, his lips parting mine further. With that first brush of tongue, I'm done.

I moan into his mouth, the sound of it vibrating our lips and teeth.

I'm about to *beg* for him to take it further, beyond the kiss—anything to ease this intense ache between my legs.

So this is what it means when the books say weak with desire.

I always thought that was the stupidest description. How in the world can you be weak with desire?

But as I hang jelly-like in his arms, my brain nothing more than mashed potatoes, I get it.

I *really* get it.

Before I can catch my breath, a wave of panic and fear slams into me.

My hands clutch Ciel reflexively. I break off the kiss and step back. I stumble and Ciel seizes my arm, trying to hold me up. The cloak falls away, but it's a distant acknowledgment.

I'm focused on the raging wall of emotion barreling through the forest.

Melody? Has that cowardly intruder dared show her face at last?

No.

Alex steps from the tree line, bare-chested from the waist up except for the bloodstained bandages. It's his fear, his panic, hitting me wave after wave.

Ciel pulls his sword.

"No!" Without thinking, I step between them. My knees are shaky from the magic, but I stay upright. I turn and face Ciel, my magic in my fingertips without any conscious command.

"Amelia?" Alex asks.

Ciel doesn't move, but he's still ready to strike.

Is this the monster from the cemetery?

He's not a monster, I tell Alex. *He's a friend, not a foe.*

Ciel moves, and I step more fully between them. "No, Ciel, you can't hurt him."

Ciel's face, which had looked as soft and drunk as mine when I first broke the kiss, is stony again. He slides the sword into its sheath.

"You've taken another chevalier," he says. It's a dangerously even voice, no doubt hiding a torrent of emotion beneath that placid façade.

"I'm her only chevalier," Alex says, and I'm surprised by the wave of jealousy that rises up in him. I scowl at him. Alex is a lot of things, but jealous has never been one of them.

"For now," Ciel says.

"Okay, whoa." I step back from both of them. "Let's make a few things clear."

They don't even look at me. They just keep staring at each other, sparks of magic surrounding them. I will zap both their asters if I have to.

"Ciel," I say, to make it clear who I am talking to. "This is Alex. Alex is my best friend. Yes, he's my chevalier. I didn't want to make him my chevalier because I don't want him to die a horrible, flaming, demon-possessed death, but if I hadn't bound myself to him, this other horrible, horrible person would have done it just to spite me."

He still isn't looking at me.

"Alex is family. I love him. I will die for him, do you understand? If you hurt him, you hurt me."

"I know what a chevalier is," Ciel says. That edge of impatience is back, but I note the relaxed shoulders. The unclenching of his fists. The white sparks at the edge of his aura dim.

I take this as progress.

"Alex," I say. "This is Ciel. He's...well, he's..."

Goddess, how do I explain who Ciel is?

"He's the guy from the cemetery," Alex says plainly. "He showed up the night the Priests died and all the demons started going nuts."

I hear the suspicion in his voice.

I step toward him, putting myself between them again. Ciel is at my back. I take a steadying breath. How will he take the news? How will Alex react to finding out he's bound himself to some fey, not a witch at all.

Alex's gaze snaps to mine, his face pinching in confusion. Did he hear what I was thinking? Great. Too late to turn back now.

I take his hand. His palm is sweaty, his skin feverish. It reminds me he is still healing and shouldn't be out of bed.

His mind takes off like a shot. *I felt you. You were upset and I came to see that you were all right.*

I'm sorry, I tell him. *I wasn't upset about that. I was upset because—*

Then I let go. I throw the door wide to our bond, to our connection. I retrace the steps, trying to form a cohesive picture of all that I've learned. I go all the way to the first kiss. To seeing Ciel in the cemetery, the way his magic rolled through me, overtaking me.

Then I move through the dreams of Ciel and me on the battlefield, of King Vinae's bargain for Ciel's life that Queen Sephone paid.

That I paid.

Alex tenses.

When the blade slides through my chest, ending my reign as The Living Queen, Alex jumps.

The journal entry of my mother finding me in the crib.

I'm not her twin. I'm not even a Bishop, my mind tells him as I put it all together in one cohesive narrative for him. The collective history of my last battle as a fey, of Ciel's choice, and the promises the Bishop women made to shelter me.

I drop my hand and step back.

Alex staggers, his chest rising and falling in great, panting breaths. "They weren't dreams. They were never dreams."

"I'm sorry." Tears are streaming down my face. "I didn't know. I wouldn't have bound you to me if I—"

Alex pulls me into a hug and crushes me. I fall apart. I'm tumbling through a tornado of feelings, the world disappearing around me. It's Alex's voice that comes through the darkness. A strong arm to pull me from the whipping wind.

I don't care what you are.

The danger—

I don't care who you are.

The king might be the one sending demons. He might be hunting me. He'll tear you apart like he did Ciel.

You won't lose me. I'll be strong.

The aunts—

The aunts love you. They've known all along what you were, and they love you.

They kept me because they had to.

No, they could have sent you away as soon as Ciel came. They didn't. Be confused. Be angry. Be whatever you are but don't be stupid. This changes nothing. Not for me and not for your family.

I'm sobbing. Full-on ugly sobbing, and I wish I could say with certainty that I know what I am crying about. About the secret truth my family hid from me, about the danger I've brought to the doorstep of the only people I care about, that maybe my coming here put people I love in danger, cost others their lives. I'm doubting everything.

Alex holds me. He speaks softly into my hair. "It's going to be okay. Whatever happens, it'll be okay." *I'll be right here.* "You're not alone."

"No," Ciel says, and his voice makes me turn and look at him. "In that we agree."

I'm surprised by what I see there, such tenderness.

"We'll help you," Alex says. I note the *we.*

They are staring at each other.

You love him? Alex asks in my mind.

My face heats. *I don't know him.*

But you remember him. I saw you...before. It's obvious he still loves you—

Whatever is going on with me and Ciel will have to wait. I think we've got more important things to deal with right now.

"Your bond is new," Ciel says.

"We sealed it tonight," Alex offers. The hostility and distrust are gone.

What do they see in each other? I wonder.

Alex answers me without pause. *I see a man who values your freedom above his own happiness. That's enough for me.*

A lump forms in my throat.

Arty's unforgiving words, *He's not ready,* slug me in the chest again. She knew I was fey. She knew our bond would be different.

I'm not afraid, Alex breathes through my mind.

But I am. I'm absolutely terrified.

The lump in my throat grows. Goddess, please. Just don't let me cry anymore. I've blubbered enough. Ciel drapes the cloak across my shoulders once more. It isn't until he does so that I realize I'm still shivering.

I share my suspicions with him. "That's why the demons came tonight. They felt my magic during the duel."

"Yes," Ciel confirms. "I felt it too. Every day you will become more and more yourself."

"Do you think someone else knows who you are?" Alex asks. He's looking between the two of us. "Maybe someone found out or saw something."

I'm about to say no, that it's impossible. The aunts are about as tight-lipped as a poppet with its mouth sewn shut. But then I think of Ibis, of the bookmarked chapter. Of a passing comment about caraway.

"Someone else might know what I am," I say, looking up into Ciel's face. "But he's a friend. I think."

Alex tilts his head. "No way. You think that Ibis is the one who told the demons you're here?"

I shiver beneath the heavy cloak. It smells like Ciel, like flowers and starlight.

Quietly, Ciel says, "If he did, then he is in league with demons."

CHAPTER 18

ENEMY OF MY ENEMY

I wish I could say that the idea of Ibis being in league with demons is preposterous. But as soon as Ciel says it, all I can think is—*Yes. Why not?* Ibis just doesn't seem like the kind of guy to hold someone's demonic nature against them, if it meant getting some rare book, or herb, or magical artifact. I think he'd be quite comfortable making bargains with just about anyone.

But this leaves me with a mountain of questions, and only one person who can answer them.

"I'll take us there by key," I say.

"This is quicker," Ciel says, and points at the forest.

Alex and I exchange a look and peer around his shoulder. I say, "I'm not sure that's the fastest way to New York."

"We will travel by tree," Ciel says. He's already stepping into the dark, leaving Alex and me to stumble after him.

Alex bends toward my ear. "Did he say tree?"

"Maybe we misheard him." I start a list of words in my head that rhyme with *tree*. I glance at Alex's bare, bloodied chest. "I don't know if you should be up."

Before he answers, I'm already trying to wrap the cloak

around him. He refuses. "Look. I love that we're bonded now, but I'm not going to wear your boyfriend's clothes. It's too soon for me."

I elbow him and he grimaces from the pain. Immediately I'm begging his forgiveness, realizing that I just hit his wound.

"Are you coming?" Ciel steps up to a large tree with a wide trunk. He places one of his pale hands on the dark trunk and waits. Then his hand disappears. *Disappears.*

I freeze. I will not be getting closer to a tree that eats people.

"We have permission to cross," Ciel says, and extends his remaining hand toward me. "You first, since you know where we are going."

"Ladies first," Alex says, nudging me. "My queen."

I mimic elbowing him, stopping short of striking him a second time. He only laughs.

"Take hold of him," Ciel instructs, patiently waiting.

I take Alex's hand. I suck in a big, brave breath and step into the dark. It's like stepping into a grave that smells of old earth and mossy bark.

Then I step out again and find myself inside The Shop on 42nd Street, holding Alex's hand as he emerges from the enormous oak tree in the center of the grand chamber behind me.

Ciel appears behind him.

I look at the ceiling, the books, the shelves of magic supplies. "Holy hellebore. How in the *world* did that work?"

An amused voice answers, "Because the fey gave us the trees."

Ibis stands beside a large bookcase, Athena at his side, her big yellow eyes watchful. Ibis steps forward into the light. He looks as if he's been waiting for us. Maybe he has been. "When the fey sealed the gates of Elysium, they needed a way to travel to Septem Terras. We remain allied tribes, after all. So they sent the birds to drop the seeds of Elysium trees. The trees propagated over the centuries and now they're the only way to travel between our realms. And it's very clever, because you must have the permission of the tree in order to pass. And a tree will refuse a wicked heart. Of course, I think this says a great deal about the fey's trust in us."

"A tree is always honorable." Ciel approaches Ibis. "Mortals are not."

"Fair enough." Ibis doesn't move closer. Athena is the one that rises from her haunches, now on all fours. The lynx has completely forgotten about us. Her attention is entirely fixed on Ciel.

Ibis, however, is looking at me. "Welcome to my humble shop, Queen Sephone of Elysium."

It's like he kicked me in the gut. "You knew? Since when?"

"When you turned up here with the bloodstone. I wanted to ask what changed, why you were suddenly radiating fey magic, but—" His eyes cut to Ciel. "I think I understand. Might this be your chevalier? Ciel, is it?"

Ciel puts his hand on his sword.

I step between them, forcing Ibis to look at me. "Why didn't you tell me?"

Ibis clucks his tongue. "You didn't introduce yourself as the Queen of Elysium, did you? Didn't say, 'Look at me and all my pretty *feyness*.' I thought it'd be more than a little rude to bring it up first."

"You gave me a moonblade," I say. "You told me not to tell the aunts about it."

His lips quirk in a devilish smile. "You didn't know what you were. I was almost certain they did."

"Why do you say that?"

His grin quirks upward. I watch him sort through his ammo, all the things he could say, before deciding on something safe. "The fact that your magic has always been stronger and more advanced than any I've ever seen in a witch your age. Half the time, I don't hear you mutter an incantation at all. You don't *use* magic like the rest of us. You *are* magic."

My cheeks heat. Ciel's fingers twitch against mine, making me burningly aware that I'm still holding his hand —or he's holding mine. I can no longer tell.

"I followed a hunch and gave you the blade." His eyes flick to my hand again, and I get the impression that he isn't thrilled by Ciel's interest in me. "What I'd like to know is how your legendary lieutenant crafted your current form."

My lieutenant.

"A body that would pass for human and channel the magic pouring from your very soul without being torn apart by its power. That's a trick I'd pay dearly to learn."

His voice turns serpentine. For the first time in my life, I see Ibis not as the handsome, bookish shopkeeper. I see him for what he is: dangerous. How much does he see of our world and keep his mouth shut?

I stick my hand in a vat of caraway and he knows exactly what it means. If a witch buys African violets and clove sticks, he probably knows just what love spell she'll cast. How many secrets Ibis must know about as we pass through his world, combing his shop with our every want and need.

He has power over us all.

"We need to know if King Vinae is behind the attacks. Is he the one sending demons? Controlling them?" I ask.

"I don't know. I'm fortunate enough to not have crossed paths with the demon king." Ibis's eyes spark. "Why don't we ask a demon? I have one upstairs. And he speaks well for a prince."

I'm flabbergasted. "You have a demon *prince* here?"

"Oh honestly, Lady Bishop. Don't look at me like that." He gestures to Ciel. "You can hardly judge the company I keep after what he's done."

"He saved her!" Alex says.

"*Ciel* murdered his own lover and threw her body to the demons," Ibis says coldly. "Let's forgo the hero worship, shall we?"

Lover.

Ciel drops my hand, but before he does, I catch a shimmer of shame pulsing through him.

Was this his dark secret? That he threw my dead body to the demons after harvesting my soul?

If he threw Sephone's—my—body to the demons, he must've had his reasons.

"A brilliant diversion, mind you, if a little heartless," Ibis concedes. "If you want to speak to the demon prince, he won't harm you, I swear it."

A demon prince. Am I really about to speak to a demon prince?

"Fine," I say. "If you think he can tell me something useful about Vinae."

"This way." Ibis turns on his heels and glides gracefully toward the back of the shop. Athena doesn't move, remaining crouched and ready for one of us to do something stupid. And she stays that way until we pass her. Only then does she take up the rear, staying close to our heels, those yellow eyes measuring each step.

The grand chamber with all the books, reeking of incense and herbs, narrows under a sweeping archway. We pass beneath the cream-colored arch into a smaller, more intimate chamber lined with chestnut-colored doors, each with a number. Odd numbers on the left, even numbers on the right.

I bump into Ibis. "Sorry."

He follows my gaze up toward the ceiling. "Oh, yes, I love that one. A beautiful woman by the name of Gisele painted that for me in the sixteenth century."

"Sixteenth century?" Impossible. If Ibis is older than forty, I'll eat my shirt.

"Yes, imagine how much knowledge a man might acquire in several centuries." Ibis winks at me.

"Less than a man acquires in several millennia," Ciel says.

Ibis barks a laugh and yanks open the door. "After you, my queen."

I peer into the darkness at the stone steps leading up, but who knows to where, because the staircase spirals out of sight.

"Really? You think I'm going to let you call me 'my queen' when I won't even let you call me Lady Bishop?"

My heart twitches. Bishop. If the aunts allow me to keep the name.

We love her, Demi told Ciel in the forest when he'd come to claim me. Demi meant it when she said it. But does Arty hold any real affection for me? Did my own mother?

My heart aches.

"After you, Lady Queen," Ibis says.

I suck in a deep breath to quell my irritation.

Alex starts up the staircase first. With each step, candles spark alive, not unlike those in the Bishop vault. I'm sure it's the same charm.

I follow Alex up, my fingers trailing over coarse stone. The walls press in on us. I can touch both sides of the narrow staircase with my arms out. By the time the floor evens out, my thighs are burning.

A wooden door swings open. Alex steps into the room. "Whoa."

Only it doesn't feel like a room at all. I've stepped into a forest.

The ground softens under my feet as I sink into the mossy earth. I turn a full circle, my brain frantically trying to process the rain-slick stones rising up on my right, so high that I can't see the peaks that disappear into an impenetrable cloud of fog. White birch trees stretch as far back as I can see, half of the lower trunks hidden by ferns and monstrous elephant ears. I hear bird call and crickets. Other insects, maybe beetles, that I don't recognize.

The moisture from the air dampens my skin. Alex's curls fray from the humidity.

A tawny blur bounds past me onto a boulder. Athena's enormous claws dig into the stone as she hauls her powerful body higher, climbing up and up until she reaches a perfectly flat landing, overlooking her lichen-covered domain. It takes everything I have not to break out into an off-key rendition of *Circle of Life*.

"These are Athena's quarters. She likes to be near the door," Ibis says cheerfully, coming around us to assume his position in front as tour guide. "My rooms are through here."

He disappears beneath an arch of wisteria blossoms.

Enchantment, I realize. It isn't really a forest at the base of a mountain. I'm sure that above the fog is a ceiling like any other. But it's crafted beautifully. All the way down to the cavernous feeling, the fresh air and subtle breeze. The smell of grass and flowers. The cool moisture licking at my skin. It's perfect. Whoever crafted this—if not Ibis himself —did so with painstaking detail.

Alex's mouth hangs slightly ajar, his neck craned back to look at the trees.

"He's waiting for us," Ciel says softly. I catch those lavender eyes watching me.

He stands at the edge of the hanging wisteria, waiting. His eyes are even more purple amidst the violet blooms. A memory stirs but doesn't quite surface. I've seen Ciel somewhere like this before—with wisteria twining in his hair.

I follow him beneath fragrant white and purple blooms. At the end of the archway is another large wooden door. Ibis says something too low for me to hear and the door swings open before he ever reaches it.

First there is a living room. A huge fireplace that resembles the obsidian hearth downstairs crackles with a burning fire. It's flanked by two red leather armchairs and a couch that looks soft enough to collapse onto.

The walls are books. No place to hang a picture, no windows, but spine after spine. The only light is the firelight, bright enough to fill the room with a warm glow. It takes a moment for my eyes to adjust from the bright, clear light of the forest to this smaller, darker space.

I bask in the smell of old books, deeply inhaling the scent as the room brightens. As soon as my eyes adjust, I realize we aren't alone.

Curled into one of the red leather armchairs is—*What is that?*

A creature. His skin is almost the same color as the

leather, red with brown splotches. His eyes are an orange I've never seen before. Burning coals. Long black nails tap against the arm of the chair.

Fire, I realize. The eyes are moving flames reflecting in watery black pools.

Ciel draws his sword.

"If you wanted to be rid of me, Ibis," the creature says, except his voice isn't much of a voice at all, more like sandpaper being dragged across a rock, "you could've politely asked me to vacate the premises. No need to hire an executioner."

"You are dangerously behind on your rent," Ibis quips with feigned indifference. "I thought you needed incentive."

The creature chortles. He clucks his tongue at Ciel. "Stop playing with your sword, chevalier. It's *arousing*."

I step forward. "Who are you?"

"I am Helvar. Half brother to King Vinae. And you are Queen Sephone of Elysium. Somehow alive."

Everything happens at once. Alex calls his magic. Ciel's sword is against the demon's throat. The demon has jumped up in the chair, back arched and hissing like a cat. Ibis has his hand on the hilt of Ciel's blade, his own magic flaring around him.

"Stop!" I yell over the outburst. "Everyone just *stop*."

"He's family to the king," Alex warns, his voice low. "We can't trust him."

"Family!" The hissing demon laughs. His nails scrape the side of Ciel's sword, a horrible screech echoing in the small space. "Family means nothing to demons, boy. But they are more obsessed with lineage than even your snobbiest witches. At any rate, I'm a bastard."

"Then why tell us?" Ciel demands. He's lowered the tip of his sword but hasn't sheathed it.

"We're going to strike a deal, aren't we?"

"A deal with a demon?" I ask Ibis with an arched brow. "How do you think my aunts will feel when they hear that you've tricked their niece into making deals with demons?"

Ibis gives a noncommittal shrug. But even to me, it looks forced. "You may be Lady Bishop, but you're also the fey queen. You have your own business in this world, don't you?"

Do I? Yesterday, my only concern was saving Alex's life. Now, I'm starting to wonder if I'm on the wrong track altogether.

"Wait." I hold up a hand. "How is a full demon in the flesh *here*, in your office? I thought only half-breeds can cross over from Hell?"

Helvar taps the gold collar around his neck. "I'm here thanks to this."

"And what is *this*?" I try to look closer but don't dare to put myself in arm's reach of the demon. And I can't see it any better in the light.

"It suppresses my demonic essence and allows me to travel Septem Terras. Unfortunately, it also suppresses all my power and strength. That's why I'm willing to help you."

The demon Helvar sits up taller in his seat.

"I'll help you, but I ask for something in return. Protection."

Ciel glares at me. "Demons lie, cheat, and fight without honor."

Helvar chortles again. "Have you *met* a mortal? Liars and cheats all around, and yet you gave them your magic!"

"I gave them nothing."

Helvar cuts his gaze to me. "Is that so, chevalier? Not even what you hold most dear?"

Ciel withdraws his sword.

"I will tell you Vinae's ambitions, but you must promise to protect me," the demon says, those firelight eyes fixed on mine.

I give Ibis a wary look.

"I've sheltered him for the last ten years," Ibis says. "Obviously, I found it a worthy cause."

This was what he'd earned exile for? For sheltering this demon? I'm trying to do the math in my head, but it isn't adding up. It's been less than ten years since Ibis was exiled. Something else then.

Helvar settles on his haunches, still perched on the red leather seat. "I alone know the form Vinae takes now and where he's hiding."

"No." Ibis clucks his tongue. "I think I know that."

Helvar glowers at him. "I alone know how to stop him from hurting you."

"No," Ibis says again. "I think I know that too."

What are they doing? Alex asks mind to mind. *Are they allies or not?*

Maybe Ibis just can't tolerate someone saying they know more than he does.

Helvar shifts on his haunches. "*I* know why he wanted the queen to begin with, why he sought her for his bride."

"You told me that yourself," Ibis says, looking at his nails.

"I'm beginning to think I should be entering a bargain with Ibis, not you," I say, and Ibis breaks into his most mischievous grin yet.

Helvar isn't ready to give up. He's practically bouncing up and down on the armchair, those black claws biting into the leather. "You don't know Vinae's weakness! You don't know his past! You don't know what he was—who he was —before he was King Vinae! You don't know what he fears more than losing his own life!"

"Now *that* is knowledge *I* would enter into such a bargain for," Ibis says, slipping his hands into his pockets. He turns to me and says, "Of course, he got me for the broken moonblade—and the story of what happened once your body was recovered."

Horror dawns on me.

The blade I held earlier is the very one that took my life.

And I don't miss the brilliant mastery of Ibis's manipulation. He just played this demon like a fiddle. By insisting that the demon knew nothing, the demon revealed what knowledge he did have, squirreled away for this very moment like this, when an irresistible opportunity lay on the table before him.

Maybe my aunts were right to talk about Ibis with arched eyebrows and wary tones. *Dangerous. This one is dangerous*, my mind warns. *And you're a fool if you ever forget it.*

I face Helvar. "I want to know everything. I want to know why Vinae broke the Southern Gate and if it can be broken again. I want to know why he wanted to marry Queen—me. Why he wanted me. I want to know his weaknesses, his past, and who he was before he was king. Tell me his fears. Tell me the story of what happened after my body...went across the gate."

I didn't have the heart to say *thrown*, seeing as Ciel flinches at the word.

"It will be a long story," Helvar says. "All of that makes quite the telling."

I don't give him an inch. "But you value your life at least that much. So you'll tell us."

"I value my life above all. I suppose there are no secrets between you and your chevaliers? No need to dismiss them?"

Alex and Ciel both tense beside me. My chevaliers. He said it in the plural. He doesn't know that my connection to Ciel is broken then? Is it a magic that can't be sensed by others?

"No. There's no secrets between us." What a joke. There are *all* the secrets between us. But instead of laughing, I ask, "Where is Vinae now? What does he look like and where can I find him?"

"He's wearing the corpse flesh of a witch girl. He wears her like a mask. It isn't all of him. Just as he sent a clay body into Elysium, he sent only part of his power into Septem Terras. He is many things, but not a fool. He knows not to show himself vulnerable before you."

"The corpse flesh of a girl," I repeat. "Melody Priest."

"That's the one," Helvar confirms, clicking his long black nails together.

I knew Melody was a demon. But I never imagined. I never suspected—"King Vinae is in my house."

I'm at the door, ready to run the whole way home, when a strong arm seizes mine. It's Ibis. "You'll want to hear the rest."

"The demon king is in my house!" I tear my elbow out of his grip. "My aunts could be back. My aunts—"

"He hasn't made a move yet because he isn't sure you're the queen," Helvar is quick to add. "Once he began to suspect you weren't really dead, he wondered if you could be here, hidden among the witches. Logic dictated it would be a powerful family, a strong genealogical line capable of cloaking your magic. He sent his prized book out into the world, hoping it would fall into your hands. That you'd be drawn to it. But he couldn't know *who* you were. If you were a boy or a girl child. Only that you would have come over twenty years ago. But there were many children of old families born the year you died." Helvar flicks his eyes to Ciel's. "It was a good show. A very good show and he was fooled for a long time."

I look to Ciel.

His face remains stony. Unreadable. But his sword is back in its sheath. That's the truth of it then. Ciel killed me and threw my body across the gate hoping that the king would be fooled. And it worked, at least for a little while.

Ciel has done so much for me, at great risk to himself.

"He could have come at any time. Why now?" I ask, tearing my eyes away from Ciel.

"High-ranking demons can come to Septem Terras only by invitation. It is part of the treaty forged at the end of The First War. But he can influence and manipulate just fine from his throne of bones. So he relinquished one of his prized spell books, knowing it would fall into the witches' hands. It seems like you haven't come into contact with the book until quite recently. But the moment it touched your hands, he knew. He knew and he took that moment to strike."

I think Melody is messing with things she shouldn't, January had said. And she'd given me the book as if she'd known it was the source of trouble. That had been just days before the murders.

January gave me that book hoping it would keep her sisters safe. What would she think now, if she knew it was the moment she called the very King of Hell down upon her house?

My heart clenches.

"How did he expect to find me?" I ask. "If I could have been any witch of a certain age, he must've had a plan."

"Your scent," Helvar says. He lowers his gaze. "Forgive my rudeness, but it is nearly impossible to hide what you are. It's sweet, almost hypnotic. Hyacinth. Lilies. I feel drunk just being so near you. You reek of magic. Now that you are no longer dormant, your scent grows stronger with each passing moment. Soon there will be no mistaking what you are. The next time he sees you, he will know."

I think of the shadows under the door. Of the creeping footsteps. Had the king been stalking me, trying to figure out if I was the queen he was looking for? But then he'd run when I opened the door to confront him. Why? I feel like I'm still missing some important piece of this puzzle.

"What does he want?" I ask. "You mentioned his ambition."

"I should think it was obvious."

"Stop playing games," I say, the first sparks of my real temper flaring. "He's in my house!"

"You haven't promised to protect me yet," Helvar snaps. "I've been generous. I want your oath before I say more."

Ibis gives me a curious look. He isn't sure if I'll promise or not. Or maybe he expects me to get the info without promising anything. Maybe Ibis has those skills, but I don't. And I want to know what I'm up against.

"No," Ciel says.

"Does the chevalier speak for you?" Helvar asks, rasping.

I look into those lavender eyes. "Do the fey never make deals with demons? Never have spies? If we were truly in a war with them, I find it hard to believe that we didn't."

Ciel says nothing, which is answer enough. I look to Helvar. "I promise to protect you."

The demon visibly relaxes. To my surprise, so does Ibis.

"I also promise to murder you, horribly, if you betray me or hurt anyone I care about," I add. "And I get to ask you whatever I want, and you have to answer honestly. So if I come back in two weeks or two years or twenty years, whenever, you have to answer my questions. If you screw with me—"

All calm evaporates from the crouched leathery creature. The demon looks at Ibis with wide, shocked eyes. Ibis purses his lips and says, "Ah, no, Helvar. That word has a different connotation here. She simply means that death will be the consequence of deceiving her."

I hope you know what you're doing, Alex whispers in my mind.

You and me both.

"Right. Betray me and you'll wish the king had murdered you instead," I say.

Ibis barks a laugh.

Helvar glares at him. "You find her threats amusing?"

"Among other things."

"Why did he want a fey bride?" I ask. A sense of urgency grows inside me. A voice in the back of my mind keeps repeating, *He's in Rowan House. He's in Rowan House. My Goddess, the King of Hell is in Rowan House.*

They're safe, Alex assures me. *They're the most powerful witches alive. They'll be safe.*

"Was it me specifically or would he have taken my sister?" I ask. Naja. The name rings some distant bell deep in my heart.

"He wanted you," Helvar says, tapping those long black claws on the leather. "You are the stronger of the queens.

They claim your mother could bear no more children because you took all the magic from her body in your birth."

I assume he means my *fey* mother, because Jocelyn Bishop didn't bear me. I glance at Ciel. He nods.

"Stop flattering her," Ibis warns. "Or her head won't fit back through the door."

"It isn't flattery," Helvar rasps, looking horrified. "It's simply facts."

"Is that the only reason he wanted me? Because I was stronger?" I ask.

Was—because whatever I am now, it can't possibly be what I was.

"He wanted you for your name."

"He couldn't have known her name!" Ciel growls, composure gone.

"Vinae had spies in Elysium. Those who were not afraid to play both sides."

"Liar," Ciel says.

"How else did we break the gate? How else did we enter your realm? Knew a great deal, did we not? Knew her stasis was coming. Knew she was weak," Helvar says, those fiery eyes fixed on Ciel's.

He looks troubled.

"Stop." I hold up my hands. "Why does it matter if he knew my name? All of you seem to know my name now and the world isn't ending."

"We aren't speaking of titles, we speak of names," Helvar says.

All I can do is blink at them.

Ciel is the one who turns to me. "When you awaken from stasis, your sister gives you three names, three gifts. During your last reign, you were Queen Sephone the Necromancer, Queen Sephone the Inceptor, Queen Sephone the Onomage. Those were the three gifts bestowed upon you at your rebirth, three gifts to guide and shape your newest incarnation."

I took so much from you. I'm sorry, Ciel's cool voice whispers through my mind.

I look down and see his fingers brushing mine. Is he using the touch to speak to me?

What am I now? If I'm not The Living Queen or The Dreaming Queen. If I'm not a necromancer, inceptor, or onomage—what am I now?

No answer.

Ibis stares at our hands.

Helvar only glances.

"The demonic world is a cutthroat one. Vinae will be murdered by the first lieutenant or knight who can manage it. Perhaps even a duke if allowed close enough. Your gifts were the perfect combination to safeguard his throne."

"I don't understand," I say.

"Onomagery—to know the name of something. You would have known any who opposed him instantly. You could unname them. Destroy them with a look. With your necromancy, you could raise the dead, control countless corpse armies to do his bidding. And as the Inceptor—oh that is the gift he *truly* wanted."

"Why?" Ibis asks. If I didn't know better, I'd say that Ibis is more enraptured by this story than I am.

"Inception. That is the most powerful gift of all. All that she can dream, imagine, made reality. A seed. An idea planted—when something is pulled from the void of noncreation and made real, it ripples through all space and time, shaping forever our reality. Vinae could remake Hell with that gift. He could remake the borderlands. Everything."

I have no doubts about Ciel's reasons now. If the king wanted those powers, then he would not stop until he had them. Ciel did what he had to do to throw the king off my trail, even if those actions shamed him. And it did shame him. I can feel that clearly in the lieutenant's cool touch.

"Is that all he wanted?" I ask. "My powers?"

Helvar flicks those twin flames up to meet my eyes. "It did not hurt that you were *very* beautiful."

Another growl from Ciel.

Ibis tsks at him. "Where are your manners, Helvar? She's still beautiful."

"Yes, of course." The demon waves this away.

"What of the gate? What's kept him from attacking Elysium again?" I ask.

"Your sacrifice. When your body was thrown across the gate, your blood sealed it. When Vinae realized this, he was furious. Not only did he fail to conquer Elysium, but with your death, your names and powers were lost. He achieved nothing. Mad, he tore your body apart, but it did not matter. Your death broke the agreement." Helvar gives Ciel a wary sidelong look. "I suppose you knew what you were doing?"

Ciel says nothing.

"If you cast Vinae from Septem Terras now, I don't think he can return. He would have used a lot of power to find a suitable host, to make a Faustian Pact, and then search this world for you. Surely the three of you, along with your fabled aunts, can cast him out?"

Helvar sounds more than a little hopeful.

"I suppose that depends on how motivated he is to have me," I say.

BLADE BORN

"He wanted Queen Sephone's powers, and you don't have them. Without those abilities, you are of little use to him. If there is anything left of the formidable queen he desired, I doubt it." Helvar looks me up and down. "Even I can look at you and see that you are not all that you were. You're diminished."

I feel Alex's desire to fight him.

Don't, I plea. *I want him talking.*

"Easy, chevalier. Be glad she is only a glimmer of what she was before. You're not equipped to channel that sort of power. No mortal is. You'd be dead now if she'd taken you in her true form. Just a taste of her magic would have destroyed your mind." He makes an explosion with his balled fists opening and expanding outward, adding a little *poof* sound for good measure.

"If that's true then why did the king even come here? Why is he hunting for me if I'm no longer of any use to him?"

"Hope is a dangerous thing. Perhaps he needs to see the truth for himself."

"And when he finds me? How do we stop him?" I ask. "You said Vinae has a weakness."

"Unless you plan to go to Hell and murder him outright, I'm afraid you are limited to what can be done to his poppet."

I blink.

"The corpse," he adds.

To Melody's body, he means.

"You can destroy the body he rides, expelling him from the world, but there is a danger he would escape before you managed it and possess another outright. Perhaps someone you love." His eyes flick to Alex and my blood runs cold. "I suggest you keep him in the corpse, if possible."

"Keep him in the corpse," I repeat. "That still leaves him on Earth. On Septem Terras."

"A skeleton key will send you to any place, will it not?" Helvar asks, his eyes fixed on my chest. Can he see the key through my shirt? I make a point not to clasp the rope cord around my neck. "If someone has a skeleton key, they can open a door right into Hell, push the king through, and shut the door before he can return. I would think that is the best way."

"And risk being dragged through herself!" Alex scoffs. "*No.*"

It's a chance I'm willing to take. And Alex must know it because he whirls on me, mouth ajar, abject horror painted clearly into every one of his features.

"No," Alex says through his teeth.

"If the opportunity—"

"*No.*" Alex looks around me to Ciel. "Tell her it's suicide. It's a disaster waiting to happen. He could push her through. He could seal the exit. And then what? She'll be in Hell. What do you think will happen to her?"

"Torn apart, most likely," Helvar says plainly. "Human flesh is a delicacy in Hell."

"I don't think Helvar would suggest something certain to get me killed if he hopes I'll protect him," I say.

"Not unless he intends to return to Hell," Ibis says. "Then it would be lovely to have a friend on standby, wouldn't it?"

Helvar is glaring again. "Think I'm on holiday, do you?"

The fire beside the demon's chair flares bright red. A spectral girl, no older than ten, rises moaning from the flames. For a horrible moment, I think it's Phelia again, wraithed and murderous. But the moment passes and I realize what I really see.

This is the spirit of the hearth, wailing its warning cry.

A high-pitched banshee wail shatters the air. We all cover our ears, save Ciel, and crouch as if the sound is something we can simply duck under. My bones vibrate. My stomach seizes, condensing itself down to a hard stone.

Then she's gone. The blood-red flames simmer down to orange. It's a normal fire again.

"What was that?" Helvar asks. "A friend of yours?"

"The Bishops' hearthstone," I say. My heart hammers in my ears. I feel like my head will split in two with its sudden pounding. "It's a distress call from Rowan House."

I'm at the door, pulling it open without second thought. I have to get home. I have to get home right *now*.

"Wait, there's more!" Helvar calls. "I can tell you so much more about Hell and—"

"It'll have to wait," I say. "We have to go."

Ciel and Alex file out ahead of me, following the path beneath the wisteria blossoms back toward the room enchanted to look like a forest at the base of a mountain.

"Amelia, wait," Ibis says softly, catching me beneath the blossoms.

My stomach drops at his use of my first name. His eyes hold flecks of hazel in the bright forest light seeping through the wisteria. His face is full of earnest as he takes my hands.

"I gave you the moonblade for a reason. *Use it.*"

"I don't know how."

In a flashflood of power, I'm knocked back. I'm entirely unprepared for Ibis's memories. Ibis is strong, of course, but this is—*this is the power of knowledge*, I think. All strength bows before it. All will fold beneath it.

Ibis squeezes my hands harder, forcing me to remain upright.

The first cohesive image blares bright against the black screen of my mind.

Ibis is in the study again. Helvar is no longer perching on the armchair but walking back and forth in front of it, their paths crisscrossing as each man delves deeper into their own thoughts.

But I smell her on you! Hell's bells, the demon hisses. *If I can smell her, he must. Then he knows. He must be here for her. And bells help us, she is the only one strong enough to fight him.*

She's a child, Ibis says.

She's as old as the galaxy! A star made flesh. The answer to all those mysteries you chase, enshrined behind a well-crafted façade. And he will take her if she lets him.

I'll give her the moonblade.

She needs more than that, the demon rasps.

Asmodeus's spell book lies open in my lap. I begin to reel back, panic rising. Ibis isn't offering information, he's *taking* it. Only I realize that isn't true. The hands turning the pages are not my hands. The knuckles are too large. The palms too square with long, delicate fingers.

Mr. Priest, there is no curse on this book as far as I can tell.

But I tell you, it wasn't there before. It's as if it just appeared in the dead of night. And look at it! It bleeds! That can't be good.

I don't know what to tell you, Mr. Priest. I would say it is as safe in your library as anywhere. I'm speaking with Ibis's voice, seeing with Ibis's eyes. And when he looks up, it's Mr. Priest standing on the other side of the counter in The Shop on 42nd Street.

Then I'm in a storeroom. My clothes have changed. The light slants differently through the windows. Glass jars of herbs and apothecary remedies sit labeled on the shelves. On a worn wooden work surface, the blood stone gleams. It pulses red.

Ibis angles a dropper of blessed moon water over it and three glistening beads fall onto the surface of the thrumming stone.

A red hologram springs forth. January appears, blood pouring from a deep gouge in her chest. She coughs blood, struggling to speak. All around her is the destroyed library. Flames licking up one of the grand cases.

Dean Prior, she spits, blood glistening bright on her transparent lips. *Prior made a Faustian Pact. He used Melody to get close to the book—*

A shrill, girlish cry pierces the vision. My blood runs cold. Elei. That must have been Elei screaming. *When I realized he only wanted the book, I tried to destroy the spell, but it doesn't burn. So, I gave it to...a trusted friend. Guard the book. Punish Prior. Avenge us.*

The connection breaks abruptly, and I'm thrown back into my own mind. I suck in a sharp breath. My face is wet. The taste of salty tears coats my lips. My chest is unbearably tight.

Ibis's face is pinched in concentration. "If Dean Prior made a pact, then he owes the demon a debt. And I can think of only one thing he would make such a pact for. Prior and the king want the same thing. Do you understand? Use that against them."

My heart pounds furiously. *A devil's pact for a bride. A devil's pact for me.*

Goddess above, a devil's pact. I remember the soot on Prior's fingers the night the coven convened, the night the Priests were murdered. The soot was probably from the Priests' own ashes.

Ibis runs a cool finger over my knuckles, holding me in place while this world, this time and place, shifts into focus. January knew there'd be trouble. She'd needed help and I didn't even notice. If I hadn't been so fixated on Alex, so eager to seize the chance to use the book for my own gain, would I have seen the fear behind January's request?

"Your book was wrong," I tell him.

His brow pinches.

"The one you let me read the day you gave me the moonblade. Chapter twenty-two says that chevaliers are little more than servants to the queen. But that's wrong."

He can't hide his curiosity. "What's the truth?"

"The truth is no one means more to her," I say, unsure why I'm exposing myself this way. Except I trust Ibis. For some unexplainable reason, I trust him, and I want his help.

Ibis gives me a sad smile. "Then I will pray to the Goddess that all three of you survive."

CHAPTER 19
HELL HATH NO FURY

W e step into the woods outside Rowan House. I half expected to see the house ablaze like the Priests' compound, but it looks fine. Lights from the large windows filter through the trees. There's a malevolent aura about it, though. That means they're inside, waiting for us. It's definitely a trap.

"We need to think about this," I whisper.

"You're breathing really hard," Alex says.

Just like that, I become aware of my flared nostrils, of my white breath puffing. I try to slow my exhalations, but my chest only tightens.

"Because I'm freaking out," I say.

This is so much...so much...I can't...Is the King of Hell really in my house? What if the aunts—I'm here, Alex whispers through my mind.

His strength, his courage, floods my limbs, but it isn't enough. This will be the first time I see the aunts after finding out what I am. What will they do? What will Arty do? Tell me she never wanted to take me? Tell me she only took me in to honor some ancient pact made by Mara

Bishop? Blame me for this misfortune, for their own murders? Am I going to be to blame for not only Phelia's death but also my aunts'?

And what in the world to do about Prior? I feel stupidly uninformed about Faustian pacts. I've always considered them idiotic, something that a sensible witch—even one as stupid as Prior—would never do. Now here I am, in the early hours of the morning, squatting in the forest outside my house, racking my memory for half-remembered scraps of information.

I'm only sure about one thing. I don't want Alex to go in there, with the demon king who can ride him like a show pony.

Goddess help me. What would be left of him when the king is done?

I open my mouth to whisper the knockout spell when Alex's hand clamps down on my mouth.

"Don't!" His face twists into a snarl. "Don't you dare!"

Surprise sparks through my bones.

"What are you going to do? Lay me against a tree like Rip Van Winkle? Come back for me after the fight? *If* you come back."

I tug at his hand, but he doesn't let go.

"Don't you *dare*, Amelia. You think I'll be okay if something happens to you? Do you think I'll just get over it?"

I can save you, he had thought during the fivefold kiss.

I can save you, I'd echoed.

Goddess help me. He's right.

Alex finally drops his hand. It's not going to be easy. It feels impossible. But I can't just sideline him. If he did that to me, I'd be furious.

"Fine. You're coming in but you have to promise me something."

He eyes me warily. "What?"

"Sephone knew how to kill the demons without her chevalier absorbing them. *Promise me* that you won't absorb a demon until I figure out how to get that power back."

"Is that true?" Alex is speaking to Ciel. "Could she really kill a demon?"

"Yes," he says simply.

"Use your healing powers, use your combat skills, but *don't* bind one to you. *Don't* absorb one. If you do, it means one day I'll have to be your executioner, and I'll kill myself before that day comes."

"That's what this is all about," he says, recognition dawning on his face. "The graveyard, all that sneaking around. You've been trying to figure out how to kill demons."

"Promise me, Laveau." My words are sharp but I'm practically begging. I couldn't sound any more desperate if I tried.

"I promise," he says.

"Now." I turn to Ciel, who's remained perfectly quiet throughout this negotiation. "How do I guard our bond?"

I glance at the house with its wide, luminous windows. "This fight will be bloody, and I can't have Alex taking the damage for me. How do I make sure I don't transfer the damage to him?"

"You have that power. You did the same for me."

"I *had* the power, but not anymore. I'm *diminished*." I try not to sound bitter. "Remember?"

"You're not diminished," he says, kneeling down beside me.

He places a cool hand on my chest. My heart knocks against his palm.

"But Helvar said—"

"You're still waking from stasis," Ciel murmurs. He's looking at my mouth while he speaks.

"How?" I press his hand harder against my thrashing, fearful heart. "I can't be any more awake."

"You have a body and a mind, but your soul is in stasis. Your soul dreams."

I have so many questions, but I swallow them down. I look at the lamplight spilling across the lawn. It illuminates the flaring head of a golden dandelion, frosted white with dew. We've already wasted too much time out here.

"We're not going in until he's shielded. Guide me through it."

Ciel takes my hand in his left and Alex's in his right. He joins them. Sweat from Alex's palm moistens my skin. *He's afraid*, I think. He's had on a brave face and has sent no hint of terror down our bond—but he's afraid.

Alex's face is a mask of perfect calm, betraying nothing. But I'm hardly going to call out his fear now when I'm terrified too.

"I cannot call up your magic," Ciel says. "It's yours alone. You must find it inside yourself."

I close my eyes.

I try to find this hidden well of fey magic squirreled away inside me. I start with a simple thought spell. An incantation for wisdom and clarity of mind. It works two-fold. It quiets the tinny screech of fear echoing through me. And it calls up my magic. Heat wells in my chest, warming the skin stretched over my breastbone with a hot flush.

"Now, place a shield around the bond," Ciel instructs me. And I get the sense that he has been my teacher for a long time.

A scrap of bright memory blinds me. Me, with a tiny fey hand resting in Ciel's palm, as I receive some long-ago lesson. He's speaking sweetly, encouragingly, about—The vision fades.

But knowledge comes with this memory as well—about the chevalier's role in reconnecting the queen with her power after she wakes from stasis. Only her chevalier and the sister queen can guide the new queen back to herself after that long rest.

"You can do this," Ciel says, his voice bringing me back to this time, this place.

"I know," I whisper, and roll the bond linking Alex's magic to mine. I throw a shield around it. A mirror at the end of the hallway. Whatever should find this dark passage will simply be reflected back to me, never reaching him.

I tear my eyes away from Ciel's and glance at Alex. "How do you feel?"

"Fine," he says. "I can still feel you."

"Then let's go." Not much of a pep talk, I know, but my nerves are creeping in again.

Without another word, we circle around the house to the back. I slip the skeleton key between the frame and door. The key twitches. Warm magic tingles in my fingertips.

I open the back door, but instead of stepping into the kitchen, I walk into my dark bedroom.

Alex clicks on the desk lamp. Ciel surveys the room with a blank face. He looks more than a little ridiculous standing in his full armor in my small room. He makes the ceiling look too low.

I double-check that my blood wards are in place before speaking. With them, no one who wishes me ill should be able to hear our plans. I whisper anyway.

"I've got my athame and knife." I grab my backpack and

toss it onto the bed. "Alex, you can use the moonblade that Ibis gave me."

I unzip the pack and find the wrapped blade still in the scrap of cloth. I unwrap the tip, which glints in the lamplight, and then hand it over to Alex. Ciel's eyes lock on the blade. There is the briefest furrow of his brow before he looks down at his hands.

"We can wrap the end in electrical tape so you don't cut your hand." I'm trying to ignore the fact that this was the blade that ended my last life. The blade that Ciel buried into my chest.

I'm wondering if that's what Ciel is thinking about too.

"Can Vinae possess you?" I ask him.

Ciel shakes his head. "No."

"Possession is not the problem. Murder is," Alex reminds us. "He didn't possess Melody. He killed her, hollowed her out, and then decided to walk around inside her."

I shudder. I find a roll of electrical tape in my desk drawer and start winding it around the end of the blade's shard until I feel like it has a decent grip for Alex.

I hand it over and he weighs it in his open palm, lifting and lowering it as if to get a feel for it.

"Does it need more tape?" I ask.

He shakes his head. "No, it's good."

"You need a weapon," Ciel says.

I raise my athame. "I have moon water in my bag."

"That will not be strong enough," he says. He reaches under his cloak and pulls out a blade. The moment I see it, I stiffen. The memory of his betrayal flashes through my mind even though this is a different blade.

Hurt flashes across Ciel's face. But his voice is steady

when he says, "Take it. It's Elysium steel. This will hurt him more."

I slip my athame into its sheath and take the blade into my hand. It feels perfect. Not too heavy, not too light. It becomes an easy extension, the length of elbow to wrist. Like it was made for this hand.

"Our plan is to wound him with blades or magic, weaken him however we can, and then hurl what's left of him through a door into Hell. Right?" I hope this sounds like a solid, intelligent plan and not a desperate move. Queen Sephone might be some immortal creature who knew how to fight wars, but those parts of her life are still closed to me.

"If only I had a ghost sister who *wasn't* a coward," I say. "Then we'd have a lookout too."

"Your aunts are downstairs," Alex says.

I cast my mind out. In my mindscape, I find them in the den, near the hearth. Not dead. But probably wounded. If they hadn't been attacked, the hearth fire would have never come looking for me.

I don't sense anyone else in the house, and that makes my skin prickle with gooseflesh. Where is the king? Where is Prior?

"The boy is here," Ciel assures me as if reading my mind. "But you will not sense the king if he does not wish it."

That seems true. Which means that Vinae is perfectly capable of sneaking up on me out of nowhere. Can't wait.

"We'll check on the aunts first," I say. I don't say, *And I'll question them ruthlessly to find out if they still love me at all or if they've thought I was a burden and curse this whole time.*

Don't be stupid. Why would they think you're a curse?

My eyes snap to Alex.

I'm whispering so low I can barely hear myself. "We agree that first we go to the living room and make sure the aunts are alive. Get them out of here if we can. *Then* we confront Vinae and Prior, and kick their asters."

"And don't die." Alex is wringing the end of the moonblade in his grip. He forces a smile, but I see the pulse jumping in his throat.

"Yes," I say. "Don't die."

I draw in a steadying breath and open the door. A shadowed hallway and wooden rail. Heart pounding so hard in my temples I think my head is going to explode.

I pause at the top of the stairs and look back. The aunts' bedroom doors and Phelia's are all closed. Alex and Ciel wait for me to go down, both perfectly poised for action on the landing behind me.

I ease down the steps, placing only as much weight on each as I have to. I clutch the banister, the new moonblade in my other hand.

When I reach the ground, I look around the steps, through the foyer, and toward the library's closed door. No one. And no shadows beneath the door. I step into the den and my heart stops.

Demi and Arty are unconscious on the floor. A smear of blood streams down the side of Demi's face. They are both blindfolded and bound at the ankles and wrists. A gleaming strip of shiny duct tape is clamped over each of their mouths.

No, no, no.

No wonder Phelia won't come. I hope the blood on their faces is from some minor flesh wound and not from a missing eye. But there is so much blood down the front of Arty's clothes. The tape over her mouth swells and compresses with each breath.

I only see the flash of metal in the corner of my eyes the second before blades clash.

I duck as metal whooshes overhead. I stumble back, losing sight of my wounded aunts.

High, girlish laughter echoes through the den. For a second, I think it's Phelia, maybe wraithed out again, but then I know who it is. Not a girl at all, but the demon king who wears her. Ciel's bulk is hiding the owner of the laughter, my faithful lieutenant pivoting himself so that he remains between us.

"Do your part, boy," the sweet voice says.

At first I think she's speaking to Alex, but Prior steps into view. A crack of magic echoes across the room and Alex stumbles, the moonblade shard tumbling from his hand.

A white hand clamps down on Alex's throat a heartbeat later. I'm ready to step in, but Alex is faster. He throws a wild haymaker punch into the side of Prior's face. It knocks him back at least three feet. When he comes up, Alex punches him again, and I can hear Prior's nose break with a sickening *crunch*. Blood gushes.

That's the most beautiful thing I've ever seen, I think, marveling at the blood dripping from Prior's soaked chin.

Alex can't help but grin at me. *I've wanted to do that for so long.*

Prior pushes himself up immediately. I feel the rise of his magic.

"Don't." I step forward. "Touch him again and there won't be anything left of your face."

I'm aware that Ciel is at my back, circling. I'm keeping my steps in measure with his, making it impossible for Vinae to get any closer to me.

Alex looks ready to hit Prior again, but that's a waste of time.

I've got him. Check on my aunts. Heal them if you can.

I harness my panic, the nagging fear that if Arty is wounded, his father might be dead. Because if not, where is he? He would have tried to protect his witch no matter what.

If he's not here it's because he *can't* be here.

"There's a problem with your pact, King Vinae," I say without taking my eyes off Prior. Magic sparks from my fingertips. Prior must see it, and surely he knows if he moves a muscle, I'll blast him clean through the wall. "Prior called you, but you promised him the very thing you came to Septem Terras for."

"Yes, I'd begun to suspect that was the case." The king lifts his nose to the air and sniffs.

Prior stiffens, the first look of confusion muddying his face. "*King?*"

The idiot didn't know who he was dealing with. Hellebore. I almost pity him.

"You didn't know it was the King of Hell you summoned?" I ask. "Then you definitely didn't know he was already looking for someone. For me."

"No." Prior's voice is thick with blood. "No. He promised me power. He promised me I could have you and—"

"It's true, boy," the king says with Melody's mouth. "You sold your pound of flesh to gain a bride, but she's promised to another."

"No, she isn't," Prior says. There's the petulant pout I've come to expect from him. Even now, in the face of imminent death, he's being an entitled jerk, as if he truly believes this will somehow shake out in his favor.

Vinae is amused by his ignorance. "I suppose there is only one way to satisfy all parties."

The king rounds on Prior, his grin stretching wolfish across that corpse skull.

Prior's chest rises and falls too quickly.

"We made an unbreakable pact!" Prior whines, having the sense to be afraid now. His words are still thick with blood. He's talking through his nose. "I want Amelia to love me and—"

"And if you can't have her, no one will," the girlish voice breaks in. "Isn't that what you said? And I can honor that perfectly. You see, it isn't some witch I want, whoever the Hell Amelia Bishop is supposed to be. I want the fey queen I was promised. I know she's hidden in there somewhere. I'm prepared to tear apart that pathetic body to find her. And once I've torn her to pieces, I can assure you, Prior, no one *will* have her. There won't be enough of her left to fight over."

Prior's mouth is opening and closing like a fish who's just found himself on a fisherman's boat deck.

Alex reaches the aunts and begins checking their wounds. I can feel his healing magic transferring from his body to Arty's. It's a warm tingling along my scalp.

"But—but what about *me*?" Prior asks with that same snot-slick tone.

"That's easy enough. I'll simply collect my pound of flesh now," the king says with more girlish laughter. "And once I take it, you won't care about this girl or any other. Not when I'm through with you."

CHAPTER 20
SOMETHING WICKED

King Vinae falls on Prior so fast that I have only one thought. *We will never win.* No wonder this thing was able to murder a whole family before they could raise the alarm. He's too fast—impossibly fast.

Melody was two or three inches shorter than me when she was alive. But the thing that slams into Prior seems so much larger. Prior's strangled cry is cut in half as the king's jaws clamp down on his throat, crushing the windpipe instantly.

Before I understand what's happening, the demon punches a hole in Prior's chest. When the heart appears, bloody and crushed in one fist, I look away. This isn't enough to blot out the sounds of chomping and slurping.

A shadow rushes toward me. My first instinct is *Phelia, no!* As if this monster can kill the dead twice. But it isn't Phelia.

The badger's pointed muzzle clamps down on my calf, hard. I scream, surprised more than anything, and kick. My foot never connects. My thought: *Why are you blaming me?* I didn't eat Prior's heart like a cupcake. Or maybe I'm just the easier target. Maybe this badger is too afraid to take on the king.

A flash of blue blocks my view, hiding my target. Dragon lands on the badger's face, talons out. His claws dig into the familiar's nose and he doesn't let go. His wings flap furiously as if he intends to cart the twenty-pound creature away somehow.

A swipe of its paw sends Dragon sailing across the foyer floor, spinning on his back. The badger's salt-and-pepper fur ripples as he bounds toward my fallen bird.

"Dragon!" I scream. I dive after him, snatching the badger's hind leg. I pull, yanking him away from my dazed jay.

The badger whirls, snarling, and bites the back of my hand.

Hellebore.

I fire three stunner spells, and the thing finally stiffens and falls over. Only then am I able to scoop up my jay.

"Dragon," I say. "Wake up. *Wake* up."

He blinks but remains perfectly still. He did this once before when he flew into a window. But now isn't the time for unresponsiveness. I'm left standing in the living room, cradling the jay. At least Alex seems to be making progress. Watching Prior get eaten isn't enough to shatter his focus. The aunts have color in their cheeks again.

Vinae stands up from the mess that was Prior and faces us, Melody's face bloodied.

"A man's heart is ten ounces," Vinae says in that sweet, girlish sing-song. "Take a couple bites out of the throat and we have a perfect pound." Vinae pauses to pick gore out of Melody's teeth. "Of course, he can't live without that particular pound. But it's not my fault he's a poor negotiator."

Laughter spills past his blood-soaked lips.

I rub a thumb down Dragon's back. *Wake up. Come on, snap out of it.* If I were smart, I'd throw the jay aside and draw the moonblade. But Dragon just risked his life to protect me.

Vinae flicks his eyes up to meet mine, and I don't see Melody's eyes, which were a soft blue when she was alive. I see matte black with a feral gleam. Coyote eyes in headlights.

"I thought you were just a jealous lover, Lieutenant," the king says, tsking. His tongue licks at the blood. "But if that were true, wouldn't you have killed this one"—his eyes flick to Alex—"for daring to chevalier with your queen?"

I flinch. The king used *chevalier* like a verb. He implied it is something one does with one's body. My face burns.

"If it was not jealousy of sharing her bed, then why? Did she tell you to plunge the knife in her back? Was her complete and utter surprise also an act?"

Ciel says nothing.

"Did she sacrifice her life to reseal Elysium? Come on, tell me. These questions have plagued me for *years*."

The back of Ciel's hand brushes mine.

Guard your mind. This is his magic. He will rewrite your truth if you let him.

I blink tears out of my eyes as if I've been holding them open for too long. And I have. I've been staring into those demon eyes and was almost hypnotized by them. My body had just started to sway, to give itself over to the king's magic. What would have happened if Ciel hadn't warned me to snap out of it? Would Vinae have crossed the room and eaten the heart out of my chest too?

I lower my gaze two inches, fixing on its nose. A line of red darkens it as the blood dries there.

The king grins. "You're still as clever as ever, my queen. And still inspiring loyalty wherever you go." Vinae's eyes cut to Alex and my aunts, who are stirring toward consciousness. "That is what they say about her in our lore, Lieutenant. Did you know?"

Ciel stiffens. Vinae seems amused by this.

"Naja didn't tell you the real reason why I came for her? Perhaps she'd forgotten," Vinae says with mock sympathy, as if he doesn't believe Naja has forgotten anything.

His eyes cut to Alex.

Don't look into his eyes, I think. It's a panicked urging, and unnecessary. Alex has already slid his gaze down.

Vinae only smiles wider. "Naja was still a child, fresh from stasis, when we broke the Southern Gate. Perhaps she had not fully awakened yet to her own knowledge."

He turns that grin on me.

"Like you, my queen. You still reek of dreams. All that delicious, unformed magic. It's intoxicating."

A moan folds into a peal of girlish laughter that makes my stomach quiver. I become absolutely certain I'm going to spill the contents of my breakfast on the den floor. I keep my stare fixed on the blood drying across the king's borrowed nose. I rub a thumb up and down Dragon's back again, silently pleading, *Wake up. Come on. Wake up and fly away.*

"If I told you the truth, Lieutenant, you would send her to Hell yourself."

Ciel lifts his sword, taking the hilt in both hands.

Melody only pouts, the girlish features pulled grotesquely across whatever is underneath. It's not bone.

That much I know. A creature is inside the flesh. A creature I don't ever want to see.

"If Naja *had* been in possession of her knowledge, she might have told you that her mother bore two daughters, *not* because she intended them to run Elysium together but because she intended them to rule Elysium and *Hell*—the two realms she created. There's even a verse about it."

Vinae comes up on his toes as if about to pirouette. Then in a rolling brogue he says:

The second born is strongest still
made to rule the realm of Hell.
She shackles hearts with loyalty,
the most relentless of all slaveries.
And in loving her, our fates be tied
the borderlands at last be unified.

Alex stands transfixed, mouth open.

It's a lie, I tell him. *It's a lie. A stupid rhyme. He's made it up. Don't listen to it.*

Alex blinks as if trying to bring the world back into focus but doesn't quite manage it.

Vinae's eyes never leave my face. "My predecessors cowered before this knowledge, fled from the gates of Elysium as if fleeing the Goddess herself. Demons can think of nothing worse than enslavement. Not I. Because unlike the others, I see myself not beneath the boot heel of some fabled queen. I see myself at her side. Or on my back beneath her. Was that how you enjoyed her best, Lieutenant?"

Magic whips out in all directions and the wind of it

blows my hair back from my face. Blades clash and metal sings. Too fast. They're moving too fast for me to track their movements. But I have enough sense to stumble back from the blur, cupping Dragon against my chest.

And the king is laughing, that high-pitched, delighted laughter of a girl.

"What kind of a marvelous queen she will be to turn Hell on its head!" he calls over the clashing swords. "Imagine it! Those beasts love only carnage and bloodshed. I cannot wait to see what hell she'll rain on us to inspire loyalty from beasts such as me."

A queen worthy of a demon's admiration. Then I'm a monster?

It's Alex's turn to pull me back from the edge.

Don't be stupid, he says. *We're loyal because we love you. We're loyal because* you're *loyal.*

Vinae drives Ciel back with a pointed jab. "I'll cut her from that clever package you've put her in. Perhaps I'll put her in the body of a child until she completes her stasis." Vinae's grin stretches too wide. "I've always *loved* children."

Dragon suddenly screeches and takes flight. His talons dig into my palms as he launches himself up into the rafters. He darts and weaves beneath the beams before shrieking toward the attic.

Startled, my heart hammers. And it's my pounding heart that alerts me to trouble.

My mind clears from the fog of magic in the room, and through the fog, I see the first sparks on the horizon of my mind. In my mindscape, something approaches. No. More than one blue-black blaze, more than I can count.

Demons! Alex hisses through our bond. He senses the approaching army the same moment I do. *He's stalling until his enforcements arrive.*

"Ciel, keep him busy!" I call out.

Without comment, Ciel's strikes intensify. The king hisses, jumping backward over Prior's remains and up onto the burgundy chaise. But I need to forget about the king for a moment and focus on getting the aunts to safety before the onslaught of demons arrive.

I slip one arm under Demi's and heft her up. I have to balance her against my hip and steady her before I can move forward. Alex lifts Arty easily. She croaks, "My cane!"

Alex bends to pick it up without letting her go.

I'm already dragging Demi toward the pantry and pulling the skeleton key off my neck. This is one of the few doors in the house, besides the library, that actually has an old-fashioned keyhole. I'm able to insert the key into an actual lock and let go long enough to adjust my aunt across my shoulder. Demi's eyes flutter open in my jostling.

"Wake up," I say, nudging her ribs. "Wake up or die."

As soon as the light around the door changes and I catch the first scent of fresh air, I yank the door open, the key still swinging in the lock. I don't close it as I step out onto the porch of the Lamberts' house.

The ominous lack of Monsieur Lambert himself.

Damsel seed. Where is he?

It's as if I've stepped from his front door into the night. Cricket song swells. The motion light on the side of the house flicks on, casting long shadows across the gravel drive.

I dump Demi rather ungracefully into the lounge chair on the front porch and turn back in time to see a fully conscious Arty hobbling through with Alex's help. She's leaning hard on her bad hip, and that wound on the side of her face doesn't look good.

But she's alive. Thank the Goddess, they're both alive.

Through the doorway, showcased by the pantry's door-frame, Ciel and the king fight. The king has an athame. Not a moonblade. The metal is dull and unremarkable. It doesn't glow with the innate light I've come to associate with the moonblades. It's probably Melody's own demon-slaying dagger. It doesn't have the reach of Ciel's sword but it's doing its own damage. A gash across Ciel's face, danger-ously close to his right eye, is bleeding profusely. And at least two more red stripes have appeared on the back of his hands. His knuckles shine bright with his blood.

Ciel feels my gaze and turns. The king takes that moment to sink his teeth into Ciel's forearm and the fey yells. Ciel lands a hard kick to the gut. It sends the king sprawling.

"Hold on!" I scream. "I'm coming back!"

Alex is trying to force Arty to sit down in the second pinstriped lounge chair, but she's hissing and thrashing like a cat. "Hellebore! Will you listen! Hell and high water. Cast hell and high water."

Alex gives me a pitiful look, his features twisted with concern in the light spilling from Rowan House onto the lawn. The sound of metal clashing and more guttural growls spill out into the night.

"I think she hit her head or something," Alex says. "She's not making any sense."

Arty whacks his shin hard and he hisses. "I'm not mad, you idiot. You're not listening!"

She jabs her cane at me.

"Hell and high water," she shrieks. "*Hell and high water.*"

Realization strikes me. "The hearth."

Arty sighs and falls back against the lounge chair. "Someone who knows how to use their ears. Bless me."

I turn to rush through the door, and she grabs my wrist roughly.

This is it, I think. *This is the moment where she blames me for all of this.*

"Amelia," Arty says, her eyes bright. "Be careful."

My heart soars. "You be careful, you old witch."

CHAPTER 21
COME HELL OR HIGH WATER

I seize Alex and pull him back through the pantry into Rowan House. I kick the door closed behind us and rush for the hearth.

Hell and high water. One of the ancient hearth spells meant to save the house when invaded by enemies.

"Got the moonblade?" I ask.

Alex shows me the severed shard peeking through the flannel.

"Good," I say, and pull my own moonblade. "You're going to need it."

I barely have time to retrieve my necklace and slip the rope cord around my neck before the first window breaks, spilling glittering glass across the bloodstained floor.

The demons are in.

The first demon to step into my path is a djinn with a ridged spine and fire in his eyes. His skin shifts with each movement. A body of sand. I remember where I saw this rare demon last—the amphitheater. Now this creature is between me and the hearth.

I swing the moonblade, and the djinn's flaming eyes

spark and he hisses at me. He jumps away, snarling. I swing again, cutting a path toward the hearth.

He shifts, abandoning his young masculine form for a swirling twister of sand. I pinch my eyes shut as grit pelts my face. I call the wind and push back, giving myself enough room to breathe.

Only something slams into me from behind. I hit the floor, bones rattling.

Teeth sink into my lower back, and I scream. I roll, lashing blindly, and the moonblade connects with a body. A Spite—nasty little flying demons with grotesquely long noses—falls back, hissing and shaking with fury. A bright slash from the blade is clear across its hind leg. Its membranous wings flutter, snout flaring. Its upper bite curls over gray, snot-slicked lips.

I spare a glance for Alex, who is fighting two Hates. He's holding his own admirably, and Ciel has added an Envy, two ghouls, and a Spite to his duel with the king. Five on one.

Demons spill through the open window, a wave of claws, talons, wings, and snarling snouts. We're out of time.

I haul myself up, swinging. The Spite lunges again, but I expect that. I bring the blade down and it bites deep into its neck. When the tip hits bone, it keeps going, slicing clean through it. It falls to the side, twitching. That leaves the djinn. He starts to dematerialize again, probably trying to blind me, but I thrust the blade forward into one of his swirling flames of an eye. He falls back, howling.

Four steps and I'm on the hearth, cool stone under my hand.

I sheathe the moonblade long enough to pull my smaller boot knife. I drag it across my palm. The skin splits, burning. I open and close my fist until blood blooms in the lines, running down my fingers in red, dripping ribbons.

I slap my hand onto the cold hearthstone and open my magic wide. The house rumbles as I sheathe the small blade. I draw the moonblade again without taking my cut and bleeding hand off the stone. It warms under my palm, responding to my blood price and my magic.

I brace myself for what's coming. I reach down my connection to Alex and send him a warning. *Hold on.*

"Come Hell! Come high water!" I cry. And I take a deep breath.

Water explodes from the hearth. A great torrential wave slams into me, knocking me back.

Two demons who were trying to crawl through the window shriek and tumble back out into the darkness. The chaise is pushed up against the window, blocking the hole caused by their rough entry. I'm washed clear across the den, across the foyer, and smack into the library's closed door.

The house starts to fill with water. By the time I manage to get to my feet despite the crushing flood, it's knee deep.

I slosh my way back to the living room.

The demons are fleeing. They hate running water. Only water demons will cross it, which is why we fight near rivers when we can. If things go south, we can cross over and regroup.

As long as water pours from the hearth, they won't come into Rowan House.

I aim for Alex. I want to reach him and see if he's hurt, but something seizes my leg and pulls hard.

I'm under the water, coughing and hissing, nails like talons biting into my upper thigh.

I open my eyes to find Phelia. Desperate and drowning.

She's screaming, a swarm of bubbles obscuring her face. She clings to me.

Save me, Amelia. Don't let me go over the edge again. Please. Please.

I pull, leap and pull, trying to drag my sister out of the fierce river current trying to drown her. But I'm not making any progress. I'm pulled deeper and deeper into the water.

Phelia's crying. *Please don't let go. It's so cold down here. It hurts so much. I'm so lonely. Amelia! Please!*

When I open my eyes, I see the demon, its black-water eyes fixed on mine, and I know the truth. I haven't been clutching Phelia. Phelia has been clutching me. The sharp bone arms are wrapped around mine with total ferocity. Her fingers are talons cutting into my arms, and her pitiful, quivering lips dissolve into a snout barely concealing rows of sharp teeth.

I'm not in the river of years ago. I'm in my aunts' house in the mountains.

In the grip of an onus. A water demon capable of using our guilt against us. It knows what wound to slip its fingers into and twist. Like an alligator, it will drown me, then eat me.

"Save me, Amelia," the demon begs, but I am no longer trying to hold on to this thing. I'm trying to swim away, and I'm only pulled deeper.

A gleaming blade cuts through the water and spears the onus. Water bubbles surround us instead of its scream.

Strong arms haul me up, and I break the surface, gasping. I'm dropped gracelessly on the stairs. My elbows and knees connect hard with the wooden steps.

"We need higher ground," Alex calls. It's his arms around me. His magic sweeps my skin, searching for wounds to heal. But there's no time. I'm sore, my muscles cramping, but I'm not dying. I wave him on and force myself onward despite my shaking legs.

"Go!" Ciel waves toward the landing. The steps underneath me are already submerged.

We clamber up the stairs. At the rear, Ciel's sword continues clashing with the king's blade. The king seems unfazed by the running water. Maybe that only works with the half-breed demons.

I catch my breath on the landing, but only for a moment. Something rattles in the wall. Pipes? The plaster cracks and a fresh gush of torrential water rips through the wall. On instinct, I shove Alex into my bedroom the second before the water slams into me.

Ciel and I are swept down the hall. I grab the banister and hold firm, arms shaking with the effort as Ciel rolls past, slamming into the closed bathroom at the end of the hallway. I let go of the banister only to grab the door frame of Phelia's room two feet down. My nails bite into the wooden jamb. I think the trim will rip off and send me sailing after Ciel, but somehow, I manage to haul myself into the dark bedroom, out of the pounding rush of water. The deluge falters. Most of it spills over the landing into the rising waters below, the ruptured pipe having obviously emptied itself.

In the still bedroom, sunlight filters through the window, giving the room a strange, optimistic look. A peacefulness at odds with the battle raging in the rest of the house.

Forget the sunlight, I tell myself. I need a door to Hell.

I pull the key off my neck and wedge it between the door and jamb of Phelia's closet. The key warms, the world turning. I'm about to pull out the key when a hand seizes the back of my neck and slams me into the door, striking my face against it. Air escapes me in a surprised cough. I'm whirled around to face my attacker.

The king's girlish hand closes over my throat, squeezing so hard I see stars. A stab of white-hot pain rips through my shoulder. I scream, only it's a strangled cry at best. My eyes roll down to find his blade shoved through my left shoulder, nailing me to the wall.

The king steps back grinning, admiring his handiwork, as I sag on the blade, still screaming. *My arm is going to come off. My arm is going to come off. Goddess help me, my arm—*

I scream until my throat is raw and no sound comes out. Only a dry, rasping wheeze escapes me.

I grab the hilt of the blade and work it, trying to get the wood to give.

The king, laughing, rips it free. I slump to the floor in a heap.

"Why do you resist me?" He twists his fingers in my hair and hauls me to my feet. Acrid breath smelling of raw meat fills my nose. Prior, I realize. He has chunks of Prior in his teeth. "Today, or tomorrow, or centuries from now, you will reign in Hell at my side, Sephone."

Goddess help me. He sounds just like Prior.

"It is written. Staying here will only bring death and destruction. You know it's true. But I can be reasonable. I can be generous. I could have slaughtered those old women. I could have torn your lieutenant's spine out with my bare hands or beheaded your brand-new pet, but I spared them. I've been patient because I want you to know that your loyalty will be rewarded. The moment you stop fighting the inevitable and join me. Why make all those you hold dear suffer along the way? You will reach the same destination because there is only one destination for you. Do you really want the road you walk littered with their corpses? Or will you come with me, head high, and embrace your destiny?"

I'm trying to draw a breath, but I can't escape that horrible stench. Like having my nose right up against a carcass in the high noon heat. Helvar had been wrong. The king won't give up on me, even if I am diminished. Could it be that Helvar didn't know about the prophecy? Or did he underestimate his brother? There's also the possibility that he lied, giving me false hope so I'd be foolish enough to confront the king. Maybe Helvar and the king work together and that bastard told me what I needed to hear to drive me right into Vinae's arms.

A hard body slams into the king's side, knocking him away from me.

I topple to my hands and knees. I drag my gaze upward in time to see Alex thrusting the moonblade into the creature's gut. It howls. It's a bone-skittering sound unlike any I've ever heard. The muscles low in my bowels go tight, and I shiver.

I have just enough strength in me to pivot and twist the door handle.

The door is sucked inward, completely ripped off its hinges. The skeleton key and smoky quartz fall in after it.

Fall in.

It takes me a minute to realize that I'm looking *down* into Hell. That somehow this door didn't open on ground level as any door in our world would, but as if straight into the sky.

Not a clear blue sky but a dust cloud. Dirt and sand whirl in a relentless wind. Vague dark shapes can be seen through the tawny haze, but I couldn't tell you what I'm seeing. Demons? A landscape? Buildings? A city?

Alex drags the howling and stabbed king to the

threshold of Hell and shoves. But in one last valiant effort, Vinae seizes Alex around the waist and pulls.

I lunge. I grab ahold of Alex's arms, trying to keep him here, in this world. His legs swing, the demon king hanging from his waist.

I try to pull him up, but my arms shake. The weight pulling at my wounded shoulder sends fresh fire rolling through me. I try to rely on my other arm but it's just as exhausted and useless.

Ciel, I beg. *Ciel, where are you?*

Alex is trying to kick the king off his legs, but Vinae isn't ready to give up. He sinks his teeth into Alex's back and Alex cries out. His fingers slip in mine.

"You promised never to give up," I tell him. But I don't know if Alex hears me over the howling winds of Hell, his eyes pinched shut against his pain.

I move around to the other edge. I jam my weak shoulder into the hole.

I twitch my fingers at Vinae. "Take me!"

I have to shout, partially because of my dry, cornhusk voice and partially because of the roar of the wind.

"You're right! I shouldn't resist the inevitable! Take me, Vinae," I beg. "Let go of him and take me instead."

He'll have to let go of Alex to grab on to me, but that doesn't seem to matter.

His face alights with victory. His fingers dig into the flesh of my forearm as the creature still masquerading as Melody seizes hold of me. The wound in my shoulder rips and hot blood rolls down my arm. I'm screaming again. I begin to slip forward. My chest is over the lip of the door. Then the top half of my abdomen.

Alex starts hauling himself up out of the hole with quivering arms, but he isn't going to make it in time. I'll be gone before he can grab me.

And besides, the king is right. Resisting will only cost me the people I love.

I pinch my eyes closed. I prepare to let go.

The king snarls and my eyes fly open just in time to see a long sharp blade slice through the king's arm. My arm burns as the sword bites into my flesh. Ciel's sword. But lucky for me, the lieutenant has perfect aim. His blade only scores me, a necessary afterthought to severing the king's grip. The weight lifts and the king falls back into the whirling sandstorm, disappearing with a howl of fury. Only a blackened hand remains, still clutching my arm near the elbow. Alex knocks it away.

Then both Ciel and Alex haul me out of the sandstorm's fury, as ribbons of my blood whip free into the sky.

The next few days pass in a haze. The same magic that was used to flush the demons from our house is used to put it back together again. The walls, floor, and all permanent fixtures are saved. Most of the furniture. But some of the more delicate items like old paintings on the walls, a tapestry, and a few books that hadn't been in the library are damaged.

Goddess—the *library*.

If I had opened the door, all those precious tomes would've been lost. Some would have survived just for the virtue of being what they are. *Bogworth's Book of Water-Witching*, for example, which is bespelled to be waterproof with the clear understanding that the witch would be working with water while using it. But so many others would be gone.

Fortunately, only some water seeped through the closed door, and therefore, only three or four inches had filled the room. The lowest shelf is five inches off the floor. I measure it myself while helping the aunts take inventory of the house.

Yes. I realize how lucky we are.

We're alive. The demons are gone. The king is back in Hell.

And the coven receives the answers they're looking for.

They make me give a declaration of truth that I really saw the King of Hell. That it was really Prior who summoned him, and I had no part in his scheme. That it was him—or the king—who killed the Priests to hide what they'd done.

I omit all mention of Ciel. I ask him to stay hidden until the interrogation is over.

In addition to leaving out all mention of the fey lieutenant and my questionable past, I also omit the truth about the king looking for an invitation into our world. I think Kaliha Yzi, who's serving as truth-teller, knows it.

But I stick to my version. Prior wanted to marry me. I refused. He made a pact with a devil to get what he wanted. I explain that when Prior came to the house to collect me, the devil betrayed him, as devils are wont to do. I conjured Hell and high water to save us, and Alex and I managed to shove the King of Hell through an open door back into Hell —though I lost my quartz and skeleton key in the process.

I tell them Alex healed me.

I miss the skeleton key and quartz. In the five days since they fell through Hell's door, I must've reached up and touched my neck a hundred times, only to find it bare.

Demi promises to give me a replacement key and crystal soon.

When they ask where the demonic spell book is, I tell them I don't know. And that's true. I handed it over to Ciel for safekeeping. It could be anywhere.

The interrogations don't end until Ibis gives his testimony. He flashes me a barely discernible wink before bowing before the coven and presenting the bloodstone. I try to look surprised and manage it when Ibis says he's found this amongst the Priests' personal effects, which had been entrusted to him for inspection after the wreckage was cleared.

They open the stone and January's Last echoes through The Shop on 42nd Street. Hearing January's hurt and angry voice cuts through me again, and I don't have to fake the tears sliding down my cheeks.

I am most relieved to find that Monsieur Lambert was investigating a lead at Arty's behest and avoided all danger because of it. He wasn't killed or maimed as I'd feared. I have every reason to believe that Arty knew what was coming and sent her demonkeeper away to keep him safe.

Maybe she has something to teach me about how to keep stubborn keepers alive.

With the house in order, the demon activity returning to normal, and Beltane just ten days away, the whole thing feels like a dream.

Flowers are everywhere. Countless vases are full of them and Rowan House itself is in bloom. Rich foliage has sprouted from the rafters. Thick vines and large fragrant flowers simply sprout on their own, spider-webbing along the walls. Every morning, I wake up in a jungle.

No one had to cast a spell for this. Rowan House loves Beltane. The only other time she gets this festive is for Yule, when instead of flowers, ribbons, and birdsong, she drowns us in holly, mistletoe, and fir. And instead of Yule's endless parade of gingerbread and caraway cakes soaked in cider, it's honey-wheat fertility bread and green-man buns.

I'm exhausted and stuffed with sweets by the time I finally fall into bed. I sleep hard, without dreams. Or memories.

It's still dark when I wake suddenly.

I pull myself up and roll toward the window. There, in a perfect patch of moonlight, Ciel waits for me. I stumble through a dark house, aiming for the back door. I have to push aside wisteria hanging from the banisters and step over some irises and crocuses that have sprouted up in the night, but somehow, I make it to the door.

Ciel has retreated a little, now standing just inside the woods. I walk barefoot across the damp grass to meet him at the forest's edge.

"Hey," I say, unsure how one opens a conversation with their fey lieutenant.

"My queen," he says, his shoulders relaxed. "Are you well?"

"Yeah," I say. "Everything has settled down here. The house is happy."

"Yes, I noticed."

He places his hand on the hilt of his sword. Not to draw it, but out of habit, I realize. "You want to stay."

"And you want me to go back to Elysium?" I ask. I've been wondering if we were going to have this conversation.

His lips twitch. "It is not my place to say where you go."

"And yet you brought me here."

Crickets sing around us.

He says, "You're right to fear Vinae will come again. He will as soon as he's able, and before he is, he'll send others."

I know he's right. It's the problem I've been turning over and over in my mind since we sent the king back to Hell.

"If he comes, I want to be here. I'm getting stronger." It's not a question. I've felt my powers growing ever since Ciel did—whatever he did with those lips of his.

"Yes, you are," he agrees.

"Then I want to be here to keep them safe. If a demon comes looking for me, I want to be here to stop it."

"You need to finish your stasis. You haven't fully replenished yourself."

Right. I forgot that Queen Sephone is supposed to be about twenty years deep into her millennium-long nap right now.

"Can stasis wait for sixty or so years?" I ask. I want to share this life with the aunts, with Alex. The time I have with them is so finite. So precious.

"You will not enter stasis while in this body." He takes my hands, the calluses of his fingers brushing my palm.

"Well then. Sixty years it is. Unless Elysium can't wait?"

"You are loved, and your return will be celebrated." He runs a thumb over my knuckles. "But a human life is but a heartbeat to us."

"What will you do?" I ask. *Stay with me, I hope.*

"I can gather the answers you seek and see if there is truth in what Vinae said. About the prophecy."

Right. The rhyme about my destiny for Hell.

"And I have a gift for you." Ciel drops one of my hands and reaches inside his cloak. He pulls out a moonblade. Not the broken one from before. A new one, bright and gleaming. It's as if the blade itself is filled with moonlight.

I take it in my palm and feel the smooth wooden handle. "This is nice."

"It will kill half-breeds. Alexander will not have to take one into his body."

My spirit lifts. "Oh. Wow. Can I have two then? One for me and one for him?"

He smiles and pulls out another.

"I *knew* you had two." I take the second moonblade and hold them up triumphantly.

I catch a glimpse of a smile fleeing across Ciel's face.

I ask, "But what about the demons who can possess mortals? We call them puppeteers. Do you have a magical solution for that too?"

"It is only part of their magic and spirit that enters the mortal. Pierce the mortal with the blade and the demon will abandon its host. Alexander can heal the wound."

I look down, admiring the blades.

A loon cries out in the dark and is answered by a barn owl.

"You are pleased?" Ciel asks, the hint of amusement still on his lips.

"Yes, but if I get stabbed with one of these, will I—" I make an exploding motion with my hand.

"No. One must know how to remove your soul using the blade. And if you died in this body, your soul would return to the fields of Elysium."

"Oh."

"We will know the moment you've returned to us. We would retrieve your soul from the fields and place it in a proper vessel."

"Guess I don't have to worry about anyone—" I make a stabby motion toward my heart, touching the point to my chest. I make fake dying noises.

His face pinches.

"I'm *kidding*." I look up into his face. "I may not remember everything, but I understand what you did for me. You saved me from enslavement—and a marriage to someone I could never love, in Hell of all places. And Goddess knows what other horrors." I put both blades in one hand and wrap my free arm around him. "Thank you."

I rest my head against his chest. I feel safe. When was the last time I actually felt safe?

"Just so you know," I whisper, "I'm not *with* Alex."

I feel stupid for bringing this up and overexplaining it, but I saw the hurt in Ciel's eyes when he realized Alex was my chevalier. The pure devastation. Overkill or not, I feel like I have to say this.

"I got the impression from what Vinae said that a chevalier bond is romantic?" I don't dare say *sexual* because my face will catch fire.

"It is the closest bond two souls can share," he says simply.

"Right, well, I just wanted you to know that I do love Alex, but not like *that*. He's with someone else. We don't see each other that way."

Ciel blinks, uncomprehending.

Goddess above.

"He's *gay*. Are there *gay* fey in Elysium? Surely. Are there male fey who like other male fey? Like—Oh, never mind. It doesn't matter. I'm trying to say that I haven't fallen in love with anyone else. If you think I want to be with someone else, you're wrong, I—"

Ciel kisses me.

My body warms head to toe. My knees weaken. No dizzying flush of magic, just old-fashioned swooning. I let myself fall into it. My free hand goes up around his neck. I kiss him deeper. When he straightens, it lifts me off the ground so not even the tips of my toes touch the earth. Both of his arms close around me, holding me to him.

He breaks the kiss first, but he doesn't let go of me. In fact, it feels like he's never going to let go.

"I understand," he whispers into my hair. "But know this: you are free to live this life how you please. You owe me nothing. You could take a thousand lovers, and it will change nothing between us."

The moon can fall from the sky. The comets can burn out their light. I will be here always, loving you.

I press my warm cheek to his cool one. "A *thousand* lovers seems a little ambitious, don't you think?"

His lips quirk again, and already I'm memorizing these features. The delicate flare of his nose. These lavender eyes. The little indention under his lip. I think I've put my thumb there before and pulled him into a kiss—when I was taller.

I feel an ache I can't describe. I'm longing for something —something I can't quite remember. Whatever we had before, perhaps.

"Ciel," I breathe. *I miss you.*

"We will have it again. In time," he promises, and sets me gently on my feet. "You need only call, and I will come."

"Swear it," I beg.

"I swear it."

Very reluctantly, he lets go of me. The heat between us dissipates. I watch him disappear into the dark, walking in that soundless way of his. I barely know him. And yet I want to run after him, throw my arms around him and beg him to stay. But that makes no sense. There is no place for Ciel in this world. Somehow, I understand this. I understand that he had to remake me so *I* would have a place here.

"Guess I'll see you in my next life," I whisper to the darkness.

I'm answered by a voice, full of mischievous humor. *Much sooner than that.*

EPILOGUE

I wiggle my body under Arty's bed, my pen knife open in one hand. Alex crawls in after me with a great deal of moaning and groaning.

Admittedly, it's a much tighter fit than when we were kids.

"Hold the light steady," I complain.

"I can't really see what I'm doing. And there are dust bunnies the size of my head under here. Now we know where the hearth puts all the dust when she's feeling lazy." He tries to adjust the light and thumps his head. "*Ow.*"

Finally, he trains the light on the wooden frame and jagged sigils appear, carved in the underside of the bed frame.

"Hold it there!" I reposition myself at a better angle. I scratch at the sigils with my knife, scoring the wood deeply until the symbols are unrecognizable.

Alex sneezes a few times and the light jumps, but we finally manage to destroy the sigils under both my aunts' beds.

Ten minutes later, we're standing on the upstairs landing, swatting the dust out of our clothes.

"Are you sure this will work?" he asks.

"We're about to find out."

I take a deep breath, trying to settle my pounding heart. My legs feel weak as I descend the stairs. I clutch the handrail so I don't tumble to my doom. We pause outside the library, listening to the aunts talking about Beltane. A hundred witches will be here tomorrow. Laughing, drinking, dancing naked under the moon with flowers in their hair. We need this celebration after everything that's happened. You can feel that need in the air.

I hope what I'm about to do doesn't ruin everything.

Alex nudges me, and I realize I've been standing here in stunned fear. He gives me a thumbs up and nods toward the door.

I take a breath and knock.

"Come on then," Arty calls.

Alex and I slink into the library. Arty is at her desk, a large stack of books in front of her. She arches a brow in question when I close the door.

"Here are some glum faces," Demi says, looking up from the book she was reading in the large window seat. "What's happened? Did you have another bad hunt?"

Bad because the demons have been avoiding us since we sent Vinae back to Hell. Of course, we all agree this is only a lull after the battle. Trouble will find us soon enough.

"No, not a hunt," Alex says, and then he looks at me, expecting me to say more.

But my mouth is so dry. All the spit has gone right out of it. Finally, I manage, "I need to tell you something."

The aunts exchange a look. Demi closes her book. "We're listening."

"Phelia." I take another steadying breath. "Phelia isn't —She's not gone."

Demi's hand goes to her chest. She looks from me to Alex to Arty. "She's a spirit?"

Now that I know my mom conceived her using magic, I wonder if she's always been more magic than girl, and that's why she stayed. But instead of saying this, I squeak out, "I think it's time you see her."

I hear a sharp gasp. I turn and find Phelia standing by the bookcase. One hand on the shelves, the other on her hip. She's mostly solid given the early evening and approaching full moon. It's why I chose today. It's best for them to see her when she's looking pretty solid and not like a creepy ghost.

"Phelia," Demi breathes.

Phelia takes in Demi's slack jaw and wide eyes. She looks up at me as if she's unsure of what's happening.

"They can see me?" she asks, and there's just enough fear in her voice that I'm certain she'll run. Arty *definitely* looks ready to run. Her back is shoved hard against her chair and both arms are clutching the armrests as if the chair is really a horse ready to buck her.

I choose my next words carefully.

"Phelia likes poetry." I wet my lips. "Sometimes she sits in the window seat with me, and I turn the pages for her. Her favorites are Gluck and Szymborska. And, of course, Dickinson. But we've also read Stein and Lorde and Lucille Clifton. Maya Angelou. We've just started Dickens."

Silence hangs in the air. All five of us just look at each other.

But more than anything, she just wants to be a part of this family again. I project this last thought directly into their minds.

Tears spring to Demi's eyes. Something in Arty's shoulders relaxes.

At long last Demi manages to say, "I like Clifton myself."

"And I like Dickens," Arty says. She isn't leaping for joy or anything, but she hasn't run screaming from the room either, and in my book, that's a win.

Phelia's face crumples. "I missed you."

"Oh, my darling girl." Demi begins to really cry now. "We've missed you too."

A tight knot in my chest loosens. Alex squeezes my hand.

This will work, he promises.

As if to prove him right, Arty pulls herself from her chair and goes to them.

Please, I think. *Please don't cast her out. If you can accept me, then you can accept her.*

Arty's voice is surprisingly gentle when she says, "Phelia, have you and your sister read anything by Gwendolyn Brooks yet?"

"No," Phelia says, still looking shy and hesitant, her small hand still on the bookcase.

Arty motions toward the shelves. It only takes me a minute to find a copy of *Children Coming Home*. As soon as Arty pats the window seat beside her, Demi sits down, but with enough space deliberately left for Phelia.

When my sister settles between them, my heart is full to bursting. Alex squeezes my hand again before releasing it and I'm left drowning in the gratitude welling up inside me.

Gratitude for all the people in my life. For everyone who has made me feel loved and wanted.

With her cane propped against her leg, Arty opens the book, thumbing to the first poem.

"Well then," my aunt says, clearing her throat. "We should start at the beginning."

GET YOUR FREE STORIES TODAY

Thank you so much for reading *Blade Born*. I hope you enjoyed Amelia's story. If you'd like to check out more of my work, please consider signing up for my free newsletter at www.korymshrum.com/free-starter-library

When you sign up, I will send you free stories from the other series that I write.

As to the newsletter itself, I send out 2-3 a month and host a monthly giveaway exclusive to my subscribers. The prizes are usually signed books or other freebies that I think you'll enjoy. I also share information about my current projects, personal news, and other relevant updates on what I'm up to.

Acknowledgments

When I tell you this book was a long time in the making, *boy*, is that an understatement. Most of the novels I write are finished from idea to publication in a matter of weeks (usually ten to twelve weeks, to be exact.) But the book you've just finished, has been one that I worked on ***for more than ten years***.

Yes. A *decade*. I still have rejection letters from November 2012 in my email from when this book was called *Water & Dark*. And that version of the book was rejected from Random House because the editor didn't think there was enough action in the story. And it was rejected from HarperCollins because the editor didn't "connect with the voice" (Amelia's).

Since then, I have rewritten and edited this book no less than five times. I would write a version, be unhappy with it, and then go write another book or three until I was ready to give it another go.

Some of the original story is still included here. Most of it is new and better and reflects how much my writing has improved over time. Why am I telling you this? Why am I bringing this up in an acknowledgments section that no one ever reads?

Just to say that if there is a story you really want to tell, or something your heart yearns to do, don't give up on it. It might take forever. It might make you want to pull out your hair. You literally might have to put it down and write twenty-five other books before you get it right (that's the exact number, folks). But whatever you do, don't give up on it.

Special thanks to everyone who read this book or a version of it: Kimberly Benedicto, Kathrine Pendleton, Angela Roquet, Monica La Porta, and Victoria Solomon. And if I've forgotten someone, forgive me. It's been a long time.

We can also thank the masterful Toby Selwyn for his editorial prowess and Maria at Artscandare Book Cover Design for the gorgeous cover, which I saw in her premade store and snapped up immediately because it was perfect for this story.

And as always, many thanks to my lovely street team. Sorry I cut it so close to the deadline on this one, but many thanks for reading the book in advance, reporting those lingering typos, and posting your honest reviews.

Every one of you make my world go 'round.

Also by Kory M. Shrum

Dying for a Living series

Dying for a Living

Dying by the Hour

Dying for Her: A Companion Novel

Dying Light

Worth Dying For

Dying Breath

Dying Day

Shadows in the Water series

Shadows in the Water

Under the Bones

Danse Macabre

Carnival

Devil's Luck

What Comes Around

Overkill

Silver Bullet

Hell House

One Foot in the Grave

Blood Rain

First Light

Castle Cove series

Welcome to Castle Cove

Night Tide

The City 2603 series

The City Below

The City Within

The City Outside

The Borderland series

Blade Born: A Borderlands Novel

Standalone Novels

Jack and the Fire Eater

Short Fiction

Thirst: new and collected stories

Final Cut: stories

Nonfiction

Who Killed My Mother? a memoir

A Well Cared for Human: self-love strategies for transforming pain into power

Poetry (as K.B. Marie)

Birds & Other Dreamers

Questions for the Dead

You Can't Keep It

Learn more about Kory's work at www.korymshrum.com

About the Author

USA TODAY bestselling author Kory M. Shrum has published more than thirty books including the bestselling *Shadows in the Water* and *Dying for a Living* series.

She is the host of two podcasts: *Who Killed My Mother?* a true crime podcast about her mother's tragic death, and a second show, *A Well Cared For Human*, which focuses on debunking self-care myths, while offering concrete strategies for improving one's mental health and personal power.

She also publishes poetry under the name K.B. Marie.

When not writing, podcasting, or planning her next adventure, she can usually be found under thick blankets with snacks.

She lives in Michigan with her equally bookish wife, Kim, and their very spoiled rescue dog, Max. Learn more about Kory and all the mischief she gets up to at www.korymshrum.com

Made in the USA
Coppell, TX
13 December 2025

65604408R00187